AN ASSASSIN'S ACCORD

MCFADDEN AND BANKS™ BOOK 1

MICHAEL ANDERLE

LMBPN

DISRUPTIVE IMAGINATION®

Copyright © 2020 LMBPN Publishing
Cover Art by Jake @ J Caleb Design
http://jcalebdesign.com / jcalebdesign@gmail.com
Cover copyright © LMBPN Publishing
A Michael Anderle Production

LMBPN Publishing
PMB 196, 2540 South Maryland Pkwy
Las Vegas, NV 89109

First US edition, November 2020
eBook ISBN: 978-1-64971-283-7
Print ISBN: 978-1-64971-284-4

AN ASSASSIN'S ACCORD TEAM

Thanks to our Beta Team:
Jeff Eaton, John Ashmore, Kelly O'Donnell

JIT Readers

John Ashmore
Deb Mader
Peter Manis
Diane L. Smith
Dorothy Lloyd
Jeff Goode
Kelly O'Donnell

Editor
Skyhunter Editing Team

DEDICATION

To Family, Friends and
Those Who Love
to Read.
May We All Enjoy Grace
to Live the Life We Are
Called.

CHAPTER ONE

The situation felt weirdly familiar, enough so that it triggered his instinct and demanded attention.

Taylor looked at himself. His six-foot-six frame was encased in a suit of mechanized armor, and he could feel his long red hair and beard being pushed up by the helmet he wore. He couldn't remember a time when that felt uncomfortable, although it was probably due to the fact that he had been clean-shaven and sported a crew cut when he first climbed into one of them, and he had simply grown into the comfortable habit from there.

After years of walking and fighting in a suit like this, he wasn't surprised that the whole feeling was so familiar. But this was a new suit. It wasn't one of the chunky, difficult-to-operate ones that broke down more often than an Alfa Romeo. And predictably in the middle of a fight.

He looked around and narrowed his eyes as they adjusted to the darkness around him.

"Come on, McFadden, get your head out of your ass!"

He snapped his head around and a familiar face registered in his HUD.

"Davis?"

"No, it's the fucking tooth fairy, and I'll take those teeth out manually if you don't scan your sector like you should, dumbass. Also, I'm a little short on quarters, so I'll do that shit for free."

The rest of the team laughed.

Right. The rest of the team because he didn't head into the Zoo without a team.

And he was in the Zoo. His gaze flicked around. The familiarity settled in with more assurance as the surroundings grew steadily more visible. His eyes finally began to adjust to the darkness. He could see the trees, the vines growing around them, and the flickers of motion that his motion sensors told him were monsters on the move. The jungle denizens, for now, kept an eye on them but weren't quite ready to attack.

Even the thought of being there had him in a cold sweat, but he forced himself to keep moving. He took his customary post at the front of the line and grasped his rifle a little tighter.

Suddenly, he froze in place, alerted by his inner sense that something was wrong. His teammates halted when he did, scanned the area, and everyone felt the ground shake even when the heavy suits had stopped moving.

"Shit!" Davis called. "We have a big fucker heading our way!"

The group knew what to do already and no one needed to be told. Weapons were aimed in the direction of the massive, dinosaur-like monster that approached as the team began to move away at an angle. Everyone hoped the creature simply wouldn't see them and would walk past. It was the only scenario that would enable them all to come out of this alive.

Taylor had a bad feeling best-case wouldn't happen. It never did. The big fuckers were hard to avoid when they trundled through.

As if in response to his thought, a massive shadow stepped between the trees and made it difficult to focus on anything else as it pushed through the jungle like it owned the place.

Hell, for all he knew, it probably did.

He stood immobile and held his breath as he waited for the beast to hopefully lumber past them.

His inner prediction proved accurate. He had already stiffened in preparation when the impossibly large head turned and caught sight of the group that tried to evade it. A brief second was required for recognition before the beast uttered a bone-shattering roar.

"Son of a bitch." Davis growled frustration and annoyance.

Everyone knew what to do. They'd been through the drills in sims before and a handful had already been through the process in real life.

All that notwithstanding, they still didn't like their odds.

"Smoke this asshole!" Taylor called and fired the grenade from the launcher under his rifle. It streaked into an arc that brought it down into the side of the creature's head. All he saw was a flash of light and a minor annoyance on the dinosaur's part as it shrugged the impact aside.

The series of explosions that followed was enough to throw it off balance and it collided heavily with a couple of nearby trees. The rest of the jungle seemed to wake with that and suddenly, a wave of roars, screeches, and hisses erupted from all around them.

"Formation!" Davis shouted and motioned for them to form a circle so they could watch each other's back. "And keep fucking moving! If any of you fall behind, you'll be left behind!"

Taylor knew the threat was far from an empty one, but they would at least try to not leave anyone behind.

Hundreds of the creatures appeared on his motion sensors as he loaded another grenade into the launcher. The bigger, badder mutant was still out there, likely circling and waiting for the rest of the monsters to have their fun before it finally stepped in.

He hated how intelligent these fuckers were.

"We have them moving in from the flank!"

His teeth gritted, he repressed every instinct to turn and help since it was his job to keep those that tried to attack from the front at bay while the group pushed forward. He could hear the heavy steps coming in behind them as the creatures continued to press in.

A moment later, he registered smoke in the air. He needed a few seconds to realize that it wasn't some kind of mist seeping through the jungle but actual smoke. Maybe that explained where all the sunlight had gone, and he felt the heat from it lick at his back.

Too many of the creatures rushed through the flames

all around him. They didn't seem to notice that their fur caught fire when they maintained their charge.

The Zoo wasn't known to catch fire, he thought with a bemused frown. Well, he wasn't in the Zoo, was he? He was in Southern California. New beasties appeared all over the place and were driven out of the wilds and into population centers. He and Tanya needed to get rid of the creatures before they could cause any fatalities.

"Tanya!" he shouted, looked around, and saw her vaguely through the smoke.

But where was the big fucker? It couldn't be too far behind them.

"Tanya, get a move on!"

She moved too slowly, and the smoke parted easily as the massive dinosaur of a creature pushed through behind her, stretched its thick neck, and snapped its impossibly large jaws at her.

It missed, but in avoiding the strike, Tanya tripped over a pile of burning branches and tumbled end over end down a small hill.

"No!" Taylor roared, yanked grenades from his belt, and lobbed them in front of the lurching creature. They forced it back a couple of steps and into the bushfire it was trying to escape from.

No, wait, Tanya hadn't met Bobby yet. And if she died on the hills of California, she never would. He reached her and skidded to his knees beside her.

"Hey, are you okay?"

She nodded and pushed up slowly. "Yeah... The fucker almost got me."

"Not if I have anything to say about it."

He hauled her to her feet and registered the heavy footsteps of the dinosaur cryptid coming up behind them again. With a muttered curse, he tossed another grenade behind his back to slow it while they made their escape.

"What the fuck, Taylor? Why are you throwing grenades around like that without even seeing what you're throwing them at?"

Was that Bobby? It sounded like the man, but Taylor couldn't be sure. He hadn't gone on the trip to California.

Wait...no, the heat was at normal levels for Vegas. The smoke came from the exhausts in the cars. It was still too blisteringly hot to stand out in the sun during rush hour in Vegas, almost hot enough to melt the tires of the cars that usually crawled bumper to bumper in a traffic jam.

Not this time, though. They all gave the armored car a wide berth. Taylor looked over his shoulder. Tanya was gone and the weight was only the bags that carried the cash they were robbing from the armored car. She was there again in the next moment, but she carried a bag of her own with her assault rifle ready and opened fire at the creatures that ran between the cars.

The monsters had finally gotten their lazy asses to Vegas. He'd always known it was only a matter of time until they did, but he had hoped they would take a little longer. But there was no need to be afraid of the inevitable. He tightened his grasp on his rifle and watched as the creatures forced themselves through the gaps between the cars. They pushed beyond the traffic directly into the rain of bullets he let loose.

One of the panthers jumped on the armored car and

waited for him to approach before it pounced. Its fangs flashed in the bright sunlight. He couldn't tell if the creature had specifically targeted him out of the rest, or if maybe it had merely waited on top of the vehicle for someone to approach, but it didn't matter. With his free hand, he drew his knife and waited for the creature's momentum to meet the blade he drove up to stab into its jawline.

Blood coated the side of his suit, and he made a mental note to double his elbow grease to get it clean again and then burn all the rags he used to do so.

"Taylor," Niki called over the comms. "You need to get out of here."

Niki? She wasn't on the heist with them. Maybe she was calling from the outside.

He turned and heard the sound of helicopters approaching in the distance, which made it difficult to not realize what she was talking about. They intended to clear the whole area out and make sure the infestation wouldn't spread.

"Wait," he protested. "I need to get out? What about you? Where the hell are you?"

"I'm pinned down," she explained. "I won't be able to reach the drop point. You guys need to get the hell out of here without me."

"No fucking way!" he snapped. "That's my move, and you know it!"

"I guess I have to take a page from your book, Taylor." He could hear her voice cracking as she spoke. "Good luck!"

"Fucking—" His response was cut short by the noise and he scowled at the helicopters as their rockets flared, dozens at a time, to wreak destruction on the city of Las Vegas. Once the missiles were finished, they were followed by bombs that shook the ground when the explosives detonated. It made it difficult to keep his feet, even with the suit working to counteract the seismic effects.

"What?" he whispered as the helicopters banked away to leave a massive crater smoking and flaming where the Las Vegas strip should have been. "Niki, are you there? Niki, answer me right now! Niki!"

Someone grasped him by the shoulder and shook him. Taylor pulled away and tried again to contact her. He needed to hear her voice again, to hear her speak through the chaos.

"Niki!"

The shaking worsened and made him feel like additional explosives impacted around him. Someone's hand clutched him and tried to pull him back, and he twisted to shove the hand away from him.

Vertigo filled his body as he spun into space and struck nothing until something cold and hard slapped him across the face. Hell, across his whole body. He shook violently, pushed up, and reached out for whatever had hit him. The whole place was suddenly dark, which made it difficult to see what was happening around him.

But the hands had hold of him again and pinned him in place. What happened to the suit?

Oh, right, he wasn't wearing one.

Taylor sucked in a deep breath and his eyes opened as he looked up from the ground to where Bobby stood over him and pinned his hands down.

"Fucking... What...where..."

The other man smirked, finally released his arms, and patted him on the cheek. "Are you having a nightmare there, buddy?"

He looked around the room. It was sparsely decorated, and even in the darkness, he could tell it needed a coat of paint. A desk stood on one side and a bed on the other, although bed might have been something of a stretch. It was barely a cot, the kind used to quickly set up sometimes when he was in the field. He had spent more than his fair share of nights on one of them and in the end, his comfort needs were fairly minimal.

Still, things would change over the next couple of weeks in that regard. He merely couldn't bring himself to part with the room he had spent so much time in. For a guy who had traveled around the world for most of his adult life, connecting to a place—any place—meant it was home.

Bobby finally pulled away and moved to one of the chairs. "What was the dream about? You shouted Niki's name while you were under, but...it didn't sound like a sex dream, between you and me."

Taylor scowled at the hefty man. "Yeah, whatever, you Jet Li lookalike. And no, it wasn't a...pleasant dream. We were...in the Zoo? I think? Then in California. And then here. There were monsters here and she...she died. I think. It's getting hard to remember."

"Well, first, I'm very sure I have a solid foot and a half and a hundred and fifty pounds on Jet Li, so we look nothing alike. Secondly…well, yeah, that's kind of how dreams go, I guess. Still, it sounds like it was rough."

He shrugged. "Right…yeah. I feel like I was in a rigorous workout. Shit."

"And you smell like you've been in a rigorous workout too."

"Fuck off, Bungees."

"I'm not kidding. You smell like shit and honestly, I'd think about changing the sheets on that bench you call a bed."

Taylor paused and peered at his shirt. Sure enough, it was soaked with sweat. He didn't need to get in closer to know that he reeked of it too.

"Shit. You're right. I'll take a shower and I'll be right down. Did you bring doughnuts?"

"Don't I always?"

With a nod, he pushed to his feet and rubbed some feeling back into where the other man had held him down. "Awesome. I'll head down to the shop in about…thirty minutes?"

"Sure, but remember that I'm your boss now and I'll be tracking your hours."

"In McFadden's Mechs only. I'll be here part-time, remember?"

"Right, right. I'll still track your hours with Zhang and Novak—"

"Ass. At least my name wasn't a mouthful."

"Says the guy who smells like one."

Bobby stood and flipped him off as he headed to the door.

"I need to put a new lock on that door," Taylor

mumbled as he yanked his drenched shirt off and threw it into the laundry bin with perfect accuracy. It was three times wider than the average basketball hoop and less than three feet away, but he still couldn't help a small smile as he headed into the bathroom.

CHAPTER TWO

It wasn't a long shower. Taylor had spent enough time in the military to learn the improperly named 'Navy Shower,' which had taught him that cleaning himself thoroughly didn't need to involve soaking in hot water until he turned into a prune.

Besides, after the night that he'd had, a cold shower seemed like the right option and he was shivering slightly when he stepped out to dry himself.

The trembling had abated by the time he pulled clean clothes on, and as he headed down to the shop, he realized he had forgotten to bolt the door the night before when he went to bed. Or maybe Bungees had found a way to open it. Despite his official qualification being that of a mechanic, the man had learned enough on the ground to have forgotten more about mechanics than Taylor would ever learn. One didn't always need the degree to gain the practical knowledge the hard way. Besides that, finding a way around a bolted door didn't seem like it would be that difficult for him.

Bobby was already busy with one of the suits that had been sent from the Zoo for them to work on, but there was no sign of Tanya, Elisa, or Vickie in the shop yet. He still wasn't sure which of them would work there full-time but they had discussed it and he didn't think it would change. Niki and Vickie would be with him—that was a no brainer —and Tanya intended to work with Bobby due to their involvement, hence the long-ass name they had thought of to replace McFaddens Mechs. Although he hadn't had a final answer from Elisa yet, she had indicated her preference to remain in the shop and avoid his type of adventures. Besides, she was good at what she did and everyone knew it.

"Doughnuts are in the break room," the mechanic announced without looking up from his work. "You might need to make more coffee, though. I didn't know you would be here today and only brought some for myself."

"Where's Tanya?"

"She's having breakfast with a friend...I think. She did say she would be a little late today."

Taylor nodded, descended the last couple of steps, and turned left into the little nook he had repurposed into a break room. It held a small electric stove, a fridge, a sink, and a dishwasher, all crammed into a location that was about thirty square feet overall.

Which wasn't that small, especially for a break room, but it certainly didn't seem big when everyone wanted coffee at the same time. Maybe him spending less time there was for the best. Bobby would undoubtedly do a great job running the business since the guy had practically done it since the beginning.

The coffee machine worked fine and it wasn't long before he poured a probably unhealthy amount of sugar into a mug of black coffee. He took a bite out of a chocolate-glazed doughnut as he stirred the beverage.

Damned if it wasn't a good cup of coffee. Taylor moved to the shop and studied the suits that had been set up on their stands, ready to be worked on. They were in varying conditions of repair but all displayed the traditional signs that they had gone through the usual mill of destruction that was the Zoo.

He leaned closer to one that looked like it had its leg chewed off and winced. "What the hell do you think did that?"

Bobby looked up from his work for a second and narrowed his eyes. "Who knows? If I had to guess, I'd say it looks like a couple of those locusts had a go at it, but the pilot would need to be more or less stationary for them to do that much damage. Is there anything on the shoulder or the helmet that would indicate that something else attacked him while they targeted his legs?"

Taylor looked up and sure enough, he could see bite marks in the helmet and indentations where it looked like maybe a panther had tried to bite through the helmet. It had no doubt held him down, which allowed the locusts to do a number on the legs.

"Do you think he made it out?" he asked and studied the suit again with a grim expression.

"Probably. There isn't much reason to go in and save a suit with a dead pilot inside. Whether he survived in the hospital or whether he kept his leg...that's a different story. It looks thoroughly mangled from my point of view. It does seem a little heartless to get his suit repaired for someone else to use, but it's not exactly the most heartwarming of tourist locations."

Taylor nodded but didn't want to say any more. He remembered more of the dream than he liked, and the memories of his time in the Zoo had begun to resurface.

Thankfully, his attention was drawn to his phone, which vibrated to inform him that someone else was taking control of the security system. There was only one person who did that before they even appeared.

"Vickie just arrived?" Bobby asked and refocused his attention on the suit in front of him.

"Yeah. She snagged the security controls without so much as a hello."

"She'll do that. You have to say hello after she's inside."

The doors to the garage began to swing open, and a Tesla pulled in as soon as they were wide enough to allow her inside. It was a nice car and once upon a time, Taylor might have wondered how a college student would be able to afford a vehicle like that, but he was well aware that she was now a great deal wealthier than most college students.

And only some of the money was illegal.

She climbed out of the car, stretched with a loud yawn, and leaned against it for a few seconds. The three-inch platform boots she preferred made her appear taller than her five-foot-six frame, although there wasn't much to be done for the lean build behind it. She had adopted a goth chic style with a vengeance, which meant black jeans with a dozen or so rips everywhere, a black shirt with a couple of obscenities written on it, and topped with her short hair and half a dozen piercings.

"Morning, Tay-Tay." She waved, still leaning against the car. "Morning, Bungees. Please tell me that's coffee I smell."

"What else would it be?" Taylor asked.

"I don't know. Bobby has been buying those coffee-flavored doughnuts lately." She held a finger with a finger-nail painted black up before the man could voice a complaint. "Don't worry, they're amazing, but they're not coffee."

"Well, it is coffee," Taylor answered and gestured for her to join him.

The hacker grinned and jogged to him—an impressive feat in the platform boots—and wrapped him in a hug.

"Fucking hell, you're a great hugger, you know that?" she asked and looked at him. "It's like being hugged by an oversized, red-headed bear."

"Yeah, yeah, whatever. Go get yourself some coffee. Maybe that'll help with your comparisons."

She poured herself a mug of coffee and added more sugar than he had before she snatched a doughnut and rejoined the two men in the shop. "So, what do you think you'll do today?"

Taylor looked around and realized she was talking to him. "Well, I thought I'd help out at the shop a little. It's been a while, what with me setting the other place up."

"Oh, right. I thought we would look for work since you're now the co-owner of a merc team, along with Niki and myself. Getting that off the ground might be a good place to start, no?"

"It's not like we're in any kind of hurry. You'll be paid anyway, and we're still setting it up so we might as well make sure everything else is running smoothly. Bobby got a new delivery yesterday, so I thought I'd lend a hand with that. In fact, you might as well earn that paycheck you're getting anyway and lend us a hand yourself."

Vickie groaned. "You know, I had a feeling you would pull that card out of the deck. I had, like…fifteen second thoughts when I was driving over here but no, I had to come and see how you guys are doing."

He grinned and motioned for her to take a seat on the bench next to Bobby. The mechanic had begun to take the suit apart and put pieces on the bench, which allowed his two teammates to start cleaning them before they placed them on a cloth-covered section where they could easily be reassembled when the time came.

"I have to admit, I'll miss working here," she admitted after they were a few minutes into the work. "She's no modern marvel of architecture, but we have been through some tough times."

"You know you're welcome to come by and visit any time you please, right?" Bobby asked.

"I know, but it won't be the same. The team's splitting up and we'll be off doing different things. It feels like the end of an era, you know?"

"Are you sure you're okay with that?" Taylor asked. He kept his gaze fixed on the delicate piece of machinery he was cleaning of all the dust that had collected in the tiny nooks and crannies.

Vickie shrugged. "Sure, and we're all moving forward and onward, but you can't blame me for being a little nostalgic, knowing that the good old times are moving along."

"Okay, fair enough. But if you feel so nostalgic, why the hell did you throw shade on this place?"

"What? You've admitted it's an eyesore. Multiple times."

"Sure, but I can say it lovingly. You merely make it sound hurtful."

"Speaking of eyesore, can we talk about the name you were working with?" Bobby asked with most of his head already inside the suit he was taking apart.

"Again, that's hurtful."

"But accurate," she cut in and focused on the mechanic. "Have you guys thought about a name yet? The last I heard, you had some long-ass name that would take Elisa a week to say for every phone call. Will you simply name it Zhang and Novak Mechs? Because the lack of alliteration is appreciated but it's still not a very…creative name."

"It's probably best to remove my name from it completely," Taylor conceded. "I'm still well-known in the circle of the clients, and I don't want them to be misled into thinking I'll be here full-time. Besides, Bobby's better known as a suit mechanic, so having his name on the company would do wonders for sales."

"Well, Tanya and I talked about it over dinner the other night, and the whole last name in the company name felt a little too corporate and Wall Street." Bobby paused in his work to wipe sweat from his forehead. "She came up with Mech Advantage. I think that has a nice ring to it."

"It's certainly better than McFadden's Mechs," Vickie pointed out. "Although again, that's setting the bar fairly low right there."

She paused to look at Taylor for a few seconds until he turned his attention away from his work.

"What?"

"It's not as fun to tease you when you don't react."

"I know."

"Ugh, every party needs a pooper."

"I'll try to ignore the fact that you said that. But yeah, I'll admit that's a good name, and with Elisa pushing it, it'll stick like…ummm…"

"Moss to a log!" the hacker suggested. "No, like shit to a shovel!"

"I had intended to go with glue, but sure…one of those. But I think the bigger question is if you'll be able to work full-time with your cousin."

Even Bobby looked up from his work with a curious expression to hear Vickie's answer to that.

She looked around, shrugged, and didn't commit to an answer for a few long seconds.

Finally, she sighed and shook her head. "Okay, Niki is the one who kept me out of the Zoo and…got me out of other problems, so I owe her a ton."

"I'm still not sure what kind of trouble you got yourself into that it required Niki to step in."

"And you never will. The point is, I think we've both grown up a great deal since then. Although I have to say, I've felt like her parent lately. The two of you aren't what I'd call mature when it comes to relationships."

"That—" Taylor paused and nodded. "Okay, that's a good point."

"So yeah, with everything we've been through, I think we would work well together. And if worse comes to worst, I don't think we'll be working, like, in the same room together much, so it doesn't matter."

"Another fair point."

He stopped working and put the piece he was cleaning gently on the bench before he retrieved his vibrating phone.

The number was blocked, which usually meant a certain AI wanted to have a word. The software Vickie installed on his phone didn't allow for any other numbers to be blocked.

"Desk, is that you?" he asked as he accepted the call.

"Taylor, it is nice to speak to you again," the AI answered.

The fact that she had been created by none other than Vickie's mentor and Niki's sister Jennie meant she was a cutting-edge piece of technology that made it easy for him to forget that he talked to a sophisticated piece of software and not an actual human.

Which meant he wasn't sure how meaningful the AI's greeting was. Well, he knew she was an AI, but it was difficult to bring that to mind while talking to her.

"Is everything all right?" Desk asked.

"I...yeah, sure. I was a little lost in thought. How can I help you?"

"Only by accepting the message that Niki asked me to pass on to you. She said that her business in Washington might take a few more days. The DOD has asked her to finalize certain admin issues that have arisen with ending her contract and the establishment of the new task force. In the meantime, she is interested to find out how work on the new base of operations is going."

Taylor scowled. He did understand that Niki hadn't had a real home since she had worked for the FBI. Even so, the property he had picked up for bananas still needed a fair amount of work. He wanted it to be ready when she got back but there were no guarantees.

As it turned out, the reason why the previous owner needed to liquidate his assets was because he had been dealing with the IRS, who had conducted a very invasive search of his assets. Walls had holes in them, toilets had been ripped out of the floor, and the whole building was left in one hell of a mess.

It wasn't quite as bad as the strip mall had been when Taylor acquired it, but there was still a significant challenge ahead of him.

"I...I won't make any promises, but I hope that with a little help from Bobby's amazing construction network, it'll be livable by the time she gets back."

"Fantastic," Desk replied. "I'll tell her the news. Is there anything else that you'd like me to say to her?"

"Uh, tell her that...well, I'm looking forward to seeing her again."

"Will do. Have a nice day!"

The line cut off and he realized that both Vickie and Bobby were staring at him.

"What?"

"You two are adorable." She grinned and nudged him in the arm with her fist.

"That was Desk."

"I know, but the message you sent to Niki...it's adorable."

The mechanic shook his head and returned to work.

"Adorable is right. Speaking of which, are you letting

your hair grow? I thought you were rocking the whole GI Jane look but now, you can almost start braiding it."

She touched the hair that fell almost halfway down her neck. "That's a pathetic deflection but...sure, why not? I won't let it grow too long—that's a headache to take care of, as you well know—but I'm done with the old look. Besides, having it too long would suck in the suits, right?"

"Well, since you'll be technical support for most of the missions we go on, I doubt you'll be in the suits too much. I'm not saying you shouldn't be ready, but from what I remember, most of the women in the Zoo had varying lengths of hair. Those who had it longer had it tied up in buns and braids and shit and it fit in the suit well enough. I'm only saying you shouldn't knock it before you try it, you know?"

Vickie shrugged. "I can always cut it if I don't enjoy it."

"Besides, shouldn't you spend most of your time in school? Getting that degree and shit?"

The hacker shook her head. "No, not really. I...well, it's on break now, and I don't think I want to go back, you know?"

Taylor narrowed his eyes and leaned forward. "No, I don't know. What's with the change of heart?"

"I don't think I need it, is all. What do I need a college degree for anyway?"

"Because Niki will kill you if you drop out now. Seriously. She'll put the bullets in you by hand."

"It's not like...I don't have a healthy fear of what my cousin can do. But what exactly will a college degree say about my credentials? Alongside all the other credentials too?"

"Getting a college degree shows—"

"Shows that I can see something out to the end. You told me, I know. But I'm already proving it by sticking it out here with you guys, right? I'll get more work done if I'm focused only on the job, and when we're finished or business is slow, I can get back to it. The credits will carry over and I'll pick up right where I left off."

He sighed and rubbed his temples. "Okay, fine. But you have to tell Niki. And you won't get that trust I set up for you until you graduate. The rules still stand."

"Of course. I won't need that money for a while. I'm set up as it is."

"I know but I want to keep the incentive there. You know I'm concerned about your future, right?"

Vickie rolled her eyes. "I know, Dad. Shit, what the hell will you talk to me about next? The birds and the bees? Because you should know that I watched that movie...*Porkies*, I think the name is, the other night."

"Don't be shitty. I'm only looking out for you. And...*Porkies*? That movie's older than you are. Twice as old as you are. Hell, it's from before my time."

"I'm merely trying to understand the older generations and I've decided that films from the time work as a perfect time capsule."

Taylor narrowed his eyes but simply shrugged. He didn't want to get into a movie argument, not with her. She was a walking encyclopedia of pop culture present and past, and she would tear him apart.

"Fine. Whatev—"

His phone vibrated again. He looked at the screen and

his squint turned into a scowl when he saw the name displayed.

"What the hell is Rod Marino calling you for?" Vickie asked and wore a glare that mirrored his.

"Let's find out." He shook his head and pressed the button to accept the call. "This is McFadden."

CHAPTER THREE

"Taylor, it's nice to hear your voice again."

His scowl deepened. He couldn't tell if the AI had meant her similar greeting, but Rod Marino certainly did not.

"Marino. How's life running a casino as a front for the Sicilian Mob? I'd say it's a dangerous business but not for the guys at the top. You are one of the guys at the top, right?"

"Well, things have been busy. Your fight brought in considerable advertising for my little place of business, you know, and it's been all I could do to keep up with the demand. People want more fights like that, and they've come down to my humble establishment to procure it. I told you I would make back all the money you took from me."

Taylor rolled his eyes. "Remind me what exactly about your establishment is humble."

"The humble innkeeper."

"Stop bullshitting me, Marino. Now, I know you only

call me when you want something from me, so why don't we get to it?"

A pause on the line tempted him to cut the call. "Well then, way to suck all the fun out of doing business. Shoot the fun in the back of the head, weigh the body down with rocks, and drop it into the river, why don't you?"

"I believe that's more your schtick."

"Hah, fair enough. Okay, I'm only calling because I want to establish a truce between our two houses. I have people who tell me I should simply kill you and be done with it, and others say I should put you to work, earning for the family. And believe me when I say these are not the kinds of people you can simply roll your eyes and make obscene gestures at. At least, not unless you want to end up in the middle of a war. Not for nothing, but these old-fashioned idiots are all...so petulant when they talk about honor and respect and bullshit like that."

"Is there a waystation between here and the fucking point? I need to take a piss."

"You should have gone before we started. So, my point is we need a truce, and it's in everyone's best interest to make sure it puts an end to any violence that may ensue on both sides."

"Hey, I'm happy as long as your people leave me the fuck alone."

"Unfortunately, since...everything that's happened, it might not be possible. You've made something of a name for yourself among my people. The kind that makes any of them think there is a position in my organization or that of others if you are dealt with appropriately."

"And I'm sure you've done nothing to disabuse them of that notion."

"You're not under any kind of protection, and while I would be hurt personally if anything were to happen to you, other dons who you may or may not have annoyed with your antics might not feel so deeply about it. Which is why I thought it might be a good idea for some kind of arrangement to be made official so I can tell people not to give you any trouble. And, of course, I can put conse-quences in to make sure they don't take it as an invitation."

"You need to get a better handle on your crew."

"Yes, because if there's anything career criminals love it's an overpowering presence telling them what to do. No, they need to know that even if you are a pain in everyone's asses, you're not to be messed with, even in the interests of the other heads of the family. Does that make sense?"

Taylor narrowed his eyes and realized that his colleagues were watching him again. He didn't know what to do with the attention and in the end, it didn't matter much. They would disapprove of any dealing he had with the man, despite the fact that their last one had earned the whole crew considerable money.

And he understood that too. They were right. Dealing with criminals like Marino was a bad idea at the best of times.

"What do you have in mind?" he asked.

"I hoped we could meet for lunch to discuss things. I know we've gotten off on the wrong foot in the past—"

"And by wrong foot, you mean you tried to have people extort and kill me and my people until I showed you the error of your ways by robbing you blind, annihilating the idiots you sent to kill me and burn my business, and beating two of your men into a bloody pulp on a live stream for the whole world to see."

"And I regret my part in that and am more than willing to let bygones be…gone by the wayside. So what do you say? Lunch today? Around…two in the afternoon? And by around, I mean you can feel free to arrive at two-thirty if you have other plans that require your attention."

Taylor looked around the room again and rubbed his temples with a long sigh. "Fine. Lunch, two-ish. Text me the location when you know where it is."

"Will do. And I hope you are having a fantastic morning."

"Do you?"

Another pause stretched on the line as Marino tried to decide if he was being sarcastic or not and finally accepted that it was moot. "Well then, I'll see you for lunch. Bye!"

The line cut off and he could already hear the eyes rolling behind him as he placed his phone in his pocket.

"I know what you guys will say," he started.

"No, you don't!" Vickie interjected.

"You'll say it would be a terrible idea for me to go to lunch with Marino on such short notice, that it's probably a trap, and that he'll try to poison me or have me shot before I get to enjoy the entrée."

"Oh." Vickie grunted and returned to her work. "I guess you do know what I intended to say."

Bobby raised a hand. "I wanted to say that he would kill you before you even sat down, but yeah, that was all more or less the gist of what was on my mind. So I guess the question is why the hell will you go to lunch with a guy who would as soon gut you and watch you bleed out while he sips an aperitif? Also, a better question is why the hell aren't we trying to kill him instead? I'm tired of reacting to what the guy devises for us. Why aren't we initiating the conflict?"

"Because people will die if we do so," he explained in a quiet voice. "We're effective and good at our jobs, so when we decide we've had enough of their bullshit, fifteen new ones will be torn through. I'd like to leave that as a last resort when we don't have any other choice."

"Okay, fair enough," the man conceded. "I still hate having to wait and see what kind of new bullshit this guy will pull out of his ass to fuck us with."

"Same here," Vickie concurred.

Taylor nodded. "Yeah, I'm a little tired of that myself."

Before any of them could voice any other ideas or opinions, they were interrupted when the door of the shop began to draw open again. This time, it was a far more modest vehicle, a Chevy Malibu, that pulled into the garage.

Taylor knew Tanya had a car but he didn't remember that being it.

She climbed out of the vehicle and paused for a moment to stretch gently and flip her black, shoulder-length hair away before she drew another box of doughnuts out as well as some coffee cups on a tray.

"I had a feeling you guys would be low on pastries," she announced as she strolled toward the bench. "It's nice to see you already on the job. Taylor, Vickie, I thought you two would be off and starting your own thing."

"Well, people are working on it and in essence, all we

would do is sit around and wait for them to get shit done," Taylor explained and took one of the coffees offered on her tray. "I decided I might as well do that here, so I spent the night and we got to work bright and early."

"Yeah, after I had to shake him awake personally," Bobby muttered, but his attention was drawn away from his work and to the box Tanya had in her hands. "Is that…"

"Yep, from your favorite place," she answered and immediately handed the box to him. "Here's where I make a joke about you looking at me the way you look at those doughnuts, right?"

Taylor peeked into the box. "What am I missing here?"

"Bobby has a new favorite doughnut place," the woman explained and settled onto a seat next to him. "It's…you know the Krispy Kreme on Silverado, South Eastern Ave? We went there while we were shopping for parts suppliers."

"Is that anywhere near where you guys live?"

Bobby shook his head. "Sadly, no, so I simply pick them up from my usual place. But when Tanya has the time, she always goes there and buys some for me."

"Well, if that ain't relationship goals, I don't know what is," Vickie commented. She reached for one of the doughnuts but pulled back when he slapped her hand away.

"Wait your turn," the powerful mechanic told her only half-jokingly.

"Yeesh." She looked at her hand. "You're like a dog with a bone. An angry dog with a bone. Angry dog with a tasty—"

"We get the idea," Taylor interrupted. "Let us know when you're finished."

The man nodded, his mouth already full of something that had a creamy filling.

"I've told him he's starting to get a little too obsessed," Tanya noted as she pulled an armor part closer and began to work on it. "There would be health issues if he didn't work it off here and in the gym afterward, but his obsession is definitely...unhealthy."

"We'll need to find you a hobby," Vickie commented. "Or...maybe only a therapist because it looks like there's a hole you're trying to fill with doughnuts."

"Duh, my stomach," Bobby rumbled from around a mouthful of pastry. "Although it's not a hole so much as a digestive system."

"The hole metaphor works," Taylor pointed out. "Technically, the whole human body is a doughnut and food passes through the hole."

"You're fucking gross," the hacker protested.

"Human bodies tend to be that way, but you shouldn't let that get in the way of a good fact drop." He raised his coffee cup as a salutation of sorts and took a sip. "I'm still not sure about their doughnuts but the coffee is good."

"That's what I said," Tanya agreed. "Bobby was too busy to notice."

"So, where's Elisa?" Vickie asked and looked around. "Has she made a decision about whether or not she'll stay here or is she still thinking about it? When we last spoke, it seemed like a done deal that she'd stay."

"Oh, Elisa has been house hunting over the past couple of days. She called me on my drive over and said that she had an appointment to look at someplace she liked, so she'll drop by this afternoon. I told her to take the day off so she might do that too, although I never could get a read on that girl. Speaking of reading, Bobby, did you talk to Taylor about that..."

Her voice trailed off until the mechanic realized he was being spoken to, and Taylor stepped in as he was still busy digging into the doughnuts.

"Uh...yeah, that's the real reason why I spent the night here. Aside from the fact that they intended to start with some loud tools at my new property very early. The...we need to get signatures on the official transfer of ownership on the business to Bungees and yeah, we were supposed to do that today."

Bobby nodded. "I'll need to introduce you to my CPA. Brent....Barlow, I think his name is? Yeah, we were supposed to meet him this morning."

"What time this morning, exactly?" Taylor asked.

The man checked his watch and grimaced. "In...about twenty minutes."

"Oh, for fuck's sake," Tanya whispered.

"It's fine, it's fine!" he insisted, put the box down, and took a moment to clean himself a little. "It's only ten minutes away by car so we should be fine to get there."

"You'd better make sure the meeting doesn't last too long," Vickie muttered. "Taylor has a lunch date."

Tanya looked at Taylor. "I feel that needs some context."

"He's going out for lunch with Rod Marino," the hacker explained, her arms folded.

"Amazingly, the context doesn't make it sound any better. What the hell are you doing still in bed with that... I'm trying to think of a better word than douche?"

"Douche fits," he agreed. "And there's a whole reasoning

behind it, mostly involving wanting them to leave us the fuck alone."

"Do you honestly trust him enough to have a meal with the guy?"

"I have in the past but even so, not really. That's why Bobby's coming with me to make sure everything's kosher. I'm very sure Desk and Vickie will monitor the situation as well, so I think I'll have all the backup I need."

"Wait, I'm going too?" Bobby asked and peered out from the break room, where he was changing his shirt.

"Yeah. I need extra muscle on my side."

"This…isn't the time to make a joke about meatheads, right?" Vickie looked around the room.

"It's always time for your jokes," Taylor answered and patted her shoulder. "You will monitor the situation at lunch, won't you?"

"Of course. I won't let you go in on your lonesome. I'm not a monster, but I still don't agree with it. You should probably wait until Niki gets back before you cut any deals with that fucker."

"We're going there to talk, not to have my girlfriend murder the guy on principle. There…might be a time and a place for that, but it won't be here and now."

"Whatever."

Bobby emerged from the break room and looked surprisingly presentable despite having spent only a couple of minutes cleaning himself up.

"Are you ready to go?" he asked.

He nodded. "Better now than after these two chew me out."

"Don't you worry. There will be plenty of chewing out on the way over."

Tanya grinned as Bobby sidled closer to her for a kiss. "I have taught you well, my young apprentice."

Taylor shook his head, joined his friend in his truck, and sucked in a deep breath of relief as the air conditioner came on to stave off the heat of the Nevada sun.

"So, about that chewing out…"

He rolled his eyes. "You know it was the right move to make as well as I do. Keeping Marino at arm's length does mean occasionally meeting the guy for a chat about how I'll physically dismantle any fucker who tries to interfere with my business."

"Right, but it's still a shit serving." The mechanic nodded. "Okay, consider yourself chewed out."

"Will do."

"Moving right along, I wondered if I could get a little insight from you on filling in the roles you and Vickie will be vacating. Not that I think anyone could take Vickie's place, and I know that if I need her help, she's only a phone call away and stuff."

Taylor turned to look at the man as he drove through the streets of Vegas. "But I guess there's nothing quite like having extra hands on deck to work on the suits with you."

"Right. Plus, you and Vickie will have to take Liz to DC to collect Niki and all the rest of the material that she was working with, so it's not like you guys will be around if there's an emergency or some shit."

"Okay." He leaned back in his seat and enjoyed the cool air coming from the vents. "So did you have anyone in mind already, or do you need my help with…like, connections and shit?"

"No, I know some people. One of the guys at the garage where I used to work is looking for something. They're renewing the show that's based on that business for another season, but he managed to get out of his contract. I guess he was as tired as I was of having a camera shoved in his face while he worked. I know the guy and he's solid, so I offered him a job. I'm waiting to hear from him. I also heard from one of the people our Heavy Metal friends worked with. A couple of guys are looking to come back to the states and want to settle somewhere…arid."

Taylor smirked. "I guess they had the same idea I had. What exactly aren't you sure about with these guys?"

"Well, you chose a very solid team on your own and I thought you might have some insight."

"It's not like I went around hunting for CVs or anything," he explained. "I found you, remember, but Vickie and Elisa basically landed in my lap, and Tanya came looking for me. So…yeah, if you trust these people to pull their weight and not be a problem, that's all you need. It's a gut feeling and one that can go wrong from time to time."

"Oh. I thought there was some kind of…NCO second-sight that allowed you to see into the minds of people and help them achieve their full potential or some shit like that."

He couldn't help another smirk. "You're giving me way too much credit here. Besides, if you want to talk about digging through dirt and finding diamonds in the rough, you might want to talk to Niki. She's the one who had to dig through resumes to find the people who currently run their own operations to kill cryptids for the FBI and the DOD now."

Bobby tapped lightly at the steering wheel as they pulled up to a red light. "Huh. I guess that makes sense. I'll have a word with her when she gets back. That reminds me —I know you guys are already more or less on the payroll of Jansen's taskforce now, but does that mean you will hunt cryptids or humans? Because from what I heard on your first job for them, you did both."

Taylor thought about it for a few seconds and shrugged. "Honestly, I hadn't thought about it much. I doubt the DOD will want us on jobs that aren't at least related to the cryptids but in the end, if we need to gun some dumbass down, we'll do it and be happy to get paid for our trouble. I guess I should have considered that before."

"But you don't have much of a problem killing humans, right?"

"Not really. But it's very different than killing cryptids."

"Oh, definitely." Bobby pushed the stick into gear as the light turned green again. "I'm merely wondering if you guys will be rivals to Academi and challenge them on jobs and shit like that."

"Who's Academi?"

"Oh, you remember the Blackwater Security guys, right? Academi is the name they took when they started rebranding in the early 2010s. It had something to do with their guys killing civilians in Iraq, I think."

"Oh, right. Those guys. No, I don't think we'll deal with those bastards, much less steal work from them. I'm not building an army of mercenaries here. We'll be a small group of very talented, highly specialized operatives who get the job done without any hassle before or during. We want to carve a niche for ourselves and won't be a threat to the rest of the folks in the business because…well, we won't."

"If there's anything we've learned over our time together, it's that trouble has a tendency to find you even if you don't look for it."

Taylor sighed. "Yeah, I guess that's fair. But you have to realize that we won't take work from every Tom, Dick, and Countries-R-Us. We'll be very focused on what's happening in or surrounding the Zoo and the stuff that comes out of it. Like…like that company we dealt with in New Orleans. You know, the one that was screwing up delivery systems for the goop products that allowed some of the more dangerous companies to get more without oversight, plus siccing mercenaries to steal our products? So yeah, sure, there were no actual cryptids involved there, but if they pull crap like that, you can bet I'll go after them with a metric shit-ton of pain."

Bobby chuckled. "I won't complain about that, especially if they tried to steal our stuff. But wait—does that mean that I will pay you for your work for Mech Advantage through your company or as an employee of mine?"

"It's probably best to keep both companies as separate as possible, so yeah, any payment I earn working for you will be paid directly to McFadden and Banks. And we'll invoice you too."

They pulled off the road and into a parking lot and Bobby looked like he was gearing up for some kind of protest.

"You'd better give me decent rates in that case." He stopped Taylor before the redhead could get a word in edgewise. "And you can't have Desk negotiating for you."

"Now, see, about her—"

"She's not a 'her.' She's not even a 'she.' She's an artificial intelligence that for some reason known only to whatever god might be out there likes to stalk you. If you put her on the job, you can be sure she'll fuck Mech Advantage over at every opportunity."

"Sure, but you do remember that I still have a partial ownership of Mech Advantage, right?"

Bobby opened his mouth to speak, shut it again, and nodded. "Okay, that's a good point."

"Exactly. How is an AI going to fuck either side over if it's invested in the well-being of both sides?"

CHAPTER FOUR

She thought she would never have to go through the security check at the Pentagon ever again. Honestly, she was supposed to be done with this bullshit once and for all. Moving to Vegas, working with Taylor and Vickie, getting herself into a position to help people and still make enough money to live comfortably on.

But no, there she was again and this time, she was searched more thoroughly than she had been when she'd visited the White House. It was almost fifteen minutes before the young sergeant—who looked apologetic throughout the entire process—motioned her through and insisted that she would have an escort to her destination.

It was ridiculous because she had been to that particular office multiple times in the past. But she no longer officially worked there so he was required to send someone with her and she would be watched the whole way to make sure she didn't deviate from where she was supposed to go. The folks working security for the DOD were nothing if not paranoid.

Niki increased her pace. She didn't want to be in the hallowed halls of the Pentagon any longer than she needed to be. Besides the fact that the whole place gave her the creeps, she also had places to be and people to see afterward.

The door was closed and she knew better than to barge in. There was no telling if the man would have guests who were discussing classified information she would be locked up for hearing. It was always best to be polite. She rapped at the wooden door three times and waited for someone to answer. To occupy herself, she drew her dark hair up and tied it in a loose ponytail and checked a nearby mirrored surface to make sure her makeup was in order. Nothing too flashy, but certain standards were required of women in places of business. Her tan skin didn't require much more than a little blush, and her grey pantsuit fit with what everyone else wore around there.

When they weren't in uniform, of course.

The door opened a few seconds later. A young man in full military attire that designated him as a Marine captain stood there and looked a little confused by her presence, although he showed no inclination to question it. He stepped deftly around her and made his way down the hall at a brisk pace.

"Miss Banks?" said a thick, thundering voice from inside. "Come on in. I was just wrapping something up here."

Niki stepped inside. "Open or closed?"

"Closed, please."

The man who waited for her, seated on the other side of an expansive mahogany desk, didn't look quite as intimidating as the younger Marine who had exited. His pale skin spoke of too many hours spent in dark offices. Thick glasses over eyes with a hint of dark rings about them completed the impression, and despite the rotund look to him as his stomach bulged over his belt and pushed at the buttons on his dress shirt, it was the eyes that chilled her spine. They were eyes that had seen much and would inevitably see far more as the years passed.

"Mr. Speare, it's nice to see you again," Niki stated and extended her hand.

He stood to take it, shook firmly, and motioned her toward one of the chairs across the desk from him. "Please, take a seat. I don't want to take up too much of your time. In fact, I would have preferred that this meeting not be necessary at all, but since your status with the DOD has changed... Well, certain I's need to be dotted and certain T's need be crossed."

"I understand. I've worked with the bureaucracy of the United States government for most of my adult life."

"As have I, and believe me, it does not get better with time. But enough disparaging the system that keeps the both of us employed—albeit indirectly in your case—and let's get back to the matter at hand."

"Right. I thought most of the requirements for my termination with you were finished already."

"Well, yes, they are except for one or two final release documents. But given that Jansen and Maxwell, your former assistants in the task force, will head a new one up themselves, I thought it was appropriate to get the paper-work out of the way. As we both know, they will work on intelligence-gathering for the most part and reach out to contractors to do most of the fieldwork necessary. They have stated that they will contract yourself and Taylor McFadden as consultant field operatives when necessary.

"Of course, you have already conducted an operation with them, but it was something of an emergency situation and we now need to ensure that everything is in place. The first contract they used for you was with...McFadden and Banks Consultants for Hire. Which...I guess is a step up from the original name you all had in mind. McFadden's Mercs is unequivocally terrible."

"How did you know about that?"

Speare shrugged and rocked back in his seat. "You'll have to be happy with me telling you it's my job to know such things and leave it at that."

She frowned and took a deep breath before responding. "Okay. So what exactly do you need from me?"

"Well, the paperwork needs to be signed by you but that's not what this meeting is about. More importantly, I need to know how to reach you if and when the need arises. Now, I know we can get you to the Nellis Air Force base in case of emergency..." His voice trailed off when he realized she was grimacing. "What?"

"Well, we might not always be at the beck and call of the DOD," Niki pointed out and leaned back in her seat. "For one thing, Taylor is coming here to DC and we might be here a while."

Speare nodded and chuckled after a few seconds. "Well, I have to say I'm not one hundred percent on board with someone with McFadden's magnetic attraction to trouble moving into the DC area, no matter for how long."

"It's less of a magnetic attraction and more like gravity."

"True, and the more pull someone has toward certain types of situations, the more I need to be aware of that person. Someone like McFadden either finds trouble or has trouble find him at an alarming rate. It's like he's attracted to it."

Niki narrowed her eyes. "What are you saying exactly?"

"Well, the fact is you are more or less the textbook definition of trouble, which I suppose explains why he's attracted to you and you to him for the same reason. The two of you will be a nexus of pandemonium until one or both of you ends up dead."

She thought about the statement for a few seconds and nodded. "So what kind of odds are we getting?"

That brought a smile to Speare's face. "That's what I always liked about you, Banks. You see the answers before anyone else and cut to the quick."

"So? What are the odds?"

"Well, there are many options in this business. You'll work internationally, so there's always the possibility of causing an international incident that will force us to cut ties with you. You might end up finding something that someone doesn't want you to find and be given the option to retire on an island with beaches, loose banking laws, and no extradition treaty. Or both of you will decide to simply hang it up after a few successful missions. It's not like you need to work for a living anymore."

"But the big money is on..."

"On the two of you dead and buried in a shallow ditch in some banana republic. That or the two of you end up killing each other."

"So that's where the money is. But what do you think? I've never known you to swim with the rest of the school."

"No indeed. Honestly, my money is on the two of you ending up in a fight you can't win. You'll both find yourself a hill to die on, and you will put up a fight that will be told about in stories around the various intelligence agencies involved for decades to come. I doubt you'll go out with a whimper or at each other's hands. Either one of you will find a job that's a little too dangerous or a little too much action, and that will be the end of it."

"Is that what you honestly think?"

"I'll never be one to say I can look into the future or anything."

"Save the political speak for the people whose feelings can get hurt."

"I'm serious. I've been around too long to think that odds mean anything in the real world. Hell, I made a fucking mint betting on my Giants to beat the Patriots— twice—even though the odds were against them."

"I'll assume that had more to do with hoping than actual studying the data." Niki paused to look at her hands and wrung them gently. "Is that what you hope will happen to us? That we'll go in a flash and end up as a legend that will forever be associated with your name?"

Speare's near-constant mild expression soured some- what as he looked at his desk. "Hope isn't exactly the right word. What I truly hope is that the two of you do your duty, help save the world a couple of times, and retire on a ranch somewhere without having to worry about alien monsters showing up to give you any trouble, but that's not the world we live in. Agents and operatives go down to the dumbest luck and for the most impossible reasons, and all I can hope for in their cases is that they do so doing something they'll be proud of and that they'll be remembered for. It's not always the kind of shit that will make the news and see them with plaques and monuments and streets named after them, but the people who matter will remember."

"Well, I'll have you know that I plan to die in bed, my hair gone white, and after a nice pot roast on a quiet Sunday afternoon. Hopefully with my family and maybe Taylor at my bedside so I can get the last word in on the dozens of arguments we've all had over the years."

"Now who's working on hope?"

Niki shrugged. "That's the plan. Things don't always go according to it, but that's what I'll always be fighting for."

He thought about it for a few long moments before his sour expression turned into an equally uncharacteristic smile. "Huh. I like that. I might use it myself."

"It's not like I have a trademark or anything. Should we work on those papers I need to sign?"

Speare took a deep breath, and his moment of introspection passed almost as suddenly as it had come on. He nodded and pushed a couple of files across the table to her. "Initial the pages and sign where indicated. Nothing too dramatic, but you'll probably want to read through everything before you put your name on it."

He was right, even if most of the papers contained legal language that she wasn't sure she fully understood. She had worked for the FBI for years and was able to pick up on the gist of it, though. Most of the documents made sure she couldn't sue anyone, that she turned in all the equipment she had used, and that there was no legal liability anywhere between the two parties before they parted ways.

It seemed like a whole pile of nonsense, but people needed to cover their asses for all kinds of inane reasons. That wasn't anything new.

There was also talk about a modest severance package that would be deposited into her account, but she cared less about that. It was a weird feeling, not having to worry about money, and one she hoped she would never get too used to.

When she finished, Speare was already on his feet.

"A pleasure as always, Miss Banks. We'll be in touch about work for you in the future."

"I look forward to it."

She didn't want to sound like she was being sarcastic, but it was something to keep in mind. They would work together in the future, and all that had changed was the remuneration and responsibility.

"As much as I enjoy your company, I do have another appointment waiting outside."

"Of course." Niki gathered her copies of the documents she had signed and made her way to the door, where a young aide was waiting. She didn't want to ask how Speare had known someone was there and simply motioned for them to go in as she started walking toward the exit.

It had been an interesting conversation, and she found that most conversations with the man were.

If nothing else, it had given her a hell of a lot to think about on the drive to her hotel.

CHAPTER FIVE

The building itself wasn't quite as lavish as most of the others that were known to populate Vegas, but there needed to be a couple of regular office buildings interspaced with all the gaudy casinos, hotels, and resorts.

Bobby looked like he knew his way around already and guided him away from the elevator at the center of the building and toward the stairs that would take them to the second floor. Taylor didn't question the choice to not use the elevator, and they stepped into a small reception area onto which a handful of businesses opened.

The mechanic moved immediately to the front desk, where a smiling receptionist greeted him.

"Good morning, how can I help you?"

"We have an appointment with Brent Barlow, at BD and Associates? My name is Robert Zhang."

"Mr. Zhang, a moment please."

She turned away and dialed on her phone, spoke to someone, and hung up quickly.

"Mr. Zhang, if you and your guest would like to sit? Someone will be with you momentarily."

"Thanks."

Taylor looked around while they waited but didn't bother to take a seat. It certainly was nicer than the exterior suggested, and most of the businesses seemed to deal with various accounting needs, although on a smaller scale than maybe what the larger casinos and hotels would need.

"How did you find this place?" he asked.

Bobby shrugged. "Tanya found it. She said she'd needed to do some business here when she first moved to Vegas. When I mentioned needing a CPA, she said she knew a guy and a couple of days later, we're here."

"Fun times."

The door under a plaque reading *BD & Associates* opened and a young man stepped out. He looked a little rushed like he was a new employee at the firm and was there to make a name for himself. That probably meant most of his early days at the firm would consist of running errands and helping out anywhere he was needed while he learned the ropes.

"Mr. Zhang?" the assistant asked and shook the two men's hands. "If you'll please follow me, Mr. Barlow is waiting for you."

They followed him for a few steps into the office and down a hallway of offices to the end and the corner office. This was usually reserved for partners in a firm, and Taylor made a mental note of that as the assistant knocked on the door and waited for an answer from inside, which came immediately. He pushed it open and gestured for the two visitors to go inside.

Brent Barlow was a stout man with graying hair, dressed in a suit and tie that, while not overly expensive, were still respectable. As was the watch he wore, as well as the shoes, which told of a man who put enough stock into his appearance to look professional but had no need to be flashy beyond that.

"Mr. Zhang, a pleasure to see you again." He circled his desk to shake Bobby's hand.

"Brent, good to see you again. Sorry we're a little late, but we had another engagement that ran a little long."

"It's not a problem. You're barely five minutes late. I only start drawing the line at fifteen minutes. People expect that type of precision from CPAs."

The two men shared a laugh, and Bobby finally turned to Taylor. "Right. Brent, this is my friend and partner Taylor McFadden. Taylor, this is Brent Barlow, CPA."

Taylor smiled and shook the man's hand firmly. "You come highly recommended by people I trust. It's nice to meet you, Mr. Barlow."

"Brent, please. As if I need a 'Mister' added to the front of my name to make me feel any older."

They followed the man to his desk, taking in the view that was visible through the massive windows that overlooked the Strip.

"That's a hell of a view," Taylor commented.

"Best seats in the house, and you can take my word for it when I say I put considerable work into it." Brent motioned for them to take a seat across the desk from him, where it looked like all the paperwork on McFadden's Mechs was laid out for them to look at. "Well, I've looked through the financial reports filed by McFadden's Mechs—"

"It's Mechs Advantage now," he corrected the man.

"We thought it sounded better," Bobby added.

The man nodded. "Well, yes, I thought the alliterative title was a little…terrible."

"A lot terrible," Taylor agreed.

"Well, yes," the CPA muttered as he studied the papers. "I'm honestly quite impressed. The work you put into filing these is the kind that people would usually hire someone like me to do, and you did it rather well. I marked off a few inconsistencies, but that's only regarding what you could make in deductions. The IRS won't mind that, of course, but it might save you money come the time to file them again for the next fiscal year."

Brent turned his attention to a TV screen on the wall next to his desk, which immediately displayed the same papers they would be working with.

"What we'll do here is examine a basic Profits and Losses sheet on the business," he explained and moved through the various invoices Taylor had added to his tax filings. "A thorough look through the financial statement reveals that Mechs Advantage made a little over eighteen million dollars over the past fiscal year. That is the gross earnings of the company through sales and services, that kind of thing. Of course, it goes through the usual grinder of costs incurred, which include salaries, purchasing of goods necessary for the functioning of the company, and all that. Overall, however, the profit margin will be hard to beat and your net earnings after twelve months are well over thirteen and a half million dollars. I've been in the business for a while, and I don't think I've ever seen a first year go that well for a start-up."

"We had a niche," Taylor admitted. "That and we had a couple of profitable government contracts with the FBI and the DOD, which contributed to a large portion of the earnings."

There wouldn't be any mention of the millions that were still being laundered through the Zoo after their little casino heist. Brent seemed like the kind of stand-up guy who would report any illegalities he found in their paperwork.

"Well, assuming the government contracts continue, I don't see why the profits shouldn't as well." The CPA smiled and flipped through a handful of other invoices. "The only other question I had regarding your spending habits is regarding security. I can see here that a great deal has been spent on improving the security system of the building you bought to house the business, and while I commend you on it being incredibly thorough, I am not sure that a... Well, even a company that deals with such expensive equipment would probably not need security systems that Fort Knox would call overkill."

"Well, we had security issues over the year," Taylor explained although once again, he felt it wasn't entirely necessary to give the man all the details regarding Marino and his goons. "I may have gone a little overboard in making sure we didn't have any of those problems ever again."

"Yes...well, they did cut deeply into the profits, more so than anything else other than supplies, but now that every-thing is set up..."

The two visitors exchanged a look.

"Yeah, that spending should be reduced this coming fiscal year, if not removed entirely," Taylor commented.

Bobby smirked. "Yeah, with him heading out, I suspect all the problems he brought with him will leave as well and give us some time to work on proper business and shit."

Taylor couldn't help a soft chuckle and even Brent smiled politely before he turned his attention to the screen.

"If you don't mind me asking, what did you do so often for the FBI and the DOD?" the other man asked as he scanned the dozens of invoices.

"Consulting, for the most part," he replied honestly. "Given my background in the Zoo, there were security issues I was asked to look into for them. They liked the work I did for them and kept calling. When my handler was moved into the DOD, she decided to bring me in with her."

"So do you think that, with you leaving, these consulting jobs might...shall we say, dry up?"

He shook his head. "Not particularly. Bobby here is as much an expert as I am, although his expertise is a little more useful overall. No one knows armor suits like he does, and in the end, he was practically running the shop already with me off doing so much consulting work."

Brent nodded. "And I understand you didn't cut a salary for yourself for this year?"

Taylor nodded. "I had other means to sustain myself, so most of the money I got went directly into McFadden's Mechs. With the buyout, that investment will be more than profitable for us both, and I think Bobby will agree."

The mechanic nodded. "I do. We're both coming out ahead in this."

The CPA smiled. "Well, as long as everyone's happy and the money keeps coming in like it did last year, I think you two will be titans of the industry before too long."

"Eh, I wouldn't go that far," Taylor commented. "We're good at our job and it's paid off, so...we'll leave it at that. There's no need to get too big for our proverbial britches."

They all stood and exchanged handshakes.

"I'll be in touch once everything has been put together," Brent assured them. "Is there anything I can get for you before you leave? Something to drink, a snack, maybe some coffee?"

"I'm good," Taylor asserted and Bobby nodded in agreement, although he needed a couple more seconds to arrive at the same conclusion. "It was fantastic to meet you, Brent."

"Likewise. Andrew will show you out."

The young assistant—Andrew, they assumed—was waiting for them outside the door before they had opened it.

"Can I get you anything before you leave?" he asked as he guided them back the way they had come. "Some coffee maybe?"

"I'm good," Taylor repeated and gave Bobby the time to agree that neither of them needed coffee or anything else before they reached the reception area.

"What do you think it would have taken for us to end up working in a place like this instead of out in the Zoo?" he asked as they strode past the front desk and toward the stairs again.

"How do you mean?" The mechanic looked around as if that would answer his question.

"I mean, like…there's always the possibility that we would have ended up as accountants, insurance adjusters, or something like that, but we risked our lives in the middle of an alien jungle instead. What kind of changes would our lives have had to go through for that kind of thing to happen?"

Bobby shrugged. "Well, for one thing, you left home. I guess if you hadn't, you probably wouldn't have joined the army. You would have gone to college and got your degree the conventional way and ended up working in an office. Assuming, of course, that you didn't pick up a career in sports or something like that."

"I was essentially a beanpole with clothes on when I left," Taylor admitted as they reached the ground floor and moved to the doors. "It took me some time in the military to put this much meat on."

"Eh, you could have gotten there in college if you wanted to. As for me…well, I've always liked working with machines, so I doubt I would have ended up in an office. My parents didn't like it and wanted me to go to med school, but I never had a mind for that kind of work. I probably would have been miserable and found a way to complete a residency somewhere and get my own practice which I would eventually sell so I could work on something I care about. Of course, I would be in my forties or fifties by that time."

"Huh." He grunted as they reached the car. "It's interesting. Our lives could have ended up much simpler if we had taken a few extra turns in them."

"Yeah, but I get the feeling you wouldn't have been happy with the simple life. Or, at least, not in most things."

He narrowed his eyes as he stepped into the pickup. "What do you mean by that?"

Bobby didn't answer until he was already inside and buckling up. "You honestly don't see it?"

"See what?"

The mechanic started the car with a smirk. "Wow, I don't think I've ever seen it this bad."

"Seen what, damn it?"

"Tunnel vision. In your case, for Niki. I never thought I'd see it in you. The two receptionists in there were checking you out blatantly and you didn't even notice. That's cause for celebration, I think."

"It's a good thing, right?" Taylor buckled himself in and watched his friend out of the corner of his eye.

"Sure. It means you have no eyes for anyone but her. You're simplifying your world, although...yeah, in Niki's case, simple might be subjective."

He frowned at his friend. "Wait, wait. Hold on. Why does my past opinion on adult relationships—which I maintain was a very adult decision for both me and them—make everyone believe I'm not capable of being monogamous when my girlfriend's not around?"

"Because women like you, and you like them in return. I've always imagined that you've seen them as candy walking around on two legs or something and you have one hell of a sweet tooth."

Taylor scowled. "Come on, man. They're not candy, they're human fucking beings."

"I know, and my point was—"

"That you guys thought that was how I saw women." He shook his head. "In the end, Niki and I both talked about it and shared in the decision. I respected her boundaries and I've always worked to deliver more than I got in exchange."

Bobby gave him a skeptical look. "You make it sound like a sales pitch."

"Isn't all dating a sales pitch?" He shrugged. "You're with Tanya now. Are you saying there wasn't a conversation about what both of you wanted out of it?"

The mechanic was silent and stared out of the windscreen for a few long seconds. "Well…kind of. It wasn't a calculated decision, as such, or that little game of cat and mouse you and Niki played all year long. Tanya was more the… I'm trying to think of a better word than 'aggressor.'"

"Initiator?"

"That works. It essentially took her sticking her tongue down my throat before I realized she was interested. I thought we would go out for drinks as…like, friends."

"Seriously? Even I could tell she had the hots for you. And I'm very sure Vickie was the one who told her to make a move."

"No shit?"

Taylor raised a hand. "Don't quote me on that. But in the end, you need to work on your self-image. I saw that in you before the two of you started going out and I'm glad she's helping you to build confidence. She's been through a lot, you know, with the divorce and not seeing her kid. She has the brains, though."

Bobby chuckled. "Agreed. And you know she thinks the world of you too, right? But she probably won't ever admit it. And I think she's kind of waiting to see how you fare with Niki, ready to step in to help the two of you before either of you do something that will fuck it up."

"Huh. No pressure, I guess."

"That's what she's like. Anyway, she's always been better than me at seeing all sides of a dispute instead of only being on the one and taking the side of the woman. If it's a tie, though, I expect her to be sister over mister."

He nodded. "Well, I don't expect there to be contention between the two of us, but it's good to know people are out there who are rooting for us to make it."

His friend grinned and stretched to pat him on the shoulder. "Now, changing the subject to the topic at hand. How do you think we will do as far as the new work coming out of the Zoo is concerned? I know we talked a good game about keeping the profits up, but it needs to be without us getting involved in another heist or keeping up with the consulting jobs."

"I think you'll be able to get more work now that most of the focus of Mechs Advantage will be on fixing mech suits. You'll be able to take more work on and get it all done without being distracted by whatever shenanigans I happen to be up to."

"Well…sure, maybe, but we'll have to see how it goes. I'll get together with Brent for the next quarterly financial review and I'll send you what he has to say about it. We'll also have to see about any competing brands that might come in. We already know there's a market here, and there are people out there who want to put us out of business. How long do you think before other companies show up with the same plan and try to take the niche away from us?"

"Well, that's where aggressive marketing comes in. None of them will have Bobby Zhang at the helm." Taylor pulled his phone out of his pocket. "Folks already know what you're capable of, and at reduced prices. It won't be easy, we both know that, but at the same time, we all know you can put a suit together better than anyone alive, honestly."

Bobby grinned. "I appreciate that. Who are you calling?"

"Marino," he asserted. "He sent me the location of our lunch and I need to tell him we'll be there in about thirty minutes."

The mechanic scowled and grasped the steering wheel a little tighter. "Damn. I almost forgot about that."

"Yeah, me too," he answered and put the phone to his ear. "Let's get this over with, like ripping a Band-Aid off."

CHAPTER SIX

When they arrived, two burly men in suits, sunglasses, and earpieces waited for them outside the restaurant. The venue was pleasant, a little Italian place near the strip but far enough away to make it seem separate.

A small artificial river ran through the outdoor section that even had a bridge people were allowed to cross and see the koi swimming in the crystal-clear water.

As was usually the case, it looked like Marino had evacuated the location so it was empty except for him and whichever guest he happened to be entertaining at that particular moment. Taylor wanted to ask how often he did that kind of thing or if it was merely a power play to make sure the person or people he was eating with knew who they were dealing with without him needing to say it.

Either way, it was a dick move all around.

The two men stepped in front of Taylor and Bobby before they could enter and talked quietly into their earpieces before they moved back and let them through without any problems.

"And here I thought they would strip search us for weapons or something," the mechanic muttered under his breath as they moved between the empty tables to the corner where Marino was already drinking something. The restaurant was not completely abandoned, as the staff were still in place.

The mob boss, when he saw them, stood and motioned for them to join him.

"Taylor—and you brought a friend. Robert Zhang, yes? I remember you from the fight."

One of the waiters approached and pulled the chairs out for them to sit.

"Might I interest you in a Bellini?" Marino asked as they sat. "As an aperitif before the meal?"

Bobby answered first. "I'm driving, so something without alcohol for me."

Taylor shrugged. "Sure, I'll take some. I'm still nursing a trace of a hangover from last night, so why not try a hair of the dog?"

The man snapped his fingers, which brought another waiter to the table in moments. "I'll need another Bellini for my friend with the red hair and...I think some apple cider for Bobby. Alcohol-free, of course."

"Right away, sir," the man answered and rushed away to fill the order.

Taylor leaned back in his seat and nodded in thanks as the drinks were delivered. "I doubt we'll have time for a full meal here. We have business to attend to this afternoon, so why don't we get to the crux of it?"

Marino smirked. "Right to it then, of course. I thought you would be in a hurry and already ordered Frutti di

Mare pasta for the three of us. It should not take too long to eat and then be on your way."

Sure enough, a second later, another waiter approached with three plates of the seafood pasta dish that had been ordered and placed these around the table.

The two guests both paused, but the mob boss began to eat immediately and gestured for them to do the same.

"Now," Marino said and cleaned his lips with a napkin. "To the crux of it. You have made me considerable money over the past few months, which I have to admit endears me to you a great deal, what with the rescuing of my *puttana* of an ex-wife and then the fight. With that said, of course, the work did elevate you to the eyes of the other heads of the family here in the US, and many of them are not as...interested in your well-being as I am."

"Cut to the chase," Bobby muttered, took a tentative mouthful of the seafood pasta, and raised his eyebrows in surprise.

"Of course. There are those who wish to see harm befall you, and those even within my organization who would be willing to do so if only to make a name for themselves. This is not new, and if you happen to beat the shit out of the wrong guy, that could start a conflict that would be beyond my power to stop. You understand this, yes?"

Taylor tried one of the shrimps and sure enough, it was exquisitely seasoned and he treated himself to a couple of mouthfuls before answering. "Sure. But I imagine you have something in mind to make sure that doesn't happen. Let me guess—you want me to work for you full-time."

Marino smirked. "As much as I would like that, I am afraid it would do more harm than good. To my reputation, anyway. No, what I had in mind was far, far from that. In fact, I think you will like it despite this animosity you feel toward me and mine."

"I'm all fucking ears."

"Yes, well, you are considered an outsider and no one—not even myself—trusts that you will have the family's best interests at heart. Thus, the farther removed you are from my business, the better. In fact, the agreement I was looking for would be to cease all hostilities. My people and I will give up on any grudges that might still be held against you, as long as you can guarantee that you will offer us the same courtesy."

The two friends exchanged a quick look.

"That's more or less what I've wanted all along," Taylor pointed out and took a sip from his drink. "Your people were the ones who dropped in on us and caused us problems. All we did was…well, make sure they knew the consequences of it."

"And rather effectively too," Marino noted. "So, does this appeal to you? A clean slate?"

"Sure," he answered. "As long as your people don't interfere with my business, mine won't interfere with yours. Is there some kind of oath you need us to take?"

"Sadly, no. Your word on a gentleman's agreement will suffice. Of course, should I have work that requires your particular talents, I might send a call to you to see if you are in any way interested."

He shrugged. "I will be expensive. More expensive than I have been in the past. Enough to make even you flinch."

"That would be a feat," the mob boss answered and took another mouthful from his plate.

"And you should know that I have an equal partner in the business with me too who would need to be convinced, and... Let's say she's not as friendly to free-market capitalism as you might hope."

"The former FBI agent?" Marino asked. "The one who was until recently working for the Department of Defense."

"That's the one."

"Yes, she was something of a challenge. I might be more afraid of her than I am of you."

"It's a smart sentiment. You should stick with that," Bobby commented. "We're...all kind of terrified of the former Agent Niki Banks."

"You guys know you're talking about my girlfriend, right?" Taylor asked and looked pointedly at them.

"Sure," the mechanic answered. "There's a difference between the two of you. While you're the kind of suicidal that makes you charge head-first into conflicts, she's the kind of psychotic that will make you charge head-first into conflicts for her."

Both Taylor and Marino paused to turn to stare at him.

The man's face flushed little and he shook his head. "You know what I mean. And I wouldn't have anyone else at my side in a fight. It's better to have her on my side than against me, after all."

The other two men nodded in agreement and turned their attention to their plates until they were empty.

"Well then." The mob boss leaned back in his seat and slid on a pair of sunglasses. "I regret to say it, but I think this might be the last time that we speak in a while, Taylor. This feels like the end of an era."

Taylor nodded. "I think you'll understand when I say

the feeling isn't exactly mutual, but I'm glad that we were able to put an end to hostilities between us."

Marino stood from his seat and wiped his hands on his napkin before he shook Bobby's hand first and then Taylor's.

"Until we meet again," he stated and patted both men on the shoulder. "Now, I'm sure you're interested in getting the fuck out of here, so don't let me keep you. Have a pleasant rest of the afternoon."

There were days on Venus shorter than what this one had turned out to be.

But when things came together and results were there waiting for him, that made it all feel worthwhile.

Dr. Carlos Santana didn't think there would be much waiting for him—at least as far as his official project was concerned. The tests had been frustratingly inconclusive day in and day out, but as he pulled the samples out of the centrifuge for what felt like the hundredth time, he could see they would at least provide a starting point to achieve results. They weren't as dramatic as he'd hoped when he started, but that didn't matter at this point.

In some ways, he was simply marking time. Turing Unlimited had been a disappointment but a few of their competitors had approached him. One, in particular, had made serious overtures, and he had been able to stir their interest in him and his abilities with minor but well-phrased snippets that suggested significant progress. It was a pity that most companies only had their eye on the billions they could make with Zoo-based youth serums.

Still, the company at the top of his list had indicated that they would encourage publication of his findings—unlike his CEO who lived life with a carrot up her nevermind and viewed publication as equal to releasing classified information. He'd be glad to walk away from her, but it would be on his terms. While he chafed under the restrictions and resented having to sneak around, he reminded himself that it would pay dividends in the not too distant future.

His assistant came over to where he took the vials carefully out of their container and put them on a tray. Anita had been a godsend. She was intelligent and caught on quickly, and he'd been able to leave much of the routine— and utterly boring—things in her capable hands. He'd also come to trust her. She was friendly without being familiar, and truly listened when he shared his ideas. He knew that because she asked the right questions.

"Any progress?" she asked as she placed a neat stack of the day's results on the desk beside him. She would already have collated and entered them, and he gave her a grateful smile. Although he didn't feel he owed the company anything, it was still good to know that someone of her caliber might be in line to take his project over—when he left, not if.

"Something a little different," he responded. "I still have countless other tests to run but we might have found at least an avenue worth exploring. It should keep the boss happy for now."

Anita grimaced and they both chuckled. Keller, the

CEO, was not easy to please. "Well, that's good news. Hopefully you'll have a little more to share with your 'friends' too when you next speak to them."

A part of him felt a little uncomfortable that he'd confided his plans and frustrations to her, but she'd given him no cause for concern. If anything, she'd been both understanding and supportive—a friend a loner like him might never hope to find, especially in a lab. He wondered if they could remain friends when he moved on.

"Our serum is still experimental," he said as she tidied the area quickly. "We can't expect to anticipate all the changes that will happen but there seems to be an indication that we can develop something that would have greater efficacy."

Anita nodded. "It's a little frustrating, though. The people providing our budget want us to come up with a miracle elixir, the kind that won't have any negative side effects. But they need to realize that any changes to the goop will merely result in...well, taking away what makes it so special."

"Not if we get it right. And stop calling it that. You know the name." He smiled as he said it, his tone teasing.

She laughed. "The name is thirteen syllables long and includes elements of French, Russian, English, and Latin to keep all the Zoo profiteers happy. I'll simply call it goop, thanks. Although AG is more professional than simply goop, I suppose. I try to use that when the powers-that-be are around. Everyone knows what Alien Goop is."

"Well, I'm still not entirely convinced that we can create a serum to aid emotional recovery," he muttered. "The rejuvenating effects have long since been established but the side effects aren't encouraging when it's ingested. It would be a fine balance between retaining the restorative benefits and minimizing the negative impact."

"Well, if anyone can do it, you can," she said encouragingly. "You've certainly made more progress than I expected, although I don't know whether to congratulate you or offer my condolences."

"Why condolences?"

"Because we both know someone else will take credit for any real discovery you make."

She was right and it was a primary reason why he was looking at greener pastures. His work was his life, and he resented the fact that his every achievement was snatched away from him. If Keller would only permit him to publish his findings—giving the company credit, of course—he'd be less disgruntled.

The CEO, however, remained obdurate and he felt strongly that he was within his rights to move on. She wouldn't like it and would throw all kinds of litigation at him, but that would take years and by then, he'd have established himself in a stronger position. Mention had been made of the head of research as a probable role, and he felt sure he'd have his new company's support if Turing Unlimited turned nasty.

He looked at his watch, then at his assistant. Their regular evening ritual was about to kick in. As always, she would gather her few belongings, tell him to not work too hard or too late, and that she'd see him in the morning, and he'd wave her off.

As she hurried through the last of her tasks, he rifled through the reports and found the one he was eager to see.

This one had nothing to do with his designated project but was merely a side project—although he hoped it would be his key to a very successful and lucrative future. He studied the results quickly, then froze and worked through them calmly a second time.

His hypothesis had been vague and more instinct than solid scientific logic. For this reason, he'd not given it too much of his attention, but Anita had listened and encouraged him to pursue it. Now, however, his heart thudded painfully in his chest and his thoughts warred between disbelief and what might be terror.

Santana glanced at Anita, who smiled, swung her purse over her shoulder, and moved to the door with her usual admonition. This time, however, the routine was disrupted when Keller stepped through the door as the other woman exited. For once, his assistant didn't close it behind her, and he caught a glimpse of her hovering in the hallway. He assumed that she thought he might need her to offer moral support and gestured for her to leave, understanding her reluctance to stay.

The CEO ignored his assistant and strode toward him, followed by two men. She was slim, with piercing gray eyes and short red hair that somehow made her look taller than her three inches over five feet, even with two-inch heels that matched the blue dress she wore.

"Dr. Santana," she stated. "I thought I'd pay a visit to see if you've made some progress."

"Perhaps, Miss Keller," he said cautiously, reluctant to promise what he wasn't entirely sure the preliminary results would deliver once they were explored further.

"Monica, please. It's way too late at night for us to stick to formalities."

One of the men who had followed her in—dressed in gray tweed and a floral bow tie—stepped closer and patted Santana on the shoulder, "Excellent work, Carlos."

"I'm not sure what we're looking at yet." *Or why you should find it necessary to swoop in like this.* The thought brought a nagging sense of alarm but he managed to keep his expression neutral. "But today's tests might have identified a possible avenue to explore to achieve our objective. I'm hopeful that they are a step in the right direction, Francis—I mean, Dr. Fusco."

"Like our CEO said, it's way too late in the day for formalities. I might be head of research around here, but I'm as invested in making everything work as you are."

"Of course. But please keep in mind that these results are merely the beginning. We have to establish that they can be repeated and aren't simply a fluke or the result of contamination. Thereafter, we will need to explore all possibilities to determine how they—"

"Yes, yes," Fusco said sharply. "We are aware of that, Carlos, but there's no harm in allowing ourselves some degree of anticipation, hmm? It's fortunate that we were in the right place at the right time to witness what might well be the beginning of the realization of our hopes."

Something about the man's attitude seemed off, although Santana couldn't put his finger on it. The right place at the right time assurance unsettled him and his instincts suggested that their presence was no coincidence. For the life of him, though, he couldn't think why it would be premeditated or what they hoped to accomplish. He'd been very careful with his communications with the other companies and had only ever discussed his plans with Anita, whom he trusted implicitly.

Even more uneasy than before, he couldn't help but look at the second man who had come in behind Keller and Fusco—someone he'd never met before, a fact that rubbed at his unease and seemed to suggest alarm bells. He was just shy of six feet tall, and his blond hair was cut neatly, about halfway between a stylish cut and a crew cut, which melded easily into the gray suit he wore. Cold blue eyes met his a few seconds after he started to stare.

The man smiled to reveal a clean line of pearly whites in a smile that looked right but sent a chill down the scientist's spine.

"Don't mind our security consultant, Carlos," Keller said and picked the report he'd been studying. "Why don't you help me with this? I don't know what I'm looking at."

Santana turned his back on the unsettling man and tried to maintain an indifferent expression.

"Oh..." he stuttered and peered at the page while he searched for an answer that wouldn't offend her. Hopefully, she would simply interpret his hesitation as him checking the details. "Well...those are results from a...from a parallel project I'm working on that I hope might...well, provide an alternative basis for our serum. I wondered if the DNA in Zoo creatures—which is AG-based—might offer similar benefits with fewer side effects. We know it assimilates DNA from non-Zoo creatures and—"

"Wait," the research director said sharply, and his frown indicated that he had begun to think this through. "Are you saying the creatures themselves might contain something that could be extracted and used as an alternative to AG?"

"That was my original hypothesis, yes," he said quickly. "We have live specimens here in the animal section, so it made sense to explore the possibilities. My thought was that we could perhaps manipulate the DNA and add it to our existing serums to diminish the side effects of the pure AG."

"It sounds logical in theory and I certainly haven't heard of similar research," Fusco said thoughtfully. "Some of the large animals contain sacs of AG, so it might be that all of them have some other sources of the regenerative DNA we could harvest. How far have you progressed?"

"Not very far, but I have only begun my research into this so it's early days. My first tests were to compare the DNA of those mutants that consumed Zoo creatures only with those that consumed earth animals."

"Why would you do that?" The director took the page from Keller, who seemed ready to speak but snapped her mouth shut as if she'd changed her mind. He scanned the information quickly.

"I wanted to see if consuming only already mutated creatures perhaps provided higher concentrations of goop-based DNA."

The director frowned. "The assumption being that ingesting earth animals might dilute that?"

"Not dilute, per se. I had hoped that perhaps we could obtain a purer version."

"Is this good?" Keller demanded impatiently, and Fusco nodded.

"It certainly has potential," he said with a trace of excitement in his tone.

Santana heaved an inward sigh of relief, but the results he'd looked at earlier haunted him. He was surprised that his direct boss hadn't seen what he'd seen.

"So when did you plan to share this…parallel project with us, Carlos?" the CEO asked, her expression pinched and suspicious. "Or are you waiting to publish it in a paper for your peers to review?"

"I…" Santana drew a slow breath, more than a little shaken now and not only by his unexpected company. Still, he reasoned, perhaps her usual paranoia had raised its head as it so often did. He'd been careful and there was no way she would know that he was considering a move to a company that had promised him publication.

"I'm aware of the restrictions on publishing any findings," he told her stiffly. "And I haven't said anything as yet as I was waiting for the first results to come through. There was little point in getting anyone's hopes up if it proved to be a dead-end."

He glanced at Fusco, who now scowled as he studied the report a little more closely. From the expressions that flitted across the man's face, he guessed he was only moments away from reaching the same terror-inducing conclusion he had earlier.

"Oh…" the director muttered and shook his head vehemently. The CEO turned her attention to him with a look of inquiry on her face. "This is not good."

"What is not good?" she demanded.

"This is… Well, it's…" He gestured to Carlos, whose heart sank. This might distract the CEO from her irritation at him not revealing the project and her somewhat pointed snark about publishing his findings. Still, he did not want to be the one to explain that her precious elixir would most likely not make her the billions she anticipated. In fact, the research might never come to fruition.

His direct boss seemed utterly lost for words—a perfectly understandable reaction—and Keller now tapped her foot as a deepener frown twisted her features.

Unfortunately, there seemed to be little he could do to avoid sharing his extrapolations. With all three people in the room focused expectantly on him, he had no choice but to soldier on.

"As I said, I...uh, ran a comparison on the DNA from mutants that consumed other Zoo creatures and those that consumed earth animals."

Keller gestured impatiently. "And? Explain your results, Dr. Santana."

He fidgeted with his hands and his gaze was drawn to the blond, blue-eyed man on the other side of the room again.

"Have you ever watched Independence Day?"

"The original or the sequels?"

"The...the original. You'll remember there was a...a scene, a countdown our protagonists were able to decipher in a signal to show there was a timetable they had to work with."

Keller nodded. "As much as I enjoy the trip down memory lane to the highlights of Will Smith and Jeff Goldblum's acting careers, I'll need you to get to the point."

"Right." He gestured to the report in his boss's hand. "The first round of tests indicated that...well, those creatures that ate only mutated animals..." He paused and drew a deep breath as he tried to still the sudden rapid beat of his heart. "They displayed a reproduction shut-down, as it were."

"No reproduction means," Fusco said by way of additional explanation for Keller's benefit, "that the fauna in the Zoo could be killed off, leaving only the flora alive."

The CEO nodded. "Okay, and that means what? Aside from all the monsters dying?"

Santana shifted his feet. "Well...the general assumption was that this was a directed attack—an alien attack on earth, right?" She snorted scornfully and fixed him with a disbelieving look—one that suggested that a scientist like him shouldn't fall prey to conjecture or conspiracy theories.

The research director came to his aid, his voice grim. "This means there are different steps to what the AG was sent here to do. When the Zoo reaches the point—assuming it cannot be controlled—where it runs out of sources of earth DNA, we would graduate from step one to step two."

She looked at both scientists and gestured impatiently with her hands. "And?"

Fusco rubbed his temples. "It means the AG is a terraforming agent. The reproduction cycle will change when the DNA structure is altered and the planet is ready for habitation."

"When everything—including the Zoo creatures—is extinct," Santana said and completed the thought. "When only the fauna remains..." He trailed off, unable to put the only obvious conclusion into words.

Keller nodded and her scowl deepened. "And can you prove this?"

"No," he answered immediately. "But it's the only logical deduction. The questions that remain is how long that will take and if we can arrest the spread somehow."

CHAPTER SEVEN

Keller sighed and Santana held his breath. She didn't look happy and he could see her thoughts flit across her features, but after a few seconds, her face relaxed and she seemed calm again. She looked intently at Fusco and the other man and an unspoken message seemed to pass between them.

"All right. Santana, gather your belongings. I'll have Smith here help you with everything tonight to get all your data and materials moved to another lab. We can't conduct any more of these tests until we're sure it happens in a safe location."

He narrowed his eyes, a little nonplussed because he'd expected a rampage of some kind. "That almost sounds like I'm being promoted."

The CEO nodded. "In a manner of speaking. You'll be moved to another facility as quickly as possible. Fusco, with me."

"But what about the creatures I'm testing?"

"They are in the containment cages in the animal section, yes?" Fusco asked and Carlos nodded. "And I assume you've noted the ones you've used? Good, then they can remain until…uh, your new lab is sufficiently secured. At which time, they will be moved across."

"Who have you told about this?" Keller demanded. "Have you discussed it with the animal section?

He shook his head. "No. I merely requested access to the specimen types I needed. The only other person—aside from those of us in this room—is Anita, although we haven't discussed the latest results."

She nodded, turned on her heel, and marched out of the room, motioning for the head of research to follow her. The man looked a little shaken and he hurried to catch up to her. They stood in the hallway outside the lab talking in hushed tones—or perhaps arguing might be better, and about him if the various gestures were anything to go by.

"Smith?" Santana asked and looked around. Anita had beaten a hasty retreat when she saw the group enter her place of work, and he couldn't blame her for that. Hopefully, they'd move her in the morning when she arrived in a suddenly empty lab.

Which left only one person in the room with him. It was the blond, blue-eyed character with the perfect smile.

"Come on," the man said and the smile appeared again. "We don't want to be here all night. I don't know about you, Doc, but I have evening plans."

"What does a security consultant do, anyway?" he asked as he began to gather the tablets and laptops he had been working on. Any other lab would have the equipment he had worked with, but the samples in the vials would not be found anywhere else. He wasn't even sure if he could replicate the results yet.

Smith proved surprisingly strong and was able to carry most of the electronics to where an armored car already waited for them. Perhaps Keller's rapid exit had been to facilitate the move, although he questioned that in some part of his mind. It seemed illogical that she would respond so calmly to something that essentially contradicted their current course—the serum was, after all, the long-awaited golden egg. Perhaps she simply wanted to keep this new possible development under wraps until they knew more?

Then again, what had she and Fusco disagreed about? He was sure it concerned him, and he wondered if the man possibly felt threatened by his work. It certainly changed the game for everyone concerned.

Santana found an electric cooler that had been set up for the temperature he needed to keep the liquid in the vials in their current state. Another period in the centrifuge would probably be needed to return them to a more workable state, but that would be a problem for another time.

"Where are we going?" he asked and climbed into the car next to the security consultant, who was already strapped in.

"Temporary storage. It's as secure as a bank vault and far more accessible if you're allowed in." He nodded at the seatbelt. "Put it on. Safety over everything."

"Is that what you're here to do?" He strapped himself in as ordered. "Tell everyone to put their seatbelts on?"

"Sure, if you can imagine that kind of thing at a corporate level."

Santana nodded. He couldn't honestly imagine it but he didn't want the man to keep talking. It wasn't like he was unpleasant to listen to. The deep voice was warm and a little too calming, but like the rest of him, something was unsettling about it. So much so that he didn't want to let his mind dwell on it for too long.

They arrived at the location, where a group of men was already waiting to take everything out of the vehicle.

"Tell them they need to be careful with that cooler," the scientist called as he reached for the handle on the door. "We need—"

Something pricked him in the neck. It felt like a bee sting but it remained in place while something burned under his skin.

"What the fu…fuuu…"

His jaw wouldn't work and his tongue felt like it was going the same way as he sagged against the door. The stinging sensation faded but it was replaced by an unpleasant numbness. He felt cold, and his body simply wouldn't work, even though he could feel hands pull him away from the door and to the other side, then out of the car entirely.

Smith dragged him along the floor.

"Hey, guys. Be careful with the cooler, okay?"

The men nodded, handled it carefully, and took it inside the building.

"You and I are going for a drive," the security consultant whispered, pushed Santana into another car, and strapped him in again. "Safety first, right?"

The scientist couldn't answer. He was held in place by the belt, and so remained upright enough that he realized they were heading to his house. It didn't look like anyone was around to help him, although he wasn't sure what they would help him with. He still wasn't sure what was happening.

The garage door opened and they drove inside. He jerked forward when the car came to a halt. Smith stepped out and once again helped him out of the car.

His car—that was his car. Why was Smith driving his car? Someone must have driven it from the lab to the new facility, but his sluggish mind could think of no reason why they should. Had Keller arranged that as well? It simply made no sense at all.

Once again, he was simply dragged inside and through the house in a way that told him Smith knew his way around it. He didn't ask where the bedroom was and the asshole found it on the first attempt. Santana grunted when he was pushed onto the bed.

"I know what's going through your head," the other man said and took a moment to wipe the sweat off his forehead. "What the hell is happening to me? And the answer is very simple. I'm sure a well-traveled guy like you would know about the blue-ringed octopus? They would have had warnings about it when you traveled to Australia. It's interesting that a tiny little beastie like that can kill a grown man in minutes.

"For you, though, I needed to be a little more creative. People managed to isolate the paralytics in the poison. Well, it's a tetrodotoxin that blocks sodium channels and causes motor paralysis. I'm not sure what the specialists did with it, but it would take you an hour, maybe two to die of respiratory arrest and...well, let's be honest, you won't live that long."

Santana opened his eyes a little wider. It had become harder to breathe now that the asshole mentioned it. Of course, that was probably exacerbated by the slow-dawning realization that Keller had not been as accommodating as he'd wanted to believe.

He tried to focus on the man standing over him. Smith had lost the unsettling smile and somehow, the harder expression was a more natural look for him. He drew a pack of cigarettes from his pocket.

"You know, your boss mentioned that you liked these old clove cigarettes. It seemed like a fitting gesture. How sad that you picked the habit again up. What has it been—almost five years without touching one of these little cancer cylinders? And when the story comes out that you got sloshed after news of your promotion, had a smoke, and fell asleep with one still burning... It'll be, like...fourth page on the local newspapers and might even get a mention on the local TV stations if the blaze gets hot enough."

Santana wanted to shake his head but like his entire body, it refused to cooperate.

"You know, it's a real shame how many smart people smoke. Aren't you guys the ones who tell everyone that shit is bad for you? Well, in that case, I guess you would know better than anyone the kind of damage it does. Still, it's understandable that the stress at work would drive you back to a filthy habit and all that. It won't be too hard to fake.

"You're no doubt asking the eternal why. Well, your bosses have been suspicious of you for a while now. So much so that they gave you an assistant—yes, that pretty little woman has been squealing on you every step of the way."

Anita was a plant? The stab of betrayal was painful and he wondered why he hadn't seen it.

"I bet you had no clue," Smith continued. "She's good, I'll say that. You poured your heart out to her and she took it all in and rushed to the bosses with every detail. Keller was all for removing you but Fusco...well, he's a little more squeamish. When he discovered she'd recruited me and we'd put this plan together, he persuaded her to give you one last chance. He somehow thought he could persuade you to not jump ship with all the company secrets. I guess you blew that, didn't you, with your fancy hypotheses and alien invasion alert?"

The man chuckled and took a lighter from his pocket. He clicked it on and stared at the flame. "As for me... Well, I'm here because your boss wanted the best. Anyone can kill a fucker. Put a bullet in their head and that's it."

Smith sat on the bed. "But the real art is to kill someone without anyone knowing they were killed. Accidents happen all the time, right? But yeah, there's an art to this. What proof do I leave behind? Did you know, for instance, that a financial analyst was killed near here a couple of years ago? She was left alive by the fire but with third-degree burns over eighty percent of her body. It took her ten days to go. She was a tough woman."

The consultant pulled out a bottle of absinthe Santana had been given for Christmas and had been taking drinks of. It was especially potent, almost sixty percent alcohol by volume.

"The problem with that one, aside from leaving her alive, was that they were able to find accelerants on her mattress despite needing to get her drunk. Bring a fire marshal in or an insurance investigator, and suddenly, it looked like murder instead of a tragic accident. It's a rookie move, honestly.

"Of course, they could find the toxin in your system—if there was enough left of your blood to test. Most of it will be evaporated and lost—turned to goo and changed. There wouldn't be enough toxin to be detected. Your absinthe will work as an accelerant that no one will question and then... Well, that's it. That's the end."

Santana acknowledged inconsequentially that the man had a pleasant speaking voice. He could have been an orator of some kind if he wanted to. Maybe reading audiobooks or something.

Smith laughed, poured the absinthe on the scientist's chest and his face, and finally grasped his hand and closed it around the bottle to spill the rest of the liquid over the bed. "Sorry, I don't usually ramble on like this, but it's very difficult to find someone to talk shop with and when you have a captive audience, you need to take advantage."

Unable to voice his growing horror, he could only stare at his killer, who wore gloves. The man lit a cigarette lazily and slid the pack into his pocket. He took a long, slow drag and grimaced before he leaned forward and put it in Santana's mouth, his head tilted in concentration.

"Don't worry, it'll be...relatively painless. Maybe some

burning around the face, but you should already have problems breathing, which should reduce your cognitive ability and your ability to feel pain. And then, if the respiratory arrest doesn't get you, the smoke inhalation will. Either way, it's not the absolute worst way to go. It's not the best either, but what can you do?"

An excellent question. The scientist couldn't think of anything he could do and breathed the delicious smoke from the pale white cylinder in his mouth. He couldn't stop himself. With each inhalation, he could see the hot embers begin to disengage themselves from the cigarette, drop to his lips, and immediately set the absinthe on fire.

It wasn't that hot at first until it spread down his neck, his shoulders, and onto the bed where the liquid had soaked in. That was when the burning brought pain. He wanted to scream but his jaw still wouldn't work.

"And boom goes the dynamite," Smith joked over the sound of crackling flames and the smoky smell of burning. "I'm sorry it had to go this way, Doc. I hope you believe in an afterlife or something. I hear it helps."

And with that, he slipped out of the room. Santana knew where he was going. The obvious way out was through the back door, where there would be no cameras, no neighbors, and no eyes that would see him leaving. He had no doubt cased his home and would have already planned his escape. The fire would inevitably spread to the rest of the house, so any drag marks or DNA would be destroyed by the blaze. No one would suspect murder. Smith was the kind of man who lived by the details and would have left nothing to chance.

Santana looked down to where his hand was burning. Funny, he couldn't feel that. Maybe the guy was right. His eyes began to close as the fire grew brighter. It wasn't the worst way to go.

Not the best, but far from the worst.

CHAPTER EIGHT

The smell of smoke would linger around the neighborhood for weeks, if not more.

Later on in the year, when the temperatures dropped and cooled the whole area, many people would light fires in their fireplaces, which made it smell like smoke anyway, but there was a difference. Burning firewood was different than a whole house burning to the ground.

The calls hadn't started to come in until the blaze had already been going for three or four hours. The neighbors were woken by the flames but by then, there wasn't much the fire department could do other than contain it and keep it from spreading to the neighboring houses and the surrounding thickets.

Being called in to deal with a body that was found inside would always be one hell of a thing. It was even worse when said call came in the early hours of the morning when the fire marshals realized there was a body inside the house. While they all assumed it was an accidental death, they needed a police detective out there to make sure.

Or in this case, two.

Another car pulled up outside the still-smoking building and a younger-looking man with his black hair slicked back climbed out. He nursed a truly massive cup of coffee which only partially helped as he walked to where the other detective stood.

"Evening, Detective Benson," the new arrival muttered and rubbed his already red eyes.

"It's morning," Benson reminded the man. "You look like shit, Trent. Which is probably about three or four steps up from where I'm at, but that's neither here nor there. I don't suppose you brought an extra coffee for your partner?"

Trent looked at the car he had arrived in and shook his head. "Fuck. I'm sorry, I wasn't thinking. I simply grabbed some from the nearest place and started driving."

The other man smirked. "Nah, it's all good. The fire department brought some themselves. It's absolute shit but it gets the job done."

"I'll try not to subject you to that again." Trent took a sip from his cup. "So, what are we looking at?"

"Some researcher—a doctor kind of character—fell asleep after going through half a bottle of absinthe and decided to have a smoke before snoozing. Before you know it, he's the very embodiment of overcooked meat. To hear them say it, they almost didn't realize there was a body in the bed until they took a closer look and realized there were some charred bones mixed in."

"Shit. Wait, so what you're saying is—"

"There's a very high chance we were woken in the middle of the fucking night to deal with an accidental death. Our luck, right?"

"Wait, how do they know who's in there if he was charred to a crisp? Wouldn't that preclude them from getting a quick ID?"

"Sure, but they assumed it was the owner of the house since the guy lived alone and didn't have any friends or social connections outside of his job."

Trent sighed. "I hate the paperwork on accidental deaths. It's, like, who are we helping? Besides those guys who keep advocating to ban all cigarettes?"

"Are those guys still in business?"

"This is Washington DC, super-sleuth. If there's any kind of cause, people will rally behind it in a desperate attempt to get more votes."

Benson tilted his head and nodded after a few seconds. "Okay, fair enough. Still, I'm not a fan of this shit."

"I hear you there. Do they know for sure who our drunk smoker is or do they not have enough to make a positive ID on him?"

"The teeth are still more or less intact, so we might be able to get an ID there. As for everything else, the fire marshal didn't look very hopeful. Still, we might get lucky eventually and find something, so they need to sift through the ashes."

Trent nodded. "You know, I shouldn't feel good about them needing to do more work than us but I do. Is there a word for that? I feel like there should be a word for that."

"There is," his partner replied and scratched the bristle he hadn't had the time to shave off. "Some...German word.

Schadenfreude, I think it is. Taking pleasure in someone else's misfortune."

"Schad…what now?"

"Schadenfreude. Think 'shad' and 'Freud' and make it sound more German."

"Oh, right. I'll make sure to remember that and use it later."

"Yeah, it makes you sound like an intellectual without being an asshole."

He laughed but it died away and the look of amusement on his face suddenly changed to one of sheer dread. Benson turned to see what the younger detective was looking at and narrowed his eyes when a BMW 850i pulled up beyond the tape that had been set up to keep people from getting too close. That didn't apply to the new arrival, it seemed, and as the people disembarked, he could see why.

Or at least some assumptions could be made. Federal agents had a swagger about them that was hard to miss. It was the kind that came with knowing they had jurisdiction in any situation they happened to stumble into.

"What the hell are feds doing here?" Benson asked with a scowl. "There's no reason to assume this was a murder, right? It's merely a dude who got wasted and picked the worst possible time to light a joint."

"Nope," Trent corrected him. "Our researcher was probably involved in some kind of Zoo science experiment. If so, they need to send these dumbasses in to make sure it's not one of the many companies working on that shit trying to get a leg up on the competition."

His partner narrowed his eyes. He'd heard people out

there had become a little too aggressive with their business policies. This had resulted in special federal task forces being set up to investigate and make sure they weren't turning the whole situation into a new and improved Wild West situation, but he hadn't thought they would show interest in something like this and certainly not this quickly.

"How...do you know?" he asked and studied the new arrivals. "Do they have some kind of marking? I don't see any markings."

"No. It's only because I happen to know one of them."

Trent nodded his head toward the woman, who now walked toward them. She was tall and thin and wore a gray and black pantsuit that could have been straight off a catwalk, including the heels.

Her dark hair was cut short in a boyish look that was certainly appealing, and from the way the man instinctively straightened his spine and improved his posture, as well as hurriedly running his fingers through his hair, there was more than merely knowing between the two of them.

It wasn't Benson's business, but he wouldn't say no to listening to prime gossip material when it landed in his lap like that.

"Whatever you do, don't trust her an inch," the other man warned him in a whisper before the woman came into earshot. "Don't worry about throwing any weight around. Answer the questions, be polite, don't stare at her tits, and for God's sake, don't ask her out."

"I'm Special Agent Rosalyn Drake, Homeland Security," she said by way of introduction and displayed her badge.

"Nice to meet you, Special Agent Drake," Benson answered. "I'm Detective Ewan Benson, this is my partner, Detective Nathan Trent. How can we help you?"

"Honestly, we're only here to make sure everything that happened is on the up and up." She tucked her badge into her coat pocket. "Whenever someone in his particular circle takes a dirt nap, we have to come in and make sure there wasn't any funny business."

"A man has died," Trent snapped. "The least you can do is show a little respect."

Both Benson and Drake paused at his protest and she finally nodded.

"Fair enough. I simply meant that you don't have to worry about any jurisdictional pissing contests unless there is foul play involved. No one will intrude unless it's very clear that it needs our involvement."

"Right." Benson cast a glance at his partner, and the agent noticed.

"He told you, didn't he?"

"Nope," he responded quickly. "Well, he implied it and I put the other pieces together. Were the two of you an item? Because if that is the case, we might have to pass this case to someone who…isn't emotionally involved in certain aspects of it."

"I think we can all be adults here," Drake answered and glanced darkly at Trent. "How are the balls, Nate?"

The detective instinctively took a step back. "All healed. If I had known you'd be coming, I would have worn a cup just in case."

"And I would have brought my armored corset. I guess we all make mistakes."

"About that whole...being adults thing?" Benson wondered if he would have to get between the two of them. It wouldn't be pleasant given the implications of their barbs.

"Come on. You have to allow us a couple of shots across the bow," Trent answered, although he still looked like he was ready to protect his genital area at the slightest provocation.

"A couple of shots across the bow," the agent agreed. "Okay, I'll go and have a chat to the fire marshal to get an idea of what we're dealing with and I'll be right back."

The woman turned and headed to where the other two agents had moved, and Benson made his finest attempt to not stare at her ass as she walked away.

"So, the two of you, huh?" he asked and turned to his partner. "I'll go out on a limb here and assume it didn't end well?"

"Sure, that's one way to put it. We were both young and hot-headed three years ago, and we ended the relationship with a fight. She took a cheap shot at the boys, and I retaliated by twisting the shit out of her nipples. Neither of us won that fight, to be honest."

"It makes sense." Benson nodded. "And it also explains why it looked like both your boys jumped into your body when you saw her."

"And she covered her ladies too."

"Okay, so is that why you told me not to stare at her tits?"

Trent shook his head. "She's quite aggressive, and if she saw you staring, she might decide to ask you out."

"I doubt it."

"Don't sell yourself short. Anyway, I might think you're a world-class dickhole but I wouldn't wish a relationship with that witch on my worst enemy."

"Who said anything about a relationship?"

"Please. One night with her and you'd be addicted. That is, right up until she busts your nuts with an uppercut."

Even Benson flinched at the mental image alone. "Okay, fair enough. Let's get this over with."

As it turned out, having connections with people in the Department of Homeland Security did pay off. Getting the doctor's name went a little too smoothly.

Still, it meant they wouldn't be allowed to merely write it off as an accidental death until all the possibilities were discarded, which meant they had to treat it like any other case.

Of course, they were able to get some sleep, but it didn't feel like enough before they needed to head out to an office building within spitting distance of the Capitol.

At least he was able to get his hands on decent coffee beforehand, which allowed him to feel a little more human as he and Trent took the elevator to the top floor, as indicated by the receptionist who told them they were already expected.

"So," Benson said as the elevator climbed slowly. "Are there any other exes I should know or be warned about? Anyone working in the White House or maybe an ex-Mossad assassin?"

Trent rolled his eyes. "You're hilarious and...well, some

of them were crazy but none quite to the level of the Snake."

"The Snake?"

"Drake. I called her the Serpent, but that felt a little... you know, pretentious. Calling her the Snake felt a little more natural and my speed."

"Don't you have a master's in law?"

"So what? I can still think of something as pretentious."

Benson nodded. "Okay, sure."

He didn't feel comfortable discussing his partner's personal life. Trent was a recent addition to the detective squad, pushed up quickly because he had a good work ethic and had put in years of school to get where he was. That aside, it still felt like the guy was from a different generation despite being only five years younger.

Talking about personal shit didn't feel natural unless there was some kind of mockery involved, and mockery was only fun when it wasn't a sore talking point.

They didn't exchange another word until the elevator doors opened again to reveal a recently refurbished but still fairly ancient office space. It explained the world's slowest elevator, of course, but it still had the look of an institution that had been around since a few years before the founding fathers got their collective acts together.

An assistant joined them immediately and gestured for them to follow her into one of the corner offices that had a direct view of the Capitol building. Two people waited for them. One was a studious-looking man with graying black hair, a pair of thick-rimmed glasses, a tweed suit, and a bow tie. Everything about him screamed academic, including the way he wrung his hands and watched the woman to his left from the corner of his eye.

She wore a blue dress so dark it was almost purple and the hem was barely a few inches lower than what would be unprofessional. Her short red hair was done up stylishly and she motioned for them to approach.

"I'm sorry to bother you, ma'am, sir," Benson said and proffered his hand to them. The woman took it immediately and the man did a few seconds later, although his gaze lingered on a bottle of disinfecting gel first. "My name is Detective Ewan Benson and this is my partner, Detective Nathan Trent. We have been looking into the death of your colleague..." He took a moment to confirm the name. "Dr. Carlos Santana?"

The woman nodded. "We were shocked to hear about what happened and are still coming to terms with it. I am the Chief Executive Officer for Turing Unlimited, Monica Keller. This was Dr. Santana's supervisor, our director of research, Dr. Francis Fusco. Do...do you know what happened?"

"Well, the fire marshals are still trying to make heads or tails of the situation, but so far, it looks like Dr. Santana had a little too much to drink, spilled that drink on himself, started smoking, and fell asleep with it still lit. It's...well, it's unfortunate but not entirely unheard of. Honestly, it's quite common for smokers."

"Oh, my God," Keller whispered, sank into a chair, and looked out the window for a few seconds while the two detectives waited in silence.

They had been through this process more times than either of them could count, and both knew a moment of silence to allow the bereaved to come to terms with what happened was needed.

"We...well..." Fusco looked similarly shocked. "Oh, God. He quit almost six years ago. I remember convincing him to give up those clove cigarettes he loved so much. He wouldn't go a day without at least going through a pack but was good about it, though. It surprised me but he quit cold turkey and didn't even use those patches. He was a little grumpier than usual for a few weeks but he was over it quickly. I don't think I've ever seen anyone that determined to move past a bad habit."

Benson nodded. "I'm sorry, but I have to ask. Do you know if anyone might have wanted to do Dr. Santana harm? Any ex-girlfriends, rivals, anything like that?"

Keller narrowed her eyes. "I don't understand. Didn't you say it was accidental?"

Trent nodded. "Well, yes, that's the assumption now, but we'd like to be as thorough as possible. Make sure that all bases are covered, that kind of thing."

She exchanged a look with Fusco and shrugged.

"Well, he's certainly had rivals, but these are all researchers or scientists," the doctor answered. "We aren't violent people. Barbs will be exchanged through papers and speeches, but that's about as far as we'll ever go. Do you honestly think someone did this to him?"

Benson shook his head, took a card from his pocket, and placed it on the table. "Again, we're merely covering all our bases for the moment and aren't making any assumptions about what happened. We'd appreciate it if you could send us a list of those rivals Dr. Santana may have been hostile with, as well as any next of kin we might need to contact."

"Shoot, I hadn't even thought of that." Fusco looked genuinely shocked and shaken, but he nodded finally and took the card from the table. "I can compile a list and I'll let you know if I think of anything else."

Keller nodded. "I'll contact HR to see if they know of any situations I might not have been made aware of. They'll send you the list of his next of kin as well."

Benson nodded. "We appreciate your cooperation. All we want is for this to be finalized as quickly and neatly as possible."

"We want the same," she assured him. "Is there anything we can get you?"

"No, thank you. We don't want to take any more of your time so we'll be on our way."

The two detectives took their leave and strode to the elevator. Trent pressed the button that would take them to the lobby and the silence held until they were about halfway down.

"Do you think they were telling the truth?" Benson asked.

His partner sighed. "I don't know. They looked shocked about it and it seemed genuine too. Of course, they could have put on the performance of a lifetime—which is possible, given what we know about the people who run these companies—but that doesn't mean they're guilty of murder."

"Hell, the chances are they are shocked and sad about how much money they'll lose over Santana's death. It's probably an accident, right? That's the idea we're going with here?"

"It was an accident. There's no other way to explain it and no reason to go any other way," Benson agreed as the doors pulled open slowly.

But despite the conviction in his tone, something contradictory nagged at his subconscious. Maybe it was the fact that Homeland Security was involved. Or perhaps because they were dealing with assholes who wouldn't mind risking a few lives as long as it gave them an edge on their competition. Or maybe it was that he was a contrary son of a bitch and always would be.

"Yeah," Trent affirmed as they headed to where their car was parked. "It was probably an accident. There's no other realistic option."

CHAPTER NINE

Vickie seemed very excited and Taylor wasn't sure why. Not many people shared his dislike of flying in a tight, confined aluminum tube and as far as he knew, everyone preferred to take a plane to the other side of the country.

In her case, she could have enjoyed a pleasant flight in first-class, a drink, a movie, and a nap in a seat more comfortable than most beds. When they landed, she would be out before everyone else without any worry about spending too much time at the airport.

But no, she was excited about going on a long fucking drive across the country. Of course, he needed to have Liz on the road since they would have to transport shit they didn't have a plane for anymore. While they could always send it via truck, he wouldn't entrust his suit to anyone he didn't know. Since everyone else was busy doing their own thing, it was up to Liz.

"Taylor, are you still there?"

Oh, right, he was on the phone. With Niki, no less.

"Yeah, yeah," he answered quickly. "We'll get there on

Thursday, give or take. Vickie and I will alternate the driving duties—or at least alternate watching the AI drive the truck—and pull over for snacks when we need them."

"Okay. I'm only asking because we have potential clients to vet when you get here so I need solid dates. It's not because I want to keep track of you. I'm not obsessive like that."

"Don't worry about it. Besides, if you want to be obsessive, all you have to do is ask Desk to keep you updated and there wouldn't be anything more to say about it. Wait, so these clients...we're not working exclusively with the DOD?"

"We might work with Jansen if they have any work for us, but we won't rely on the DOD exclusively. We don't need the work so we can afford to be selective, but we won't be that selective. We're doing this shit for a reason, after all. Right?"

"Right, right. There's nothing wrong with that. I only thought...no, never mind."

"What?" Niki sounded like she was trying not to laugh. "That we would be joined to the DOD at the hip? I quit my job because of that, so no thanks."

"Fair enough. I look forward to meeting these clients of yours."

"Drive safe."

He knew he didn't need to point out that he wouldn't do much of the driving himself. The automated truck lanes were some of the safest land-transport options in the world and she knew it. Unsafe driving was the exception, not the rule.

"Will do."

She hung up before he could, and Taylor turned to where Vickie was completing the preparations for departure.

"Who was that?" the hacker asked.

"I was letting Niki know about our itinerary. She says she might already have clients set up for us when we get there and wanted to make sure there was a schedule for us to work with once we arrive."

With a nod, she climbed into the shotgun seat as he turned Liz on. "Has she vetted them yet?"

"No, but I doubt Desk would let her get involved with anyone without a thorough check involved. It's probably already in progress."

She nodded again as they pulled out of the shop and started heading out. Liz was difficult to navigate on the tighter streets, but it became much easier once they left the confines of the city.

"I've planned our stops for the trip," she announced, looked up from her computer, and answered the question she assumed Taylor deliberately didn't ask. "It'll be at least thirty-five hours driving and probably up to forty, so we should have planned stops here or there. Leg-stretching and snack stops all along the way. Besides, we are carrying a couple of hundred thousand dollars' worth of equipment, which is so unique that it would take Bungees more than two or three months to replace, so we'll have to be careful."

"Why don't we simply spend the night in the truck? That way, we don't have to worry about security since we'll take care of it."

Vickie turned to look at him. "Why should we? That might do in a pinch and the occasional nap for when we need to stay on the go without stopping, but we're beyond that now. We're in no rush, and there's no need to push ourselves to work hard and subject ourselves to a brutal schedule."

His head tilted in thought, he finally decided he agreed with her. "Which begs the question, of course, of why you chose to come on this trip in the first place. Taking a first-class flight is well within your means now. I need to get Liz there and I'm more comfortable on the road, but that doesn't explain why you didn't simply go with the easier and more comfortable option."

The hacker narrowed her eyes at him. "Come on. Do you think I'd ever pass up on the opportunity for a road trip with my Tay-Tay?"

"I'm fairly sure I'm Niki's Tay-Tay."

"Ugh, not in the same way, you pile of bricks. If you need a way to make the distinction, you can think of yourself as my Tay-Tay and her Taylor...or whatever cutesy nickname she has for you."

Taylor smirked. "Thanks to you, I think everyone calls me Tay-Tay. Besides, your cousin isn't one for cutesy nicknames."

"Her Taylor then. Whatever, I don't want to know anything about your personal lives." She held a finger up to stop him from speaking. "About that part of your personal lives, that is. It's not like you can hide anything from me, but the fact is I intentionally avoid that kind of shit, understood?"

He nodded. "Okay, understood. And I don't need to be reminded about how you're Big Brother's big sister, so if we're moving right along—"

His phone rang and the sentence remained incomplete. He had connected it to Liz's Bluetooth, which meant he would have to disconnect and take the call on his device if he didn't want it to go through the speakers.

That didn't appear to be necessary as the screen told him the number was blocked.

"Morning, Desk. What have you been up to?"

"Good morning Taylor, Vickie. I hope you are well."

She grunted. "It sounds like Jennie's worked on giving you some conversation upgrades. Remind me to have a talk with her about that."

"Noted and registered. And to answer Taylor's original question, I have performed background checks on the contact Niki wants you to meet and a few alarming issues have arisen."

"Alarming issues?" The hacker pulled her laptop up and connected it to Liz's Wi-Fi. Taylor could see her making a handful of other connections as well before she seemed ready to proceed. She had explained the process of not letting anyone track her actions online. He had followed her talk of VPNs, but when she started talking about randomizing her connection, he immediately knew he was out of his depth. The girl was good at her job and that was all he needed to know.

"Yes," The AI answered. "Irregularities that raised red flags on my network. If you'll connect to my servers, I'll be able to show you what I mean."

It could not have been more obvious that Desk was talking to Vickie there, and he zoned their conversation out quickly. If she found something she thought he should know, she would draw his attention and make sure he knew about it before letting Niki have a meeting with the characters.

As it turned out, the research seemed to take its sweet time, and Taylor was essentially alone on the road trip once more as the two continued to dig into the red flags they had discovered. Enough time passed that he could see Liz's tank starting to run low. He wouldn't let her run on fumes ever as long as he could help it, so with the tank a third full, it was time to refill.

That and they needed to restock their supplies and snacks. He pulled them off the interstate and down one of the side roads that led him into a nearby gas station.

"I'll fill her up again," he announced. "And pick up some snacks. Do you need anything?"

Vickie didn't answer and he doubted she even heard him. It was common enough that he had long since stopped taking the phenomenon personally. She was a gal of focus and sheer will and sometimes, it meant she was too busy with one thing to keep her eyes on anything else happening around her.

It was a part of who she was, and he wouldn't give her any problems over it.

All he could do was support her while she supported him. He climbed out of the truck and put the pump in quickly to refill the tank. It took a little while for it to reach the brim. His companion stepped out of the truck after five minutes, still listening to what Desk had to say through an earpiece he couldn't remember her connecting to his phone.

She still seemed a little too engrossed in her work for him to engage, and Taylor turned and entered the shop to pay for the gas and pick up the snacks they would need for the rest of the trip.

Well, need was a little strong. Want felt more appropriate. He made a selection from the sweets and savories on display, as well as a few that were sour rather than anything else, along with the necessary selection of drinks. Unless they stopped for lunch, this would keep them going for most of the day.

The young man behind the counter raised an eyebrow as he approached with the bill for the gas as well as the stack of foods and drinks.

"Road trip?" he asked, scanned the purchases with quick and bored precision, and bagged them deftly.

"You know it."

"Where are you guys traveling to?"

"DC."

"No shit? Wouldn't it be quicker to, uh…fly there?"

"I'm not big on airplanes."

"Good stuff."

It was nothing more than a casual conversation. The young man was clearly bored out of his mind and wanted to be anywhere else in the world. He was desperate for something to do and someone to talk to who wasn't on his phone.

Still, it came to an end, and Taylor pulled his wallet out. The biggest chunk of the bill came from the gas, which left him with a little over twelve dollars from the snacks. He placed a selection of bills on the counter as his gaze drifted to Liz.

Vickie was still outside, but she was no longer alone. Another truck had pulled up next to her, and two local workers had climbed out and now tried to talk to her. She put her hand to her ear to indicate that she was talking to someone else, but it didn't look like the duo were getting the message.

"Keep the change." Taylor growled his irritation, picked the bags up with one hand, and strode out before the youth behind the counter could get a word in edgewise.

It was a quick walk to Liz, where he deposited the bags of goodies in the back seat. He could hear Vickie talking.

"Desk, hold on a second," she said. "Listen up, bubba, because I'll only say this once. Apparently, one of the shortest words in the English Dictionary—two letters long and also means the same thing in dozens of languages all over the fucking world—was too long and too complex for you. Even the visual cue of me shaking my head to show I was busy and not interested wasn't enough. Now, you can leave with a firm hell no, or you can—"

"Can what, little lady?" asked one of the men sporting a soul patch and spikey brown hair. "Come on. If I allowed every girl who didn't say yes right away to get me down, I wouldn't get anywhere."

"You have to be a little pushy sometimes," the other one added, his long black hair tied in a loose ponytail. "No doesn't always mean no, you know?"

That was the point where Taylor was done. As much as he knew she could handle herself in the face of a couple of pushy assholes, she couldn't expect him to stand back and simply let something happen.

He slammed the door of the truck shut sharply enough to catch the attention of all three, and both men's eyes widened when they saw him advancing on them.

"How's it going?" he asked and patted Vickie to make sure she knew he was asking her even though his gaze was locked on the harassers.

The hacker nodded and moved to the truck as he stepped between her and the two who had now begun to inch back.

"This is your one and only warning," he stated and kept his voice low since there was no point in escalating things. "You two can fuck off and leave my daughter alone, or I will tear your arms off and shove them so far up your asses you'll be chewing on your fingernails. You have ten seconds to make your choice."

They didn't move immediately, and he looked at his watch to drive the point home. Five seconds ticked past before both sprinted to their vehicle and drove away in a cloud of dust. It didn't matter that they had come to the gas station. They could find somewhere else to get their needs serviced.

"Your daughter, huh?" Vickie asked with a broad grin and folded her arms.

"It felt like it would have a little more weight that way. And it's not that far off from the truth, right?"

She smirked and opened the truck door again. "I wish. Hey, did you get the Coke?"

"Cola or -caine?"

"Cola, you dumb shit."

"Yeah, it's in the back. Do you mind putting the drinks in the minifridge there?"

Her gaze was one of astonishment. "Liz has a minifridge? What the hell doesn't she have?"

"Come on, a truck having a minifridge isn't that uncommon," he admonished her.

Vickie turned, wrapped her arms around him, and hugged him close. His eyebrows raised but he didn't say anything and instead, squeezed her in return.

"Thanks," she whispered. "Although you do know I had that shit handled, right?"

"Sure, but I don't think we had the time for you to disassemble their entire lives and lay them out for everyone to see." He waited for her to disengage before he climbed into the driver's seat. "Besides, you have a sadistic side to you. I'd rather you focus a little better on the people we're gunning for. Speaking of which, did you and Desk find anything that Niki might want to know about?"

"Oh, shit—Desk." The hacker connected her device to the phone call that was still going. "Right, where the fuck were we?"

"We were discussing details of Niki's contact," the AI asserted through the speakers. "And honestly, I feel you should make as good a time as possible to DC to deliver the information we've gathered to her."

"Why don't you share it?' Taylor asked.

"Because my status in the FBI and DOD servers would draw attention if I were to transfer this much data, no matter where to. And with the Wi-Fi connection on Liz, it wouldn't be possible. With that said, I will pass the message along that not all is as it appears with Niki's contact, but I still urge you to make it to DC in as short a time as possible."

He nodded and swung out of the gas station and onto

the road to the interstate. "Okay. So Desk, do you think you can take Liz over and get us going a little quicker?"

"I thought your vehicle already has an AI driving it," she noted.

"Sure, but it's very basic and won't be able to push us faster. The other option would be for me to take the wheel and put on my best lead foot impression, but I have a feeling you would be able to get us there faster and with less chance of us ending up in a fiery crash."

The AI considered the option for a second. "All right. Let me know when you arrive at the connected section of the interstate and I'll take the controls from you. And I do appreciate the faith put in my driving abilities. I will not let you down."

"Don't get any tickets," he instructed. "And maybe get us there a few hours early? All while getting to Niki's meeting without letting her know yet? If you can do the last two, I'll pay whatever tickets that end up on the record."

Desk made a noise on the line that almost sounded like scoffing. "As if I would ever get you in trouble with my driving. And if there were any problems, I would simply take care of the records."

Sure enough, as he sidled into the automated lanes, the control of the vehicle was taken from him and they increased speed to barrel down the straight and smooth lines of the road ahead of them.

"It makes me wonder why we didn't try this before," Taylor muttered, unbuckled, and turned to head into the back. He handed Vickie one of the bottles of Coke and retrieved a bottle of water for himself from the minifridge.

The beer was cold. Sometimes, that was all one could ask for. Karl handed his friend Jerrod one of the bottles and sat next to him. The afternoon performance on stage was about what could be expected—not as bad as the morning performances but still well below what could be expected in the evening.

Still, it was a good time either way. Watching a bad performance for free could be as enjoyable as watching a good one, especially when the beer was cold and the company was good.

Neither of them seemed up to the task of heckling and having fun with the pretty country star wannabe on the stage, though. All they could do was stare directly ahead and take occasional sips from their beers as they considered what had happened earlier.

"Okay, so...what else could we have done, right?" Karl asked finally once they were halfway through their beers. "The guy was fucking huge. And you see that tattoo on his arm? That's from the army. He knows how to throw down. And...well, that threat...it's not a pretty visual, you have to admit."

Jerrod shook his head. "Not...nope. Just nope."

Both took another sip from their beers to put some distance between the mental image and themselves.

"Dude...the fucking Jason Momoa-look alike seemed like he could have picked me up by the scrotum with one hand and choked me with the other."

"Yeah, I guess," Karl admitted. "That's the kind of situation where the rules for camping in bear country apply, you know?"

"How do you mean?"

"Well, you're slower than me, right?"

"Sure."

"The rule for camping in bear country is always to bring a friend who is slower than you."

Jerrod needed a few seconds to realize what was being said before he narrowed his eyes. "You're a fucked-up son of a bitch, you know that?"

"What? I'm your friend and everything, but I draw the line at nutsack asphyxiation," he countered. "And if he caught you, that would have given me the chance to escape."

The youth with the long hair in a ponytail gaped at him for a few moments and shrugged. "Whatever. But I wish you could have come up with long words like that when we were talking to the chick. You know, before the were-bear arrived."

CHAPTER TEN

Preparing for a meeting always had her nerves on edge. Niki didn't know who the person was. While details were available, in this day and age—where almost anything could be faked, altered, and hidden—she didn't put much stock on what she could find.

Of course, there was little that Desk, Vickie, and Jennie couldn't find if they put their minds to it, but there was also the problem of sifting through all the bullshit to find the actual data.

She was still waiting for them to come through with it, which meant the conversation would be in a public place and with as many cameras and witnesses possible. The fact remained that there were people out there who would watch her whether she liked it or not, and it was about time she started using them to her benefit.

Even so, she wouldn't go in until she knew her contact had arrived. There was no point in making a target of herself any earlier than she needed to.

Her phone vibrated and she pulled it out. It wasn't a call

and instead, Desk was sending what looked like a dossier on the contact she had asked the AI to investigate.

The picture looked about right and on par with what she already knew. The woman appeared to be in her early thirties with the kind of build that was deceptively strong and well-covered in most of the images. Short black hair appeared to be the most common, although there were instances of blonde, red hair, and even dreads at one point. All these pointed to a woman who could alter her appearance as smoothly as she changed clothes.

Niki pressed the button on her phone that connected her to the open line she always had with Desk.

"What am I looking at here?" she asked. "Seriously, no one has…what? Five names, all with corresponding socials, and financial histories."

"Unfortunately, those are the five names we were able to find and there might be more," Desk alerted her. "As far as we were able to tell, her real name is Dorothy Littleton, but she's also gone by the aliases Stephanie Undercoat, Alissa Asbubs, Melissa Anderson, Nicole Renee, and Rosalyn Drake. There are many professions listed, but none of them appear to be for more than tax purposes. She even has government-grade credentials on several defense agencies in three different countries."

"If I were to place a guess on what her real job is, I'd say it's some kind of fixer." She scowled and ran her fingers through her hair.

"Fixer?"

"You know, the kind of person who's called in to deal with a certain type of problem. It looks like she's working on multi-country issues related to Zoo projects. Are you sure these credentials aren't real? How come no one has caught on to this level of infiltration?"

"It's very unlikely as that level of cooperation on an international level is fairly unheard of. But not...utterly impossible. The central theme she appears to work toward seems to be something called the United Society to Protect Indigenous Peoples."

Niki frowned and checked the dossier again. "So...wait, what? Is that about Native Americans? Sponsored by the Sioux Nation or something?"

"Not as far as I can tell. In fact, the indigenous peoples referenced in this case are those of this planet. As in all of humanity and the indigenous peoples of this planet."

"Oh, okay. Do you know where she is?"

Desk paused for a second to run a trace on the woman. "According to eyes inside the restaurant, she is already at the location in question. Do you want me to cancel the meeting? Make alternative arrangements?"

She shook her head. "We're already committed here so any changes in the schedule will spook someone like her. If we already have eyes on her, I think I'll be safe. And if not...well, vengeance will be swift, right?"

"That would be correct. I must advise against this course of action, however."

"Noted."

With a sigh, she moved from her surveillance position a few blocks away from the restaurant in question. She wasn't the best at this kind of thing but she liked to think she could identify a physical tail if one was there. Desk would easily locate an electronic trace, which meant her bases were more or less covered.

She stepped into the restaurant, where the Maître D' was already waiting for her, and she smiled politely as she approached his station.

"Hi, I'm here for the Renee party?"

The man nodded and motioned wordlessly for her to follow him to one of the far corners of the room. As expected, the woman was already waiting for her, seated with her back to the wall. Niki noted that she was in a position to see anyone who approached the building as well as anyone who entered. She also had a good view of the back entrance and the kitchen, while she remained in a place that was not the first one where gazes settled when someone stepped through the door.

It was very unlikely that the position was chosen at random, all things considered, and she strode directly toward the table. She waited for the Maître D' to pull her seat out for her before she sat across from the woman.

"I'm not sure what to call you," Niki admitted once the man was out of earshot, off to collect another menu for her. "We both know that the name you gave me—Nicole Renee—is bogus, right?"

Her contact smirked, placed her menu on the table, and folded her hands over it. "Sure, but it is a favorite. I couldn't resist."

She nodded. "So, what do I call you? My intelligence suggests that Dorothy Littleton is your real name?"

The woman tilted her head and regarded her calmly. "As real as any other, I suppose. Dorothy works for me. I do prefer Nicole, though."

The Maître D' returned, toting a menu and a tall glass

of beer, and placed both on the table. "The drink is from the gentleman at the bar, with his compliments."

Niki narrowed her eyes. It was a Lager, her favorite, and a Sam Adams no less. Very few people knew it was her favorite brand and one that likely needed to be asked for specifically.

"Uh...no thank you," she answered and shook her head. "Let him know I'm taken but thank you."

"Of course."

The man retreated to relay the message with a calm dignity that suggested he'd assumed he would have to.

Nicole—or whatever her name was—shook her head. "I assume that's your friend McFadden at the bar looking out for you? And that offer of a drink was to make sure all was well and there was no intervention necessary?"

There wasn't much else for Niki to do but shrug.

"I have to say," the woman continued. "The two of you are smooth operators but he is a little difficult to miss, wouldn't you say? I did homework on you, exactly as you did on me, and a former Zoo operative like McFadden will always stand out. Still, it's nice to know something good is happening for the two of you. I can't say the same, given that my type fluctuates between warm and willing to used-up and broken."

Niki narrowed her eyes at the woman. "And by 'used-up and broken' you mean..."

"Oh." Nicole brought her left hand up and indicated her ring finger with her thumb. "I'm already attached to someone, ring on finger. Or formerly attached to someone with the ring still metaphorically there, if you know what I mean."

"And what if they're attached to someone but with no ring?"

The other woman shrugged. "If you like it, put a ring on it. No ring means he or she is fair game."

It was surreal. She recalled hearing this kind of talk before but those times, it had come from a six-foot-five-ish redheaded and bearded giant of a man who tried to convince her that his way of living life was appropriate. While she knew on some level that he wasn't the only one to think that way, it was weird to hear it from someone else.

She would have to ask her how she knew about Taylor. Or maybe not. She didn't want to be catty like that.

"Well, Dorothy," she continued and made a point to use the woman's real name in the hope that it might unnerve her. "Why don't we get to the topic that brought us all here together? What do you need a merc company like ours for? We both know you're more than a little connected."

Nicole didn't let much slip but Niki noticed a stiffening of the shoulders in the woman across from her. She was used to being the one who was the smartest in the room. Having the tables turned like that made her uncomfortable, but she recovered quicker than the ex-agent liked to see.

"If you insist. I was quite enjoying the small-talk part of the conversation. I was hoping you'd play along, ask me who I was having fun with, and whip out a couple of anecdotes about your particular thoughts on the morality of sleeping around. But if you're simply going to sink the showboat, I won't bother. To business then."

"I think that'd be best."

"In that case, I guess we should be as honest with each

other as possible." Nicole took a sip from the glass of white wine in front of her before she continued. "I'm looking for a team with very unique experience, the kind your team possesses. Being a little over-zealous and possessing a little nationalistic pride wouldn't hurt either."

Niki folded her arms in front of her chest. "We plan to help, not hinder, so if this is your attempt to manipulate us into bullshit, I suggest you give it your A-game. If you intend to hire us to help some rich assholes get away with putting the world in danger, we'll pass. If whoever hires us thinks they can try to pull one over on us, we'll pass as well. In short, you either come clean about what you want us to do, or we'll do what these boots were made to do."

"Huh?"

"We'll walk."

"Oh. Vintage reference."

"Thanks."

"Well, from what I can see, you guys do expensive work and you'll only do it with people who can pay."

"Only if those people are straight with us about what they want from beginning to end. If they aren't, it makes me think they'll knife me in the back at the earliest opportunity, and if they intend to do that, I'd prefer they do it to my face."

"Knife you in the back?"

Niki nodded.

"To do it to your face?"

Her second nod was as assertive as the first. "It's as reasonable as shit, right?"

Nicole responded with a soft chuckle before she nodded. "Quite reasonable, yes. You should know that merely because I know the names doesn't mean they might not try something, though."

"At this point, I kind of expect it. Have you ever been to the Zoo?"

The woman's composure slipped, this time more obviously than before as her face twisted a little like she tried to push a bad memory down. "Three times."

"Have you ever been inside?"

The woman shook her head. "Nope, you?"

"I've been close a couple of times but never went inside."

Nicole's face scowled in agreement. "That alien savagery is barely enclosed by millions of tons of concrete and firepower. Honestly, the best thing to do would be to nuke it and keep at it until there was nothing but a massive wasteland. Much like what the Sahara was already but on fire and with a hell of a lot of radiation, I guess."

"Since you know that, you'll know that until someone wrecks the jungle for good, people like myself and Taylor will be in high demand. Don't think anyone who tries to fuck us over will see anyone else take their work, so you might want to send that as a message to those names you know. If they want reliable work from people who are good at the job, don't fuck with us. Got it?"

Her contact took another sip from her wine and tilted her head with a neutral expression. "That's fair enough. You do make an excellent point."

Niki smiled and raised her hand to call the waiter. "Would you kindly tell the gentleman at the bar that I'll have that beer now? And if you could bring another chair for him to join us?"

"Of course."

The woman raised an eyebrow. "Does that mean I'll get to meet McFadden in person?"

"Implying you haven't already?'

"No. I've heard what he's been up to in and out of the Zoo and I've looked forward to meeting him."

She shrugged. "But remember that, ring or no, I will gut you and strangle you with your intestines if you even think about flirting with him."

Nicole didn't appear to have heard her and instead, had focused her attention on the heavy footfalls that indicated Taylor already approaching.

"Do you think I'm joking?" Niki asked.

"Not for an instant," her companion replied, her head still tilted. "But you can't blame a girl for ogling, right?"

"That ends the moment he sits here and we might be able to work together."

"Understood. This may surprise you but I am perfectly capable of being professional."

Taylor arrived with two pint mugs. He put one down in front of Niki and the other at his place once the waiter found another seat for him to join them. The server also set out a napkin and a selection of silverware for when they would eventually order something to eat.

Niki was aware that the man could clean himself up quite admirably when he had a mind to, and the perfectly tailored summer suit looked like it was intentionally cut to leave enough to the imagination.

Or maybe it was merely her imagination that needed to be reined in—although the way Nicole continued to watch his every move made her doubt that was the case.

She grasped the knife in her hand a little tighter and

wondered if she could get away with quietly fulfilling her promise to the woman without drawing any attention.

But when he sat, a physical change came over the woman. In an instant, there was no sign that she was in any way attracted to him. She shifted casually in her seat and regarded him with a polite expression.

"It's nice of you to join us, Mr. McFadden."

"Well, it was a little boring trying to follow the conversation from the bar and try to listen to what you guys were saying. I thought it would be a good idea to come over and see if you needed help."

"Well, since you're here, we might as well have a chat about what kind of business we'd like to do together." Nicole took another sip from her wine glass before she continued. "My name is Nicole Renee—"

Niki coughed. "Supposedly."

The other woman scowled and continued without missing a beat. "And I'd like to bring your team in on the work performed by my organization. First and foremost, I've been called in to look into the death of a researcher at a local corporation contracted by the Pentagon. The death was officially ruled an accident, but I have my suspicions that it might have been an orchestrated hit made to look like an accident. He—"

"Wait," Taylor interrupted. "What organization did you say you worked for again?"

Nicole fixed him with a stern look. "I didn't. Banks wants me to be as upfront and honest about what will happen, but that doesn't include sharing the names and identities of my employers. The people I work for are very insistent on their privacy being respected, and if that is a deal-breaker, I'm afraid it will be the end of our association."

Niki frowned at that and she was ready to stand and end the meeting. She didn't like not knowing who she was working for. While she respected people wanting their privacy, she doubted they would have anything to think about when it came to putting them on the line. She didn't like people playing cloak and daggers.

But Taylor—almost looking into her mind—placed a hand on her arm before she could stand.

"What are you talking about?" he asked. "About the accidental death, I mean."

"There are people invested in making sure no one tries to interfere with the testing that takes place around the world," the woman explained. "Of course, no one wants anything to get out and start spreading, but some testing is...well, considered safe. Not too many people like the idea of companies turning the whole situation into the Wild West, killing each other for a leg up on the competition."

"People are killing scientists?" Niki asked.

Nicole shrugged. "Most of the time they merely kidnap them and steal secrets, that kind of thing. The only victims we have are people who can and have done the same thing dozens of times on the corporate level, and while we try to stop them...well, they can get violent. So, when someone dies, whatever the cause, we pursue any avenue necessary to make sure nothing was done to them. Most of the time it's simply some old fart who bites the dust from a dozen different kinds of ailments, but you'd be surprised how many times it turns out that their endings were…coerced by outside influencers."

"They were murdered," Taylor concluded simply.

"Sure, but we could never prove it, not in a way that would stick in a court of law. And even if there was any actionable proof left behind, the people involved would merely resign and so cut off any investigations, and the people who took their places would keep doing the same thing, maybe after paying some kind of a fine. Corporate goons love their wrist-slaps, after all."

"So what do you want us to do, exactly?" he asked as he leaned a little closer and took a sip of his beer.

The woman retained her calm and somber expression. "Investigate. Dig into this kind of thing. Banks has done a fantastic job of it so far, and we thought if she was no longer confined by the rules government operatives need to play by, you'll be able to pick up in a way that we have been…well, if I'm honest, we've failed to a large degree. The people I work for have some pull, certainly, but they prefer to work from the shadows. Intervening directly and openly would deprive them of that."

"So, you want us to do what your people want to do but out in the open?"

"Something like that."

Niki still doubted she could trust the woman as far as she could throw her, which wasn't that far—at least not if she wasn't wearing a suit—yet there was something appealing about digging into the possibility of someone trying to kill scientists. It brought the added bonus of finding out who was responsible and making sure accidents happened to them too.

The chances were they would merely help someone else do the same thing, but in the end, it was better to be on the inside of this than not. Her inclination to be involved improved when she considered that Desk and Vickie would be on the case, digging into who these private people might be.

"And what kind of compensation could we expect for our efforts?" she asked and motioned for the waiter to approach. "We're not running a charity here, after all."

"Of course not," Nicole answered, picked her menu up, and ran her gaze over the offered specials for a second. "We'll offer an advance payment for your services of twenty-five thousand dollars—a check for which I already have with me if you choose to accept our offer. You'll then define your price according to your personal billing practices."

"Are you sure you can afford our billing practices?" Niki asked.

The woman shrugged. "That's not ultimately my responsibility. They'll pay your first invoice, if only to avoid garnering a bad name among the…community."

"The community of spies for hire?" Taylor asked. "Yeah, that's one hell of a niche."

"It's small but tight-knit," Nicole informed them. "And word of someone refusing to pay will spread quickly. More importantly, that will be a problem with anyone of your caliber. There's no point in making enemies of people like you. Everyone knows about the skills held by the likes of the Ginger Giant over here, but a select few will know to fear the investigative skills of the former Agent Banks— and those of the members of her family."

Niki narrowed her eyes. "My family? That sounds... suspiciously like it could be intended as a threat."

"Of course not." The woman shook her head firmly. "My point is that there are certain people who know the other members of McFadden and Banks have skills that are equally as impressive and are no less to be feared. They know better than to fuck with you. Now, should we get food orders in? I'm fucking starving."

A little mollified, she looked at Taylor, whose powerful shoulders raised in a slow shrug.

"Food sounds good," she answered.

CHAPTER ELEVEN

It wasn't the kind of restaurant Taylor would willingly patronize as a matter of routine, although he wouldn't go so far as to say it was terrible. The venue was about on par with somewhere he would take Niki on a date—the kind that involved dressing up nicely like their first date.

While he couldn't see himself dining there too often, it was an option for something special—an occasion like an anniversary or something.

Nicole looked perfectly comfortable like she ate there all the time. The plates that served a herb-crusted salmon were cleared and replaced with smaller, white plates with molten chocolate cake and a couple of scoops of vanilla and honey ice cream. He very soon realized it was the kind of decadent sweetness Nicole Renee—or whatever her name was—had a weakness for. She hadn't cared much about anything else they'd ordered, but she was insistent that they choose the molten chocolate cake with ice cream.

The woman undoubtedly had a sweet tooth. He wasn't sure what that meant, if it meant anything, but it was certainly something to note about someone they knew so little about.

And sure enough, she dove into the dessert like it owed her money and savored every mouthful with far more enthusiasm than either Niki or Taylor displayed.

He couldn't deny her the simple pleasures in life, of course, and as long as nothing was poisoned, things seemed to have gone better than he feared they might.

"So," Nicole started although she still worked on a mouthful of cake. "Where did the nicknames start? Okay, they're fairly obvious, like Ginger Giant—and there was something about a leprechaun in there too—but you have to think people would simply move on from them after a while, especially given your history."

Taylor raised an eyebrow. "What history are you talking about?"

"You know, heading into the Zoo eighty-three times—which is impressive, by the way—plus all the work you've done around here ever since you left. Given that, you'd think there would be a little more…"

"What, respect?"

"Sure."

"It's not that there isn't respect. It's the fact that despite whatever I might have done in the past, we're all equals in there. No matter the experience, we need to be reminded that the Zoo isn't impressed by how many missions I run. Well, except for maybe trying a little harder to kill me once I'm in there. That might seem a little too intelligent to someone who's never been in the jungle or never faced a cryptid, but there's no way I'll underestimate what these critters can do. Either way, it's kind of an instinctive way to make sure everyone involved keeps their feet on the ground, as it were. It isn't something anyone thinks about, though."

She nodded, and he could see Niki's eyes narrowed at her. Both had treated the meeting with the kind of professionalism he had come to expect, but as the other woman began to relax, she talked less about business, and that was annoying his partner for some reason.

"Interesting," Nicole said. "It would seem that as a group, people who go into the Zoo are more focused on the short-term than anyone else. I suppose it makes sense when you think about it. They are unsure if they'll survive from one day to the next. That kind of uncertainty faces us all but it generally lacks the kind of...certainty of uncertainty that the Zoo does."

"Did you have a point?" Taylor asked and fidgeted with his cake.

"I did, but I may have forgotten it. Oh, right." She shook her head. "My point was people who have that kind of short-sightedness aren't those we want in charge of the whole operation. It might be great to keep people alive and more or less sane in there, but out here in the real world, we need actual long-term thinkers. Because as much as we might want a quick solution to this kind of thing, it doesn't look like there'll be one. Even nuking the shit out of the place will create numerous long-term problems for the area, and given that radiation doesn't appear to be much of a problem for what's growing in that fucking jungle, it might not even work."

Niki tilted her head. "It sounds like you've given this a fair amount of thought."

"If you stick around this business long enough, you start looking for solutions that will last longer than a bullet to the head of the nearest cryptid. And the more you try to think of a way out, the more depressing the realization is that we're in this for the long haul."

"In that case, the short-sighted bastards in the Zoo are the best at staying sane," Taylor noted, finished his cake, and washed it down with some of his beer. "You can go ahead and think about long-term solutions, but until one pops up, you need people like us to deal with the short-term problems and make sure you don't have your arm eaten by a monster while you think up the answers to the problem."

Nicole smirked and nodded. "I never said soldiers on the front line weren't necessary, mind you. And the kind of soldier who goes to the front line as many times as you did and walks away with your life and enough money to retire on… Well, let's say I'm surprised that you choose to do this kind of work instead of writing books and helping out in movies, acting in a couple yourself and having women throw themselves at you left, right, and center—Ow!"

The woman reached down to her leg. Taylor didn't have to be a detective to realize that Niki had kicked her in the shin. Again, he felt like there was more to the story than he knew but there was no point in digging into it any further and pissing Niki off besides.

"The thought occurred to me," he admitted. "But in the end, even a short-sighted foot soldier like myself realized there isn't much benefit to turning my back and letting everything keep happening to the world while I sit around and do nothing. The best I can do is help out in any way I can."

Nicole was still rubbing her sore shin while Niki acted like nothing had happened. He had a feeling that any attempt on his part to intercede and try to talk either woman into keeping things calm, more or less, would backfire.

They wouldn't listen to him anyway so he took another sip of his beer and avoided eye contact with both. He wouldn't get involved in this, not if he planned to leave the meeting with his shins intact.

"Well," the woman said when she finally gathered her composure. "All I can say is I'm sure both of you would result in a revolution in the movie and TV industries if you ever elect to go in that direction. Until then, of course, you are in a position to help me and my employers, which will always be appreciated."

"Are there other people you could call in for this kind of situation?" Niki asked. "For one thing, wouldn't local law enforcement be the best to bring in on this? They already have something of an in on that."

"I tried that once," Nicole explained, finished her dessert, and leaned back in her seat as she took a deep breath. "It started out fun, but things got a little too involved for my tastes and I had to back away before things got too complicated."

Taylor nodded and leaned closer to Niki to translate. "She got romantically involved with the police officer in question and things became too complicated. Plus, they broke up badly so she now thinks it's a bad idea all around."

His partner raised an eyebrow. "Yeah, getting in bed

with one of your contacts in the field does seem like it can only end badly."

"You're one to talk," Nicole snapped in response.

Both Taylor and Niki opened their mouths to retort but instead, looked at each other. The woman made a good point, although she wasn't exactly wrong when she said it had no way to end but badly. Or, at least, the chances were that it would do so unless the woman decided to leave whatever organization she was a part of to simplify her working relationship with the guy in question.

That and about fifteen other variables that had come into play to get them as far as they were, alive and well, more or less.

"Well, in my case, I got involved with a local police officer who was looking into a similar case," she explained. "And it ended up in a situation where both of us were a little too aggressive about shit, and when it came right down to it, we weren't very good at anything other than the sex. We had no common interests, nothing we liked about each other's personalities, and neither of us was willing to put the effort in. I had an excuse since I was using him for my job, but what was his excuse?"

"I'll assume it has something to do with wanting to be in a casual relationship with a woman he knows is simply using him," he suggested. "Most guys can tell that if they have a functioning brain stem. They merely don't care."

Nicole shrugged. "Well, whichever way you slice it, the relationship was a terrible idea. We both agreed on that, and after a fight that got a little too physical, we parted ways. Surprisingly, I ran into him again on this case of the dead scientist. It wasn't as uncomfortable as I thought it would be, although he undoubtedly held a grudge."

"What did you do to him?" he asked.

"I crushed his nuts."

Taylor winced instinctively and shook his head. "Yeah, that'll get a guy to hold a grudge all right."

Niki smirked but turned her attention to the woman opposite her. "What did he do to you? I assume that turning him into a eunuch would have been something of a...shall we say, last resort?"

The other woman nodded. "I had him in an armlock and he used his position to...well..."

He raised an eyebrow, genuinely interested to hear about what sounded like the fight of the century. "Well?"

"He went after the girls." Nicole motioned to her chest to clarify. "Grabbed the nipples and tried to twist them the fuck off."

His brain tried to assimilate that. The empathy was there and the thought made him want to cover his chest a little better, but it wasn't quite on the level of what she had done, at least to his mind.

"Is that...comparable?" he asked Niki cautiously.

She nodded. "Oh yeah. The dude was asking for it. I would have gone for the throat punch myself and stamped on his balls once he was on the ground, but in the end, it's basically the same thing. It's an invitation for the fight to get dirty and not in the fun way."

"Well, there are people who are into that kind of stuff," he commented. "I won't kink-shame here but okay, it sounds like both of you were...not right for each other."

"Amen to that." Nicole grunted and took a deep breath.

"But anyway, that's why I'm currently on a break from local law enforcement and looking for people on my side who won't give me so many problems. Which brings me back to you. What do you think about the offer? The money is about on par with what Taylor received from the DOD when that was still happening, and it'll only go up the longer you work. Besides, there's no guarantee of crazy shit happening. There could be nothing. Our scientist might have accidentally set himself on fire after a celebratory drink and smoke, but on the off chance that there was something off about it, we'd like to have someone with your credentials on the case."

Niki regarded her thoughtfully. "And by something off, you mean…"

"The kind of thing that gets the knickers of voters, investors, and the population in general in a twist." The woman finished her sentence for her. "You know, aliens at the front door, that kind of thing."

"Aliens…at the front door," Taylor muttered under his breath.

"You know," Nicole explained. "The monsters bred in places where they shouldn't be and inevitably end up in a situation where they break out, rampage through the scientists who had the hubris to breed them, and spread out into the local populace. It happens far more than you think it does."

"Oh, I'm aware," he asserted.

"No, I mean you truly have no idea how often it happens. And not only here either. I've put fires out all over the world, and if you take the deal, so will you."

"It sounds like a stressful existence."

"Yeah, it's the story of my life. So, are you interested?"

Taylor glanced at Niki, who had long since finished her food and drink and looked like she was only waiting for the bill to come before getting the hell out of there. He could understand that much, at least. The meeting had started to drag somewhat, although they were using it to give Vickie and Desk the time to dig a little deeper into this woman. Nothing came through on their phones, though, which either meant there was nothing for them to look into, or there was too much.

"We'll take the offer," Niki said finally. "We're looking to expand our client base anyway. And the down payment on our services will be appreciated too, as well as you picking the bill up for this meal?"

Nicole smirked. "Naturally. What kind of a schmoozer would I be if I made you guys split the bill with me?"

She waved to catch the waiter's attention, motioned for the bill before he came too close, and waited while he went to arrange it so he could bring it to the table.

"So, this was the schmoozing?" Taylor asked and looked around.

"Yep."

"You'd think she could have upped her game a little," Niki noted. "Don't take it the wrong way, you got the job done, but a little constructive criticism never hurt anyone."

The woman grinned as the waiter arrived and she handed him a black credit card. "Yes, well, this is my first time…schmoozing like this. Most of the time, it's merely manipulation and back-alley dealings where they don't know much about me, but it seems that's not a very good long-term strategy."

The bill was returned with her card, and Nicole tucked it into her jacket pocket before she drew a manila envelope out and placed it on the table. "Well then, I look forward to doing business with both of you. Now, if you'll excuse me, I have calls to make."

She stood and strode away quickly like she had already planned her exit from the moment she arrived and left the other two at their table for a few more minutes.

Niki pulled her phone out and scowled when there were no notifications on the screen. "Is that good or bad news?"

"In a situation where more information is better, I'd say it's bad news," Taylor answered, stood from his seat, and paused to stretch his arms. "But there's no point in any conjecture if we don't have facts. Let's head to a secure location and call Vickie to see if she can fill us in on what we don't know about this woman."

His partner nodded. "On that topic, I think we'll need to find us digs around here if we'll work in this area. Not that I don't appreciate the work you did finding us a house to move into in Vegas and the work going into it, but we'll probably need to find some kind of headquarters in DC."

He tilted his head thoughtfully as they stepped out of the restaurant and proceeded down the street. "Agreed. If you think about it, the chances are we'll be in and out of different places in the country—and hell, probably the world too—so this might need to be a common factor in our future dealings."

There wasn't much else to say on the topic. She knew he was right and they would start working on that, but it wasn't the most important thing to think about at the moment.

"What do you think about her?" she asked suddenly, and he focused on her and raised an eyebrow.

"What do you mean?"

"Your general thoughts. Anything you might have had on your mind while talking and didn't feel comfortable discussing in front of her."

That sounded like a trap if ever there was one, and he wouldn't walk into it. It was best to simply stick to the obvious. "I don't trust her. Her loyalties won't be in keeping us out of any frying pans or fires we might run into, so we need to be the ones to look out for our asses on the assumption that no one else will."

"Do you think she'll try to screw us over?"

"If it's a choice between us and whoever her clients are, I'll say yes. Again, we'll have to put ourselves first when push comes to shove. Let them take their money elsewhere if they don't like it."

She looked at the envelope in her hands. "Well, yeah, but as long as they're dishing it our way, we might as well take advantage."

CHAPTER TWELVE

This was more or less what she expected her work to be while in business with McFadden and Banks. Vickie was trained to deal with real and difficult problems, but the reality was that her skills lay in the technical world and she was happy with that.

Well, maybe not as happy as she would have been inside the Michelin-Star restaurant, dining on salmon and having a cold beer but still, they did have to enjoy a couple of good ones here and there. Way too many times, while she was waiting for them, they had to fight their way through literal alien monsters.

"Alien monsters," she whispered in the back of Liz, parked three blocks away from the restaurant.

"Did you say something?" Desk asked in her earpiece.

"Yeah, it's only…alien monsters," she repeated. "It's one of those things that should be cool, but the more you say it, the more it feels…overused. I'm glad we call them cryptids now. Otherwise, all other descriptive names they'd have for the fuckers would sound off and weird."

"If you say so." The AI sounded like she didn't know how to respond to her rant and was programmed to say that line every time when presented with the kind of conversation where there was nothing else to say.

It was an odd part of human interaction that had always fascinated Vickie, and one Jennie had managed to nail in her development of the software. The way people didn't understand what was being talked about but did understand it was being spoken of with passion and therefore discussing and disputing it would not be worth the effort.

Of course, having an AI pull that trick was a little unsettling. She had spent too much time worrying about Skynet coming to be comfortable with an overly intelligent AI.

She shook her head and leaned a little closer to her screen, a simple trick that she had learned to help her focus better. "What am I looking at here? All I can see is a list of dates and transfer registrations. Did you pick up the wrong file?"

"Possibly," Desk answered. "The name of the researcher they were asked to look into has been sealed after his death, which isn't that uncommon since most of the data will be transferred to others who will take his work over later on. There is no notification of when the reassignment will happen, however, so all I have is the data on when and where the data was transferred."

The hacker scowled. With that context, the numbers she was looking at started to make sense, and it looked like all the data had been transferred to the same IP address.

"Can you give me access to the address?" she asked. "I

think I could probably sneak the files out without anyone realizing what I'm doing. Besides, if there is the possibility that alarms would be raised, would they be able to track us and give us any trouble?"

Again, the AI sounded like she wouldn't contest what she had to say, which was fairly intelligent of her. It took Desk a few seconds to finally speak again. "The IP address attached to the files is not accessible."

Vickie's head snapped up and her eyes narrowed as she double-checked what Desk was doing. "Did they isolate the transfer? Scrub the address after they transferred it to another location?"

"There is no sign of the data being transferred out of the physical location of the IP address," Desk answered. "And the address is still there. I simply cannot access it."

She scowled. "So…it means they've isolated the servers and sealed them from anything but physical, wired access. Yeah, I had a bad feeling we would run into something like that."

"Something like what?"

"A speedbump. A wrench in the works. Something that someone put down to make sure our job would be that much more difficult while we try to save the world or some shit."

"Yes. But in my admittedly limited experience, it would appear the people who are willing to go to such lengths to cover their tracks generally have something they want to keep hidden, which means we should continue to dig into that."

"Right, but we can't do anything from here." Vickie

scowled and stretched lazily in the back of the truck. "The chances are Taylor and Niki will want to take any field-related duties anyway, assuming the idea is to sneak in ourselves and obtain the info. It seems like a brute force strategy—the kind he favors, honestly."

"Either that or we could infect the computer software of someone who would have access to the servers on a regular basis and simply use the trojan to take what is needed through an unwitting third party."

"Either way, it'll be much more complicated than we'd like." The hacker picked up the bag of chips she had been eating from and peered sadly into the bottom of the reflective interior. She would have to restock. "Do you want to give them the good news or should I?"

"You should probably do the honors," Desk replied. "I have a feeling they would want me to keep digging into this Dorothy Littleton character."

"Have you found anything concrete on her?"

"No, but if there is anything to be found, I will. It's only a matter of time."

She wasn't sure, but that was the first time Desk had ever sounded frustrated. Maybe she should talk to Jennie about when the latest upgrade was installed.

"You have to admit, an apartment won't be the best location," Niki stated firmly. "While admittedly, ease of access and centralized locations are always nice, we'll have to deal with a situation where our Internet access is hampered by a horde of other residents. And you can be sure the householders will be more likely to cause a problem if they realize we're running a black operation out of their building. Have you ever had to deal with a co-op board?"

Taylor shook his head.

"Well, let me tell you from personal experience, they are a fucking nightmare at the best of times."

"Okay, so an apartment is out. Renting a house can be excluded for the same reasons."

"What...well, yeah. Homeowner associations are as much of a headache."

"So what do you think we should do? We can't run our black ops out of the fucking hotel."

"Well, I thought we could find an abandoned warehouse or strip mall like you did in Vegas. Property around here shouldn't be that difficult to find, right?"

He shrugged, a little bemused as he hadn't thought about settling anywhere near Washington DC. Ordinarily, he would have spent a couple of weeks doing market research to find the right place at the lowest price, but it wouldn't always work out that way. Not unless he wanted to set franchises up all over the damn place.

It could be an option for the future, but while he was doing well financially, he wasn't doing that well yet.

She sighed. "It's something to think about but it looks like you have something else on your mind at the moment, so out with it."

"Not really on my mind." He shook his head. "But if you're looking to change the subject, there has been something I've wondered about ever since we left the restaurant."

"Again, out with it."

"Well, do you want to talk about the kick?"

"Kick?

"You know, when you kicked Renee or Nicole or whoever she is in the shin under the table? You weren't exactly subtle about it."

"Oh, right. That kick."

"I didn't want to question your decisions, but if you feel like explaining it, I'm all ears. You can feel free to change the subject if you don't want to."

Her shrug contained no awkwardness. "It's not that uncomfortable. I thought it was very clear the woman was a dog and decided it was a good idea to keep her on a leash, that's all."

"A dog? As in we should have looked around for a tail?"

"What? No, of course not. How did that even occur to you?"

"Dealing with alien monsters created by a jungle that was in turn created by alien goop forces one to keep one's mind open about almost everything. What do you mean by dog?"

"Like…hound dog? The kind that's always looking to hump? That kind of thing? I know the term usually only applies to guys since there are some less than appropriate names for women who are sexually active, but yeah."

"Oh. Wait, what do you mean by that?"

"Only that guys are more famously…applauded for their promiscuity, while women are shamed for it. Generally speaking, of course. There are always exceptions here and there."

"Okay, fair enough. And yeah, the gender roles have always been a little twisted. Even if things have lately taken a turn for the better due to efforts around the globe."

"Right. But I guess there is still stigma attached to it, which is why people turn to terms generally used for men to apply to everyone, right?"

"Right. So...wait, you were...keeping her on a leash, metaphorically speaking. Does that mean you merely kept her houndery in check in general or was there something a little more focused about your efforts that I should be aware of?"

"Well, she admitted that she was more than a little interested in you when you were approaching the table," Niki confessed. "Hell, she practically acted like a crazed fangirl when you were walking over. I did tell her that if she tried anything, I'd make her regret it—"

"Wait, make her regret it?"

"I'm paraphrasing, but yeah."

"Oh, okay."

Niki narrowed her eyes. "What?"

"No, nothing. It's only...you were always good at coming up with vivid imagery to go with your threats. I would have been a little disappointed if all you said was that she would regret it."

She smirked. "I think I said something about...yeah, I would gut her with the restaurant's knife and strangle her with her entrails, something like that."

He couldn't help a grin. "Yeah, that sounds better. It's not the best you've ever come up with but still damn good."

"Please tell me you're keeping a top-ten list we can go over later?"

"You know it. But back to the topic at hand."

"Whatever." She rolled her eyes. "I've never thought of myself as the jealous type, but I guess I might be. If she started getting flirty with you, I would make her regret it."

The grin remained on his face as they continued to walk at a leisurely pace to where he'd parked Liz. "I have to say that's kind of hot."

Niki didn't quite look as amused as he was. "Yeah, yeah, like I know you're still getting adjusted to being in a monogamous relationship. And yes, there's no ring on your finger, so I might not be as trusting as I could be, but can you blame me for being a little possessive?"

"Nope. I've been what you call a dog but there's no need for a ring on my finger to stop me from being one of those assholes who cheat in a relationship where it'll hurt one of the members." He tugged gently at his beard. "With that said, though, if you'd feel better if there were a ring involved, I wouldn't be opposed to that."

"Yeah?"

He shrugged and drew them to a halt so they could speak face-to-face. "You know, the original point of the rings was meant to be a part of the dowry, which meant the guy was paying the father of the bride for possession. I think there was a point where the ring was meant to be a way for the bride to be able to pay her way back to her family if the wedding fell through."

Niki raised an eyebrow. "It sounds like you did a little research into this type of thing."

"You know, a guy reads shit and it sticks." He indicated for them to keep walking. "I'm sure it was the De Beers diamond cartel that pushed the use of diamonds in rings after the 1930s when the price of diamonds collapsed.

They started using the 'Diamonds are Forever' slogan that turned it from a rare splurge into a necessary thing in engagement rings, which in turn pushed the diamond prices skyward."

"Huh." She grunted and regarded him thoughtfully. "I've never been that kind of traditionalist gal. And the whole blood diamond trade certainly put a damper on my aspirations for the situation, but still. So are you telling me you're a liberated man? Willing to be the property of a woman? How progressive of you."

Taylor smirked. "Not really. What I'm saying is that if it helps you feel a little more confident about my commitment to you, I'll wear a ring for you. Or...get you one for you to wear, or whatever situation you'd like it to be."

They continued walking for a few minutes in silence. It looked like she wasn't quite sure what to say to that.

Finally, she shook her head. "Let's start with finding a location to establish our headquarters. All this emotional shit makes my head hurt."

Taylor snickered. "So you're all for being possessive and kicking other women in the shin and threatening them with death and mutilation if they so much as look at me the wrong way. But when it comes to talking about where the relationship is going, that gives you a headache?"

"Yeah, and can you honestly say that thinking about it doesn't give you a headache?"

"I think there's too much blood rushing the other way for me to have a headache."

"So...you're saying seeing me all possessive over you is..."

"Yep."

She grimaced but he caught a hint of a smile coming to her lips as they approached the truck. "Oh, shut up. We both know you've spent way too much time thinking about odd and wacky ways to twist relationships around."

"Sure. And the problem here is?"

"No particular problem, but we're in something a little more…civilized here, so you'll have to adjust to it. And I guess I will too."

"We're both works in progress," Taylor agreed. "There's no shame in admitting that. We merely need to keep on working."

Niki smiled at that thought before she knocked lightly on the truck's door. It took Vickie a few seconds to answer. She pulled the door open for them, her face a little flushed.

"Well, it's good to see spy girl over there didn't try to poison your drinks," the hacker commented and ran her fingers through her short black hair.

"Well, if she'd tried, I have a feeling you would have suited up, charged in, and been ready to kick ass and chew bubblegum," he replied as he climbed into the driver's seat. Niki took the shotgun seat, while Vickie remained in the back where her improvised setup was situated.

"Well, it looks like we have a job," Niki stated and shifted in her seat.

"Yeah, I've looked into this guy our spy girl wants us to investigate." Vickie turned her screen so the other woman could see it when she twisted to look. "Dr. Carlos Santana. Born in San Juan, Puerto Rico, graduated from high school three years early, and was offered scholarships all over the country. He chose the biology program at Cornell and got his

BS, Masters, and doctorate there before he was offered a research position at Glass Door Innovations, owned by parent company Greer and Greer. Since then, he's been moved from lab to lab, all owned by G&G, but hasn't ever remained in one facility for longer than five years. He's an only child and has no wife or kids. His parents live in Nashua."

"Who owned the house that burned down with him in it?" Niki asked.

"It's owned by G&G, and he was leasing. From what I've seen, part of his package was to lease different locations from them for a certain amount of time until he settled on a place he liked. All his past lease payments would count as a down payment. It's an interesting arrangement and one he negotiated for hard. It looks like they wanted him fucking bad."

"Do we know what he might have been working on?" the other woman asked. "If the police didn't find anything to indicate that it was murder, we won't get past them stonewalling us without serious motive being involved. We don't know about means or opportunity, but if there's a motive, that might encourage someone to dig into the other two."

"Well...no, we don't know what he was working on," the hacker explained, her tone reluctant. "All his research material was moved off-site. The physical copies were shipped to a secure location, after which I kind of...may have, uh, definitely lost them. Whoever was in charge of disseminating it knew to randomize everything to make sure nothing could be tracked. All the digital files are ready to be transferred to other researchers, but there's no set date on when that will happen so it's being stored on a secure server."

"Let me guess," Taylor interjected. "It's the kind of secure server that is isolated from anything but physical access. You can't dive into it from here so we have to find a way to do it in person."

"I have taught you well, young grasshopper." Vickie bowed awkwardly from the back of the truck. "Give the man a cigar or whatever because the fact of the matter is that we'll need to throw some serious curveballs if we want to find a way into that fucking place."

He leaned his seat back a couple of inches and scowled. "Okay, I don't know anything about anything when it comes to the technical aspects of what you do. Or anything else about what you do. Honestly, you might as well tell me that everything you do is magic—"

"Stay on point," Niki chided.

"Right. So do you need someone to head in there and insert one of your...famous dongle fixes into the server? That sounds like spy work to me, am I correct?"

"It sounds about right," she agreed. "There might be a couple of other options. We could possibly sneak a trojan onto a computer that will have physical access to that server, but that will take a little...shall we say, finesse? First, we'd have to find out who might have access to that server and if they are able to bring any software-carrying devices within broadcasting range. Many places don't even let people carry smartwatches into secure server rooms these days."

Taylor could see his face scrunch in the mirror. "All that

to say Niki is probably the one with the expertise on how we'll find a way in, right?"

"Well, I was never exactly a spy myself, but yeah." Niki sighed and rubbed her temples. "We have a ton of work to do."

CHAPTER THIRTEEN

Vickie scowled at Taylor.

The man seemed unable to sit still. He fidgeted with everything he could get his hands on, which on Liz's steering wheel and dashboard was a considerable number. There were buttons to press, switches to flick, and devices to click, and he had manipulated every single one of them at least three times in the thirty minutes since they had parked.

He'd changed the radio station, adjusted the temperature, and fiddled with the mirrors and the windows to the point where she could almost feel steam coming out of her ears.

She reached out, placed a hand on his arm, and brought the giant of a man to a halt. Both his hands settled on the wheel as he turned to look at her.

"I know you're worried," she said and tried to keep her voice from showing the annoyance bubbling beneath. "Nervous, even. But I have work to do, and it'll be impossible to do it with you trying to find a good song playing on the radio for the fifteenth time. It'll be even more difficult if I have to go out and find a sedative to put in your coffee."

After a long, deep breath, he relaxed slowly into the driver's seat. "It's not that I'm nervous. Well, maybe a little. You never know what'll happen around here, but I do know Niki's more than capable of handling herself."

"So chill the fuck out." She patted his shoulder, which she realized was still tense enough that it might as well have been granite. "Niki is good at this shit or we wouldn't have let her go in there in the first place, right? She wouldn't have gone in if she didn't think she could pull this off, and she is a woman who, above everything else, knows her limits and knows when it's time to let someone else do the heavy lifting."

Taylor nodded, but she could feel none of the tension leaving his shoulders.

"I'm serious. I will get valium and inject you with it if you don't chill the fuck out. You being all weird and still is almost worse than you fidgeting with everything in reach. Almost, mind you."

With another deep breath, the mountain of a man finally let himself relax an inch and closed his eyes. "I don't feel right sitting this one out. I'm the guy who's the most comfortable on the front lines, throwing punches and shit. Sitting around and letting other people do all the work feels wrong."

"I know, but you're part of a team and that means letting other people do shit and help you. Besides, you're not sitting this one out. You're the backup team if Niki runs into trouble. You're as vital to the mission as any of us since knowing you're ready to charge in and get her out is probably the reason why she was so confident in her ability to infiltrate the facility in the first place."

She had to admit, it was a little heartwarming to know that Taylor was worried about her. And a little hilarious to know he was angry about not being the one to jump feet-first into the mission like some kind of action hero.

But in the end, she was running an operation and she did need to focus, which was difficult when the people in her ear chattered away like they were at a coffee shop.

"Guys?" She hissed under her breath as she advanced to the front door. "I hate to interrupt what must be a truly Hallmark-worthy moment happening back there, but do you think you could keep quiet on the comms?"

"Oh, shit," Vickie snapped. "Sorry, but Taylor was making a mess and I was trying to focus, and it wasn't working and—"

"I don't give a shit!" Talking like that was acceptable outside the building, but it wouldn't fly once she was inside where people could hear her. "Stay focused and help me with this because I didn't have the time to memorize the blueprints for the whole building. And Taylor, babe, do as Vickie says and chill the fuck out or I will tell her to inject you with something."

"Noted," he muttered.

Niki took a deep breath and let a superficial calm fall over her. Vickie was right—she did know she was capable of infiltrating a building. She had done it before in her early days with the Bureau, back when she had no connections and all kinds of pressure. There were times when bullshitting her way into locations was the only way she was able to get the intel her superiors needed.

It wasn't strictly legal, but she managed to get most of the intel from people who literally handed it to her, so it wasn't technically illegal either. She hoped the same would apply in this instance as well.

With that said, if she said her hands weren't sweating and her mind wasn't rushing through every way this could go wrong, she would be lying.

She stepped into the building, her heart thudding loudly enough in her chest that it was hard to hear anything else, but she had control of herself. There was no need to panic. She was merely another worker heading in for another day. Like everyone else, she would put her nose to the grindstone in hopes of getting enough on her year-end bonus to treat herself to a week in the Bahamas in January.

That was all. She was simply another employee who marched through the halls every day.

Vickie had made sure that she was on the company roster. She had been added to the system as Alice White, an accountant working in the fine foods division on the fourth floor of the building owned by G&G and populated by the various subsidiaries they were in charge of.

She had gotten a building ID, complete with markers that showed her checking in around nine in the morning every day and checking out around five in the afternoon, with a handful of vacation and sick days taken during the three years she had worked there. The hacker had even managed to spoof a 401k account the company had matched her deposits on for all three years.

While she had a long list of things to say about Vickie—not all of it good—one thing she knew for a fact was that the girl was good at her job.

Still, she couldn't help the feeling that each one of the security guards who manned the reception desk knew she was an imposter. Of course, that would be fun to watch too since getting her out was Taylor's job and he wouldn't spare any assholes who tried to detain her. Still, he wouldn't hurt them too badly since they were only doing their jobs. Probably.

Niki moved closer to the desk and waited patiently in line as the rest of the folks coming into work were checked by security. They scanned their ID cards at the small glass gate and there was a hint of a delay as the guards checked their credentials before they opened the door for them.

She did recall that there was a small weapon safe under the desk, out of sight but ready to be used if someone ever tried to force their way in.

Her deadpan, tired expression in a couple of reflective surfaces around her caught her eye and she sipped idly at the coffee in her hand. It was decaf since she didn't need anything to rattle her nerves at this point.

It was her turn at the scanner and she slipped the card under it. Her heart skipped a beat when the scanner didn't beep like it had with the others. Vickie hadn't fucked up, right?

"Wrong side," one of the guards muttered when he leaned forward to see what the issue was. "Flip it and... there you go."

Niki did as she was told and tried not to look too relieved as the man slipped back in front of the screen that displayed the credentials the hacker had put so much work into.

"Shit weather we're having today, huh?" the man asked as he waved her through the gate.

"Yeah, but it should clear up over the weekend, and that's all that matters, right?" she replied smoothly and stepped through the open gate.

"I guess. Have a nice day."

She hadn't paid attention. Did the guy talk to all the people coming through or was she a special case? Was it only because she was a looker and he wanted to develop a rapport or had he played for time for his partners to get through her cover?

It didn't look like it. None of the five guys behind the desk looked stressed or tense in any way and merely wanted to get the morning rush of people coming in out of the way so they could go about the rest of their day's work.

After another sip of her coffee, she checked her watch and moved with the other staff toward the elevators. It was the little mannerisms that counted. Remaining still and tense was a rookie move. Normal people fiddled and moved around, fidgeted and sighed, and everyone else would notice if she acted a little too icy as well as if she acted too frazzled.

When she stepped into the elevator, she slipped into the traditional dance of avoidance people did without noticing every time that they entered one and pressed the button to take her to the fourth floor.

Everyone else had selected the higher floors, which meant she was the one to step off first.

"Not to sound like an eighties action movie cliché or anything," she whispered, "but I'm in."

"Keep going down the hallway," Vickie instructed like she could see what was happening. "Take the third left and your office is the first one on the right."

Hell, she probably could see everything that was happening. The girl having access to security cameras was practically a given, especially in the less-secure areas of the building.

Niki followed the instructions, headed down the hallway, and noted that no other people walked around the area with her. It was the middle of a work week, meaning there should have been dozens of people manning the various offices around her.

"Hey, Vickie?"

"Yeah?"

"Where the fuck is everyone?"

"Oh, the fine foods division was recently restructured with most of the staff either forced into some vacation days or sent to other branches, and they haven't populated the offices with the replacements yet. It was the best place to slip you in without anyone noticing and anyone seeing that you're not at your desk."

"Where am I?"

"Trying to get to the secure server rooms."

"Oh, right. Duh." Niki stepped into her office and saw a desk, a computer, and an office chair but nothing else. "I guess it's a good thing no one will see me here. There's no sign that anyone worked here, ever. Not even a plant."

"Look, I can spoof your credentials. I can get you a 401k so legit that the company is forced to automatically match your contributions and no red flags were raised. Hell, we'll probably be able to take all the money out and come out of this with a cool two hundred grand in profit only from this part of the operation. But as much as I can do—and that's a long goddamn list—there are some things I can't do. On that list is making pictures, personal items, and mother-fucking plants appear from thin air."

She grinned. "Okay, fair enough. So, how will I get to the secure server levels? I don't think I saw any security around the emergency stairwell."

"There's a reason for that," Vickie grumbled. "Those doors are sealed at all times unless a fire alarm goes off."

"Could you get one of the doors to open anyway?"

"I could but they've been set to trigger those alarms if someone forces the door open too. It's a very effective system. You know, if they ever have a fire or something."

"So…how can I get down there?"

"I…I had hoped you would find a way down yourself," the girl admitted. "There are only two access points to the server room, and that's the elevator and the stairwell. The elevator shaft has motion sensors throughout to make sure no one goes up or down except the elevators, and all the air ducts are too small for a human to fit, so…none of that Die Hard shit. Which means, short of setting off the fire alarms…"

Her voice trailed off for a second, and Niki could almost hear the gears in the young hacker's head turning.

"We're setting off the fire alarms, aren't we?" she asked and sighed deeply.

"Unless you have any better ideas?"

She didn't. "Do you know how that'll make the security teams react? If they'll call the local fire department or handle it themselves?"

"I'm looking at their evacuation plan as we speak... Okay, this indicates that the security team inspects the site of the alarm before they call the fire department. It seems there have been numerous instances of people burning shit in the microwaves in the break rooms on...shit, all the floors. That should give you time since they'll evacuate the building too, but you'll have to be at the door when it opens or you might be forced out of the building with the rest of the staff. How quickly can you run down the stairs?"

"If the operation depends on it? I think I can work up the speed to get down there in time."

"I hope so. Get to the stairwell doors. I'll set the alarm off on the thirtieth floor in...five minutes."

Niki once again did as she was told, made her way out of the office, and returned to the elevators, where the sealed doors of the emergency stairwell were waiting. "Wait, why the thirtieth floor?"

"The elevators will automatically drop to the first floor and be locked there until the alarms are deactivated. That means the security team needs to walk all the way up to the floor to check it after they make sure the evacuation has gone without a hitch. You...should be fine."

That wasn't exactly the most inspiring pep talk she'd ever heard, but she didn't need one. She moved close to the doors and ran in place for a few seconds to warm up as she waited for them to open.

Bright red lights flashed almost exactly five minutes

after Vickie said they would and a few seconds later, the doors began to swing open automatically. Niki immediately squeezed through the opening and descended the steps three or four at a time. Worrying about missing a couple and falling the rest of the way down would have been smart, but she couldn't give too much attention to excessive caution.

It was only four flights to the ground floor, but her lungs dragged for air the moment she circled to check that none of the security guards were inspecting the door yet.

None were, and she sprinted past it and took the extra two flights of stairs that led her past the underground parking lot and toward the secure server level. She had managed to make notes of where their target was on the blueprints. There were three underground levels. Two were for parking lots and the one below was for the secure servers.

When Niki reached the lowest level, a sheen of sweat coated her skin and her muscles burned as she pushed through the door. She wouldn't have much time, and if she was able to get out by evacuating with the rest of the building's population, so much the better.

She came to a skidding halt on the waxed floors as she rounded a corner and almost collided headfirst into someone who was running almost as quickly to the door to the stairwell.

There wasn't enough time to see much about him. All she could see was a uniform and a radio at his hip, which was enough to tell her that the man across from her was a security guard.

Or, hell, it could have been a woman for all she could recognize.

She extended her right hand to catch the guard's before it could reach the radio. Her left balled into a fist and launched into his gut.

His breath expelled in a rush as he doubled over. He wore some kind of body armor, but Kevlar didn't do much other than spread the impact of her fist across more of his stomach, and his solar plexus still screamed for attention.

Niki had retained a grasp on the man's hand and twisted it quickly to force him off balance as she jerked her body to the side. The sudden maneuver launched him over her hip and into a nearby wall.

He wasn't unconscious but he was stunned enough that he didn't resist when she removed his radio as well as his phone and any other means of communications.

"What...the fuck?" he asked and tried to regain his wits.

"I'm very, very sorry about this," she whispered. "There's no real fire so you'll be fine. Hopefully. Probably. Anyway, people will come here to make sure you're okay in a short while. For now, don't be a problem."

She pulled the handcuffs from his belt and looped them around nearby piping before she locked his hands to it. The guard didn't look like he understood a word she had said but it still felt important to say.

"Holy shit, Niki rolled the guard." Vickie chuckled through the comms. "Do you think he'll be okay?"

"He'll be fine," Taylor answered with a low laugh. "Wait, play it again."

"Can we focus?" Niki snapped. "Where am I going?"

"Oh." The girl tapped her keyboard for a few seconds.

"The first door to your left will be the server room. Put the dongle I gave you in the nearest USB port and leave it there until I tell you. I need to get our trojan in and out."

She nodded and moved toward the door. It was still open and from the looks of the desk in the corner, the security guard had worked there before the alarms activated. She looked around for a few seconds, still feeling like the adrenaline would burst out of her body at any second, and finally found a USB port.

"Okay, so how long do I wait here?" she asked with a grimace at all the electronics.

"As long as it takes," Vickie replied. "It shouldn't be long, though. I'm opening a back door that allows me access. They'll close it as soon as they find the guy you trounced, but I should be able to—hold on, you have incoming."

"Shit!"

CHAPTER FOURTEEN

There wasn't much space for her to hide. The server room was cramped and the only space she could get into was behind the door.

It was a childhood tactic but it was her only option aside from scrambling under the desk.

Niki circled quickly and stepped behind the door. She hadn't come in with a weapon since the blueprints had told them metal detectors had been installed at the front doors. Maybe she could have picked up a taser or whatever these security guards were equipped with on their belts. That would have helped.

Maybe pepper spray too.

She could hear footsteps approaching the door and her entire body tensed in response. Her mind hadn't yet managed to formulate even a rough plan of what she could do, but she had a feeling it would come to her in a rush when the time came. Taylor and Vickie remained silent, likely not wanting to distract her or maybe trying to find some way to help her.

The door opened and she pressed back against the wall. Booted feet stepped inside and stopped as the guards tried to identify something in the darkened server room. She held her breath to avoid being heard in any way as the three men surveyed the area.

Taylor would have been able to handle the three of them but she was another story. She could disable one or maybe two, but three would be too much.

Her gaze lowered to the closest man's belt and a can of pepper spray secured there.

An idea began to form. It probably wasn't a good one, but it would be a matter of time until they decided to check behind the door.

Vickie still needed time, though.

Niki sucked in a slow breath. Her pulse ticked like a time bomb waiting to go off.

"I'm good. Get the dongle!"

She had waited for the hacker's signal and surged into action like she'd been shot from a gun. Her body powered into the nearest man with enough force to thrust him forward into his two comrades and allowed her to snatch the pepper spray from his belt. As the three tried to extricate themselves and recover from the confusion, she yanked the dongle from the port.

Something snapped as she pulled it out and she wondered if she'd broken something, but Vickie probably already had everything she needed and wouldn't need to use the device anymore.

Hopefully.

Niki backed to the door, took the safety off the spray canister, and pressed the button with her thumb. The air in the room felt like it turned to fire in that split second, but she darted through the entrance and slammed the door shut.

The sound of the lock clicking into place told her Vickie was still watching her back. She could hear shouting from inside the room as the men realized what had happened and why they were suddenly blinded.

The hope that they hadn't been able to see her face was a reasonable one, as well as the fact that she'd caught less than a whiff of the pepper spray. Her nostrils burned slightly and her eyes stung with a few tears, but that could be explained by allergies if anyone asked. She moved past the man she had left handcuffed.

He had slumped and sprawled awkwardly, looking like he was unconscious or maybe suffering from a concussion. She hadn't meant to hit him too hard but she had judo-flipped him into a wall. There was no way to tell what kind of injuries she'd inflicted.

"Sorry," she whispered again, used her sleeve to wipe a couple of tears that had escaped her irritated eyes, and drew a pair of sunglasses from her pocket as she jogged up the steps again.

The sounds of movement above fortunately confirmed that people were still evacuating the building. She darted out of the stairwell and pushed into the crowd, making sure no one noticed her sudden appearance. The security guards waved them through the doors and out of the building.

Inhaling fresh air would have been so much better if her nostrils didn't feel like someone had rubbed them down with literal fire. She jogged away from the group that had assembled outside the building. Most seemed to try to find out what had happened to interrupt their work-day. Maybe it was the single most interesting thing that had happened to them all month. Or maybe this was a common occurrence, given how often the smoke alarms had been triggered in the past.

It wasn't difficult to slip away. A fair number of people did, perhaps to get more coffee or to play hooky for the morning and claim that the incident lasted longer than it did. If she was stuck in an office building day in and day out, she knew she would find almost any opportunity to take time off simply for a change of scenery.

Once she was out of eyeshot of most of them, she jogged to where Taylor had parked the truck, yanked the passenger-side door open, and climbed in.

"Mission accomplished," she rasped and looked around for a bottle of water before she realized her two team-mates were both silent. "Right? We did get the intel we needed?"

Vickie shook her head a couple of times before she turned her attention to the computer. "Uh…yeah, yeah, we got what we needed. Most of the data was heavily encrypted, but I have Desk working on that. Are…are you okay?"

"I'm fine," Niki lied and gulped from the closest water bottle before she removed her sunglasses to pour some over her eyes. She realized they were still staring and shrugged. "I caught a whiff of pepper spray when I maced the guards. It's nothing serious but it hurts like a moth-erfucker."

Taylor nodded and as her eyes started to clear, Niki

could see him slowly slide a pistol into its holster, hoping she wouldn't see it.

"What?" she asked. "What happened?"

"Taylor wanted to go in there to get you out," the hacker reported and straightened her shoulders. "I told him you had it handled and he only needed to intervene if you were in real danger. I knew that wouldn't happen immediately since none of the guards going in there to check the server room were armed with anything but that pepper spray and shit. He disagreed and wanted to go in guns blazing anyway, so I locked the doors. I think he was about to shoot the windows out before I told him you were out of the building."

The man did look annoyed and worked up but also a little ashamed as he put the holstered weapon into the glove compartment. "I still think I should have been ready and waiting outside. In a situation like that, you don't want to be late getting the help into the building, right? Fuckers like G&G aren't known to play with kid gloves when it comes to protecting their intellectual property."

"Yeah, I wanted to ask about that." Niki paused to try to wash more of the spray residue from her face. "Why in the hell does a company like that have that level of security in place? You wouldn't think a firm that deals with biology research would put so much money into security, right?"

"Companies like G&G own thousands of patents in fields like food production and pharmacology that are worth billions of dollars," Taylor explained. He still looked like he was ready to break out of Liz and charge into the building. "They protect those patents with security that some governments might call overkill. The fact that Niki was able to get through their lower levels of security shows exactly how good she is. Believe me, if any of those guards had realized someone was breaking in, we'd be dealing with SWAT teams. And that's why I wanted to be in there just in case."

"Well, we got in, got the shit, and got out alive and… more or less well." She poured a little more water over her eyes. "How long do you think it'll take for Desk to get through that encryption?"

Vickie scowled. "She didn't say and honestly, seeing it, my guesstimate is that it might be a while. We'll keep working on that shit, but we might want to start looking through other avenues. Changing the subject, how the hell did you know about the kind of security these companies have, Taylor? I know it for…you know, reasons. I've had some experience with the assholes in the past but how did you know?"

He started the truck. "They had some merc companies working out of the Zoo. It turns out those guys like to boast about their backers when they've been drinking for a while, and I like to listen. So…Niki, it wasn't that I didn't trust you to get yourself out of the situation on your own, you understand? It's… Well, it's that it's better to be safe than sorry in these cases. And it's better to have backup closer than farther, right?"

Niki smirked and patted him on the shoulder. "I'm well aware that all you wanted to do was protect me, big guy. Thankfully, this time, I didn't need any of it but you keep that shit ready. I'd like to see you bull-rushing a SWAT team and tackling them while I sneak away."

Taylor smirked, pulled the vehicle onto the road, and

pressed slowly on the accelerator. "I swear, this relation-ship will turn my hair gray prematurely."

His partner tilted her head and studied him closely. "Hmm. That wouldn't necessarily be a bad thing. You'd rock the papa bear look, even with red hair. Or maybe because of the red hair."

"I hate to interrupt," Desk announced over the truck's speakers. "I thought you would like to know that while your escape was a little messy, you are in the clear. The police have already been contacted but as far as I can tell, they are looking for a woman with dark hair who was seen leaving the building, which...well, I don't need to tell you it's hardly the most complete description. I managed to scrub all images of your presence in the facility, so they shouldn't be able to identify you. I'll continue to monitor the investigation as it progresses but you should be safe for now."

"Good to hear, Desk," Niki said as the burning in her nose and eyes began to recede. "How are you doing with cracking that encryption?"

"It is challenging," the AI admitted. "Military-level encryption might take me some time to break through, assuming you want the data we collected to be intact when we finally get it."

"We do!" Vickie insisted from the back seat.

"In that case, it will take me some time. While you wait, however, I have received communications from a PR representative from Granger Tech who wants to talk to the newly established McFadden and Banks about a possible business opportunity. They asked if they could confirm a meeting with either one or both Niki and Taylor for tomorrow morning."

"Granger Tech?" Niki asked.

The hacker raised a hand before she tapped her computer. "Uh...Granger Tech, founded three years ago, a new arrival in the weapons market but making some waves. They won bids on a couple of minor government contracts last year."

"Okay," her cousin muttered. "I think we can make the meeting but we shouldn't go into it blind. Do you think we can get intel on them before tomorrow? Nothing too deep and nothing that will get you caught. We only want to make sure this isn't the kind of company that'll get us involved in the wrong kind of business."

"I'm already on it," the girl confirmed and gave them a thumbs-up.

"And I will continue my efforts," Desk announced. "I am glad you were able to escape the building without extensive injury, Niki."

"Thanks, Desk," she answered. "Me too."

CHAPTER FIFTEEN

"What are you thinking?"

Taylor looked up from his coffee and shrugged casually. "What makes you so sure I'm thinking anything?"

Niki rolled her eyes. "You have that look on your face—the kind that says you have something on your mind you want to share with me."

He raised an eyebrow and took another sip of his coffee. "Damn, I can't believe I'm getting predictable. I was always told this day would come but I hoped it never would."

"Stop deflecting and spill."

"Honestly, I don't know what to think about this Granger Tech." He scowled deeply and tugged irascibly at his beard. "Vickie saying there's nothing in there about them that raises any red flags makes me more suspicious. Weapons companies don't have clean records like that."

"Technically, I think she said there's no reason why they would have any problems with us, so there's probably nothing to be worried about."

"That's what I mean. It could be a trap."

"Or it could merely be some folk who want to make use of our services. We're looking to expand our client base, and this is something we'll have to do if we want to have more people working with us."

Taylor nodded. "You can't blame me for being a little paranoid, though."

"No, I can't," Niki replied. "But this is why they agreed to meet us at a neutral location."

They stopped talking when they heard the sound of people approaching the conference room they had rented for a couple of hours for the meeting. Granger Tech had offices in the city, but no one felt comfortable meeting there. Since McFadden and Banks didn't have any offices of their own, they found a location that was willing to house the meeting for an hourly fee.

It was nice. The place was set up for the kind of corporate collaboration that likely was the lifeblood of the city of Washington DC.

With that said, Taylor wondered if it wouldn't be a good idea for them to acquire offices. All they needed was a small location that didn't cost too much from which they could run their operations and use it as a corporate base.

But that was a matter for later. It sounded like their potential new clients had arrived, were being shown in by the people who owned the location in question, and were offered coffee and food, which some of them accepted.

They didn't look much like the weapon merchants Taylor had seen in the past, most of whom were the kind of fat cats who had been around Washington for a while. They came from old money and their families had been gaming the system in their favor since the founding fathers.

These representatives looked fresh, young, and ready to fight for a new position. There was always an infusion of fresh blood with every generation in Washington, and as far as he knew, it invariably ended the same way with the newcomers either being pushed out, ground out, or bought out.

Still, it was nice to think these guys had a chance. They didn't look like they were there to maintain the status quo but rather like they wanted to shake things up a little.

The man in charge—who was testing the coffee—looked like he was barely into his early thirties and wore a flashy dark-blue suit with his hair slicked stylishly. He looked more like a salesman than a businessman, although he knew he was the Senior Vice President of Public Relations for Granger Tech.

"Sal Colman," the man introduced himself and shook Taylor's hand first and then Niki's before the former motioned for them to all take their seats. "First, I have to say it's a real honor to meet you, Mr. McFadden. We've all heard so much about you and what you did in the Zoo—and what you've done here in the States since you got back."

Taylor scowled but tried not to look too displeased. For one thing, he wasn't sure how much the man could know about his recent operations given how paranoid the agencies were about confidentiality. Either he had a highly-placed informant—which stirred all kinds of problems and ramifications—or he was simply feigning knowledge to butter him up for a pitch. "Thanks, I guess. You can call me Taylor, though."

"Of course, I'm sorry." The visitor laughed nervously. "We wanted to talk to you about the possibility of going into business and an offer I think we'll both benefit from. See, there are many people you've encountered in your operations who have paid attention to the weaponry and equipment you've used since you broke out on your own. We've looked into market research that has shown empirically that sales for the TrueGuard Mark XVII have gone up by eighty-three percent since it became known that you used it.

"Independent operatives and the military talk, Mr. McFadden, and the accouterments for the suits sold have matched your preferences almost exactly all across the line. This has forced TrueGuard to push a deadline up to introduce their new Mark XVIII to cash in on its newfound popularity."

Taylor narrowed his eyes. He couldn't deny that he liked the Mark XVII and looked forward to trying the new model when it reached the market, but he hadn't been aware that anyone had paid attention to the suits he had worn. But there had been occasions when he'd interacted with both merc groups and soldiers, so it wasn't unlikely that they would have taken note without him realizing it.

"What are you saying, exactly?"

"Well, I guess what we're saying is that you've become something of a kingmaker when it comes to which suits will be popular in the private market. All the governments are tied into contracts with the lowest bidder, as I'm sure you're aware. Those are all political, but we're going for the dark horse, and we want to break out big in the market of private investment.

"We have some of the top engineers in the field making very effective changes to the way the mech suits are being designed to make them more user-friendly, more powerful in the short-range engagements, and pack more heat for the longer-range fights, all while working with the same prices the big guys are selling. Now, of course, we can't pull off the production bulk the larger companies like True-Guard, Pegasus, Calleans, and Fencer can, but we know our quality is enough to put us on the map. What we need is someone to break us into the market we're trying to reach."

"You...want me to promote your suits and weapons?" Taylor asked and raised an eyebrow skeptically.

"Something like that would be where we want it to lead but more importantly, we would like you to test the new designs we will put on the market in three months to make sure they're what the potential clients will be looking for when it comes to suits. We have complete confidence in our engineers and testers, of course, but there's nothing quite like the word of someone who's been there and done that."

They had a whole presentation prepared that included the sales on the suit he was using compared to those on the other suits on the market. Of course, they didn't compare the tank-type suits or the lighter hybrids, only the regular combat suits. It made sense since the larger and smaller suits weren't sold in quite the numbers that the more combat-oriented suits were.

"Our designs have been fitted with new and improved

magnetic-mobilization technology that reduces the dependency on hydraulic systems to facilitate the power functions of the suit. The reduced requirements allow the hydraulic system to be better focused and thus results in better sensitivity and dexterity on joint movements through the rest of the suit. This should give you the edge on close-quarters combat and finer control of your weapons, which assists in longer-range shooting, if necessary."

Taylor frowned as he considered this and nodded. "Okay, I think I've seen that somewhere before."

Coleman continued like he hadn't heard what he'd said. "In addition, we have also designed suits that have additional mechanical limbs that would, while being AI-controlled, also assist in combat situations and mobility in tough terrain."

"We've definitely seen that before," Niki muttered under her breath.

A flash of annoyance crossed the man's face as he nodded. "We have put a handful of prototypes out for sale, and from what we've heard, they are quite popular in the Zoo—and very useful as well. I understand if you think it might be too much to get used to when you're already accustomed to the design of another suit, but all these new additions are far more functional than you might think, as well as quite user-friendly. We can almost guarantee that once you're used to them, you won't settle for anything less."

He nodded. "Sure. I can't promise anything until we've put the suits to the test. I'm fairly sure we've seen a couple of your prototypes in action in the field, and I think a mechanic friend of mine has been able to work on and improve a couple. If they are that effective, it should be interesting."

"That's all we can ask for at this point," Coleman insisted and flipped through a handful of vids that showed the functional effects of the suits they were selling. Taylor knew better than to buy into hype videos, though, since too many times, they were tested in sterile conditions and the failures were cut out of the film that was shown.

Still, if they had displays of the suit ready for the show, he wouldn't turn that down. Sal Jacobs had the kind of suits they were talking about and was likely in possession of their prototype. If this meant he was looking at the combat suit version of what the kid used in the Zoo, he was all for making that shit more popular.

The team began to head down the stairs and Niki nudged him gently in the ribs.

"What?"

She tilted her head with a somewhat disgruntled smirk. "You didn't realize it, did you?"

"Obviously not. What happened?"

"You guys all geeked out over the suits and they acted like your fanboys, all while they basically ignored me. The other co-founder of the company."

Taylor raised an eyebrow, and after a few seconds of thought, he realized she was right. "I guess they must have thought you don't know much about suits and likely wouldn't be as interested in working with them. Erroneously, which means they should have done their research a little better since anything that involves me working here in the States would have your name stamped all over it.

That's if their sources of information are real and accurate."

Niki nodded. "I swear it's how you people react when you look into those new VR games about the Zoo. You simply zone everything out. You know that Testosterone Titties has sold over fifty million digital copies?"

"I'm sorry…Testosterone Titties?"

"You haven't seen it? It's that game about super sexy ladies who go into the Zoo to fight monsters. They wear suits that have boob plates. You know, the armor that's—"

"I know what boob plates are."

"That and the boob physics are completely off, but it doesn't matter. I can rock these ladies for all they're worth—"

"Damn straight you can."

She smirked at his wink and continued. "But when it comes right down to it, you'll always be more distracted by the weapons that make everything go boom instead, zoning everything else out."

"I'll work on that. But you have to admit, the things that go boom are quite…uh, distracting."

"I know, and I'd be lying if I said I wasn't distracted too, but still. Keep your head on your shoulders. These guys are trying to sell you on something. And don't think for a second they wouldn't fuck you over if it meant pushing their sales numbers up."

"Agreed." Taylor nudged her in the shoulder. "Now, would you be an adult and go and check the fun things that make other things go boom with me?"

Her laugh was light-hearted. "Well, all you had to do was ask."

They followed the team down the stairs and had to pick the pace up to catch up with them as they reached the parking lot. He now realized that, along with the limo that had brought the PR team to the meeting, a truck waited as well.

"Oh, this doesn't bode well," Niki whispered.

He knew what she meant but wanted to give them a chance to prove him wrong as they approached the vehicle. The doors were already swinging open electronically to expose what they had brought as part of the presentation.

"Oh, fuck me." He sighed and rubbed his temples.

Inside, he could see three suits, already put together and hanging from harnesses for display. He had to say these guys had panache and showmanship, but there were a couple of things they needed to get straight first.

"Well, then." Coleman was beaming at the triumphant reveal of the suits. "Which one do you want to try first?"

"Honestly, I won't try any here," he stated calmly. "Those suits tend to make something of a mess when people are working the kinks out for the first time. Secondly, you brought...what, six? Seven and a half tons of futuristic mech suits, with what looks like fully loaded and functional assault rifles, rocket and grenade launchers, and other assorted weapons to a pitch meeting?"

"There's nothing like showing the real thing to get people on board, wouldn't you say?"

"Sure, right up until someone shows up and appropriates it while it's parked out here." Taylor shook his head. He wanted to admire the craftsmanship of what looked like impressive feats of engineering, but there was no reason for them to have brought it to the pitch meeting.

"What else would we have brought except for the real thing?"

He shrugged. "Design plans, functional pieces—the kind that would fit in a briefcase—and maybe your lead engineer to answer questions or explain significant advantages. I appreciate the display but I won't test these here."

"That's...fair," Coleman admitted. "When and where do you think it would be appropriate to try them?"

"We've got our hands on an abandoned warehouse in the outskirts of the city. Our tech expert should already be there setting it up. What do you say sometime this afternoon? Once we're ready for you, bring the truck around and we'll give the suits a test in a secure, safe location."

"Uh, maybe..." Niki interjected.

He nodded at her in agreement. "Okay, safer. More controlled, anyway. There's less chance of accidentally blowing a hole in some building or another."

"That's fantastic, then!" the man announced. He grinned from ear to ear and ran his fingers through his short brown hair. "Shall we say...three? We can have everything ready by then."

"We'll be ready," Taylor told him and shook his hand. "I'll send you guys the address."

The group returned to the limo as the truck closed again, and it wasn't long until the entire team had left.

Niki broke out laughing once they were gone. "You have to hand it to them. They are...enthusiastic."

"They like to show their stuff, which means they have considerable confidence in it," he conceded. "I guess it's up to us to see if that confidence is well-placed."

She still didn't understand why people insisted on having these meetings in person. It felt like it was more a matter of habit that none of the old farts wanted to get rid of, but at the same time, they were all well into their sixties and seventies. Most of them spent very little time working at the company and only arrived for board meetings. They always filled the conference room with the smell of coffee and talcum powder—the source of which Monica didn't know and didn't want to know—and each meeting left her with a bad taste in her mouth.

Every one of them could have transferred their duties to a proxy or attended the meetings online, but none of them wanted to. They needed to come in and listen to the CFOs and managers drone on for hours in person.

Still, it was a necessary evil. She had committed to more than she could count on her way up the corporate ladder, and there was absolutely no reason that she couldn't add another to the list.

She wore her bright purple pantsuit with matching heels with her hair done up in a rigid bun, all of which contributed to the fact that none of the geezers had spent any time on her. Her tenure with the company had been long enough to know it was a mistake to appear in anything they might find appealing, and that knowledge did help to raise her spirits somewhat as she picked her pace up so her two assistants had to rush to catch up with her.

It wasn't until she was about to pull the door of her

office open that she realized someone waited inside for her.

He was a tall man in a dull gray suit and had the look of someone who had been an NCO about a decade before. Still as fit and trim as the day he exited boot camp, he sat ramrod-straight in his chair—the kind of man who needed to be ordered to relax, and even then, it was an uphill fight. He looked like he would be uncomfortable in anything but a uniform, although maybe that had something to do with his hair being cropped short. About regulation length, she assumed.

"Mr. Cornwall. How nice of you to come by," she stated crisply and motioned for her assistants to remain outside as she shut the door to her corner office. "Can I offer you something? There's a wet bar behind you if you feel like taking the edge off a little."

"I'm fine, ma'am," he insisted. "Thank you. I'm afraid I've come here with some bad news."

Monica raised an eyebrow but took a moment to place a handful of ice cubes in a crystal glass before she filled it the rest of the way with the scotch she had in a decanter. "Oh? What kind of bad news?"

"The worrying kind," he admitted. "As head of security for Turing Unlimited, I thought I should deliver this information to you personally and before it reached the rest of the board."

She took a seat behind her desk and sipped her drink calmly before she nodded. "Go on."

"There was a breach at one of our secure facilities in DC."

"A breach? Which facility?"

"The one run by G&G. The secure servers were supposed to be protected by some of the best security companies in the country, but something...went wrong. The security team was disabled and the infiltrators were able to make off with an unknown amount of data. They were able to scrub their presence digitally so we only have a vague notion of a dark-haired woman being the infiltrator, but even then, our men aren't sure."

"Was anyone injured?"

"One man is in the hospital with a concussion. Three others needed treatment for injuries sustained from pepper spray but should be all right."

There was no way she would show her true reaction in front of Cornwall. To call the man a straight arrow would put all other straight arrows to shame, and if he knew what was contained on those servers, he would immediately quit and probably turn them over to the SEC, the FBI, and any other agency that would lend him an ear.

All she could do was take another sip from her scotch. "Well, there's that at least. Do the techs know what was taken?"

"They're combing the files, but it looks like whatever was taken was copied and transferred via a physical connection. I...I'll admit that I'm not sure what they were talking about but it seems it's quite difficult to trace. If...if I could ask, ma'am, should I write a resignation letter?"

She looked up from her desk and stared at him in momentary confusion. Of course he was worried about being fired and he would do it in a way he considered to be honorable. She could respect that but there was no need.

"I don't think so, Cornwall," Monica replied and placed

her glass on a coaster on her desk. "This wasn't your fault, and while I do expect you to continue to pursue it, there's a reason why I brought you in as our security chief. It's because I know you'll put every effort into making sure it never happens again and that those responsible are brought to justice."

"Of course."

He wasn't the most political fellow but he was an ingenious soldier. Now that he had a target, there wasn't much in the world that could stop him from getting to them, no matter how evasive they were.

"Honestly, it's kind of flattering to know there are lazy companies out there that are willing to put everything on the line simply to get their hands on our secrets. And assuming they're that lazy, I guess it means they'll be much easier to find."

"Of course, ma'am."

"I have a couple of calls to make and I'll look into the possible details myself." She nodded toward the door. "I'd like a full report on the situation before the end of the week, please."

"Of course, ma'am. I'll let you know if there are any new developments."

He pushed to his feet and all but marched to the door while Monica watched him leave. She waited until the door was shut before she took a long, calming breath.

"Fucking shit," she muttered on the tail end of a long breath out. Feeling a little calmer, she snatched her phone up and pressed the button that would connect her to one of her assistants.

"Miss Keller?"

"Be a dear and set me up with a secure line, please?"

"Of course, ma'am."

The line beeped and dialed a couple of times before indicating it was ready to make the call, and she quickly punched in a number she had already committed to memory.

It rang three times before someone answered.

"Hello?"

She forced a smile, an old trick that made her voice sound a little more positive. "Good morning, Bob. I hope I'm not interrupting anything."

A moment of silence lingered on the line before the familiar voice continued. "Nothing very important. And you know I'd rather you call me Robert, right?"

"That's why I call you Bob."

She wasn't a fan of the sign and countersign lingo, but the man insisted on making sure there was no possibility of either of them saying anything on a compromised line.

"So, I heard about that barbeque you're throwing," she continued and recalled the code she had spent hours memorizing. "I hope you didn't burn the ribs again. You know I hate it when you simply pick them up from Dreamland."

"Damn, I did burn them to cinders, unfortunately," he replied and sounded genuinely regretful. "They were utterly inedible, trust me. Maryanne didn't want anything to do with it and almost swore off all meat when she saw the results. I set a timer and everything, but it still didn't go right. I didn't catch them in time, I'm afraid."

Monica sighed and wracked her brain to remember what the man was talking about. The target was burned and there was no sign that the local law enforcement thought it was anything but an accident if she translated it right.

"Right," she muttered and hoped she hadn't misunderstood anything. "Well, you should know that my Aunt Karen wanted to make it to your barbeque, but her car got stolen right out of her garage. It seems like someone truly wanted that Datsun, although I'm not sure how much good it'll do them. Still, we have the local cops looking around and trying to find it, but you might end up having to pick her up and give her a ride to your place when the time comes."

She made it about as clear as she intended to. The data had been stolen from in-house, and the chances were that she would need him to cut off any and all loose ends, including whoever the thieves were.

He paused, likely translating her code as well. "Well, that's unfortunate. Do you think you could wire me the gas money beforehand?"

"We'll see if we need you to give her a ride, then we'll talk about gas money."

Despite everything else, he was a businessman and she couldn't blame him for wanting money to be kept on retainer.

"All right, then. You give me a ring if you need me for anything else. I'll make sure the brisket is to die for."

"Well, things might be a little busy on this end but I'll let you know if an opening appears. I'll see you around, Robert."

"And I appreciate you using my preferred name."

She wasn't sure what that meant exactly, except that he

wanted to meet, but it didn't matter as he hung up. The man had spent too much time reading spy novels, but if this was the game he wanted to play, she would have to go along with it. He was the best in the business, after all.

"Okay." Vickie grunted in irritation and put her headset down. "Why the fuck would this woman need to get on a secure line to talk to her friend Bob about a barbeque?"

Desk needed a few seconds to realize she was speaking to her. The AI was spread thin while working on decoding the data, and the girl knew she could expect a reduced response time.

"Do you think there are actual barbeque plans she wants to be kept secret from anyone listening in on the switchboard of her building?"

The hacker shrugged. "I suppose it's a possibility but one that's very fucking remote."

"Agreed. The most likely scenario was that she was discussing something in code. It would be difficult to decode the conversation without some kind of cipher, but given that she made the call less than a minute after her head of security informed her of our efforts yesterday, I think it might have something to do with that."

"Probably, but what do you think they were talking about?" She replayed the recording of the conversation. "Burnt to a crisp? Ribs? Do you think they're talking about Dr. Santana? Because if they are, all I have to say is ew. Seriously fucking gross."

"I doubt they would have eaten the scientist."

"Maybe not, but the mental image alone makes me want to throw up."

"The reaction is quite appropriate, but in the conversation, they do discuss the burning to a crisp. It would not be enough to stand in a court of law but even so, I believe we have found our perpetrators."

"Well, found is a little subjective. I wasn't able to track the call past the switchboard. But the CEO being involved in the killing does seem like it's enough knowledge. We could put an electronic trace on her—see if we can catch her meeting any unsavory characters who did the deed."

Desk processed the possibility for a few long seconds. A little too long.

"It would be unlikely that she would make such a mistake, but it is still a possibility. I'll get on that."

"You're a little overtaxed as it is," Vickie noted. "Why don't I take care of that?"

"That would be appreciated."

The girl shook her head. "Do you think this is enough information for us to update spy lady? Or do you think we should keep digging and see if something else pops up?"

"I would suggest maintaining the advantage of knowledge for as long as possible, or at least until the point where it becomes more advantageous to share the information."

It was a good idea, even from an overworked AI. "Yeah, I guess. I'll talk to Taylor and Niki too and see if they have any thoughts. They're part of this company too, you know."

"The two other founding members?"

"Sure, but it was always my idea, so I'm the original founding member, no matter the name they put on it."

CHAPTER SIXTEEN

There weren't many cop stereotypes he liked to perpetuate. Considerable work went into making sure they were cleaning their act up, so none of the bad shit was taken up anymore.

With that said, one stereotype was true. All men who worked the kind of hours they did needed the spark of energy that came from a caffeine and sugar combo, and there weren't many places that delivered on that combo better than the local doughnut shop.

That and the fact that the owner had a standing twenty-five percent discount to all police officers who frequented his establishment. It was fairly ingenious since it meant the business would always have a police presence, every day of the week and any time of the day.

But there was always something to be said about not being too predictable, and Nathan could almost feel the point ramming him in the balls when he saw someone waiting at the counter.

It was weird that he could recognize her simply from

her ass—or, rather, the way her ass looked in a pantsuit. It was probably a little sexist of him too but at this point, he didn't give a shit about that.

He cleared his throat, consciously avoided looking like he was trying to protect his genitals, and advanced to the counter.

She heard his footsteps, turned, and smiled when she saw him approach.

"Morning, Nate. What are the chances of running into you here?"

"Fairly good, given that I come here every day around nine for breakfast. Which you would know, right?"

She smirked. "I don't know what you're talking about. I merely remembered someone raving about the quality of the coffee and pastries here and I thought I'd give it a try while I was in DC. Wouldn't you know that they give that same quarter-off discount to Homeland Security agents?"

"You heard that from me." Nathan tried not to sound too petty or angry and realized that he failed miserably. "I was the one who told you about this place, so your timing in coming here couldn't have been a coincidence, which means you came here to find me. Is this only you being a bitch or is there some news my partner should hear about? Because he's waiting outside in the car."

"Honestly, this is me trying to get back on a semblance of your good side." She turned to collect the order that was pushed across the counter. He recognized his usual order of doughnut holes and chocolate glazed, along with a cappuccino and a black coffee with seven sugars for Benson. "Thanks, Tommy, you're the best."

He scowled. "That looks suspiciously like a bribe, which means you want something. What do you want?"

"Well, I wouldn't call it a bribe."

"I'm out."

She reached out and caught him by the shoulder to turn him. "Okay, okay. Look, I'm sorry. No more games. I'm having a problem with a case—one you and your partner are in charge of—and I need some unique insight."

Nathan narrowed his eyes. "Wait, do you mean that fire? It's already been ruled an accidental death. They're having the funeral in a couple of days and cremated the poor bastard for some reason."

"That's the problem I have. So why don't you call your partner in and we can have a conversation between the three of us."

"Because he might see the perky tits, round ass, and sultry mouth and let that distract him from the monster inside."

"Sticks and stones, Nathan."

"I don't hear you denying it."

"Still, it's hurtful."

He picked the coffees and doughnut box up, fully intending to return to the car. But he was a police officer above all else, which meant that if the HS agent had something to add to what others had already ruled was an accidental death, it was his job to hear it, no matter how monstrous the source was.

With a sigh, he walked to one of the tables and put the coffees and doughnuts on it before he retrieved his phone and pressed the first number on his quick dial list.

"What? Do you need help to carry it all to the car?" Benson asked when he answered his phone.

"No, I think we'll sit in for this one. Someone here wants to have a chat, and I can't believe I'm saying this but I think we'll want to hear what she has to say."

His partner thought about it for a few seconds and sighed. "Fine, but if we're late for the roll call, I'll blame you."

"Nope, you'll blame someone else."

"Who?"

"Come inside and see, dumbass."

He could see his partner climb out of the car, lock it, and walk across the parking lot to the shop.

When he arrived, he startled when he saw Rosalyn seated across from Nathan and calmly sipping a cup of coffee.

"What the fuck?" he muttered as he approached the table and sat beside his partner and across from her. "What's going on here? Are you looking to torment my partner some more?"

"Far from it," she replied and sounded like she had expected the question. "I'm here to talk about a case you guys closed as an accidental death. You remember, the guy who set his house on fire?"

"Right, the guy who got drunk, got smoking, and took a nap that lasted much longer than intended." Benson nodded, collected his cappuccino from the tray, and took a sip. "That's a closed case. The funeral's happening in a couple of days. The ironic thing is that they cremated the bastard. Is that irony?"

"I think it's merely a coincidence," Rosalyn pointed out.

"Either way, some evidence has come to light that indicates it might not be as open and shut as originally thought."

"I thought we went over this," he retorted. "You looked at the scene yourself and even talked to the fire marshal. There wasn't anything to indicate that it was anything but an accident."

"Sure." She paused and took a sip before she continued. "But this was a guy who, by the word of his bosses, was powered by sheer will. He was nothing but a perfectionist at work, and from the looks of the photos he had online, his home was the same way. The man quit cold-turkey and suddenly, charges appear on his credit card buying in three different places?"

"Stress at work might have been getting to him," Nathan pointed out. "You never know what'll make an addict relapse."

"Sure, okay, but who the hell falls asleep with a lit cigarette anymore? They have the warnings on the cartons, for fuck's sake. Also, he somehow happened to slosh a five-hundred-dollar bottle of absinthe all over himself—which he was supposedly drinking without a glass—and all over his bed. That happens to be one of the most flammable spirits out there."

Nathan looked at his partner, and both men acknowledged a hint of niggling doubt. They both hated the feeling.

"Okay, those make a fair number of coincidences," Benson conceded. "But coincidences happen all the time, and you wouldn't come to us with this unless you had more than a string of conjectures."

"So are you telling me that neither of you believes this could have been a murder and not an accident?" She leaned forward like she was trying to goad them into admitting something.

Nathan felt like she attempted to probe them for information by telling them shit they already knew. As much as he felt that trusting her was a good idea, a dull ache between his legs reminded him that it probably wasn't.

Benson finally answered. "There's a lot wrong with it, so if there were any evidence of foul play involved, of course we would need to investigate it properly. Assuming you have any such evidence?"

Rosalyn raised an eyebrow and toyed with her coffee cup. "But all the evidence points toward an accidental death, and if the evidence says so, we can't go against it without the question of bias coming up in court."

"Bullshit," Nathan snapped. "Do you honestly expect us to believe you came here fishing for information without having some knowledge we lack? Seriously, we all know fires are generally the best at cleaning any trace evidence that might have been left behind by a perpetrator. Hell, the medical examiner couldn't even run toxicology tests on what was left of the guy due to the fire causing too much damage. We don't even know if he was drunk or not. But unless you have any evidence that could tilt it over the edge of plausibility, there's nothing we can do."

Rosalyn tilted her head and fixed him with a firm look. "Well, that's good enough for me. Unfortunately, I don't have any evidence that there might have been foul play involved. Only...conjectures and theories—possibilities. But I have a team gathering shit, and if they find anything, you can bet you'll be the first to know about it."

She stood, and Nathan pushed to his feet as well,

leaving Benson with the coffees and doughnuts while he followed her out.

"You're not bullshitting us, right? All our personal history aside, we're here to do a job and I know you wouldn't get in the way of keeping people safe and alive, right?"

"Right," she answered and turned to face him. "And again, I don't have anything concrete, but I wanted to make sure your gut instinct said that something stunk about it. Because all our personal history aside, you have good instincts for this kind of thing. And again, if my team does find anything, I'll know I'm bringing it to the eyes of people who will be open to the possibility."

He nodded. "Well, we'll never turn help down from Homeland Security. And...I appreciate it. Your comment about my instincts, that is."

Rosalyn looked around and let the awkward silence drag on for a few long seconds. "It wasn't all bad, right? There were some good things about us?"

He honestly hadn't expected the conversation to turn in that direction. She had never been the kind of person who indulged in introspection, but maybe she had changed since the breakup.

"I think the only good thing I can remember from our relationship was that the sex was incredible. But when that was over, we simply weren't compatible. We fought like cats and dogs or became passive-aggressive, which ended up coming to a head with the...incident."

She sighed. "Yeah, I guess you're right."

"It was good to see you again, Rosalyn," he said and realized that he meant it, despite everything.

"You too. See you around, Nathan."

He turned away and heard her walk to her car, open the door, and start the engine. As she drove away, he returned to the table where Benson was still waiting for him.

"Do you want to talk about it?" the older man asked as he took the seat she had been in.

It was still warm. Weird.

"Nah," he lied. "I'm fine."

"Is that why you're walking like you need to cover for a nut shot coming in at any time?"

Nathan cleared his throat. "I said I'm fine. Let's head to the station. We're probably already late for the sarge's roll call."

They needed to acquire actual offices in the DC area. It was already a busy day, with a ton of shit to do before they could focus on getting the work done.

Niki didn't like meetings. They always felt like a waste of time since the real focus was to make sure everyone was always on the same page. If people weren't on the same page in shit, it meant they weren't doing their job right.

But she wouldn't bring that up. Besides, it had been a while since she'd run into Jensen and Maxwell and it would be nice to hear from them again.

Even if it was over yet another meeting, this time a lunch held in one of the hundreds of places that were elevated to a decent enough standard for the thousands of business lunches conducted in the city on any given day.

The restaurant Trond had suggested was having a

special on halibut, and she said they would order that once the rest of their party arrived, although the waiter should go ahead and get their drinks ready.

"Do you think this is a good idea?" Taylor asked.

"What?" she countered. "We can both agree, working with the DOD will always be something of a headache, but I thought you would look forward to seeing Jansen and Maxwell again. They did a good job prepping you for that fistfight you got yourself into, right?"

"First, I didn't get myself into that fight. I merely finished it as emphatically as I could."

She snickered. "I know, but it's still fun to tease you about it."

He rolled his eyes. "Secondly, I was talking about ordering a beer for both of us since one of us will have to drive and we have those suits to test."

That gave her pause and she shook her head. "Right you are. But we ordered the beers already."

"You can go ahead and take them," he answered, seeing where her mind was going. "I'll order a soda or something."

Niki grinned and nudged him in the shoulder as they saw Jansen and Maxwell both enter the restaurant. The men told the waiter who greeted them that they were expected and they were directed to the table.

Maxwell was a little shorter than Taylor was, which made him as difficult to miss as he had about twenty pounds of muscle on him. His build and height matched the look of short hair and a neatly groomed beard.

Jansen was a little less conspicuous. He came in at a more average height and weight, which made his clean-shaven look matched with the short blond hair all that more regular.

But there was nothing ordinary about the two men who joined them at their table. Before they could sit, Niki pushed to her feet and wrapped them both in a shared hug.

"It's nice to see you guys again," she admitted as she finally broke the contact and motioned for them to take their seats. "I have to say that while I like working for myself, the support staff doesn't quite rise to the challenge."

"Hey!" Taylor exclaimed.

"Are you saying you have the connections and work ethics of these two?"

"Me? No. Vickie does, on the other hand, and she's probably listening in on the conversation too."

Her eyes widened and the new arrivals grinned.

"You done fucked up now," Jansen pointed out. "Get ready for embarrassing high school pictures to surface somewhere."

Niki nodded. It was fair and she had asked for it by speaking without thinking, although she started to work on the apology she would give the girl while they placed their order.

"How have things been going with your task force?" Taylor asked Jansen and took a sip of his bubbly water.

"Filling Niki's shoes will never be an easy task," the man admitted. "But moving forward, I think we'll make significant progress in preventing the bad shit from happening. There's still too much red tape, especially in our international dealings, which we might need your help with."

"I assume that's why you set this meeting up," Niki stated.

He nodded. "Yep. We've had some jurisdictional issues with our friends up north. The Canadians are importing some of the Zoo products, and they don't want anyone from the Pentagon to investigate their problems. While I can't blame them, it must be mentioned that they lack certain qualifying elements in dealing with potential problems and the locations of one or two of these make them a definite threat to the US. They don't want direct influence from the Pentagon, but they were more than happy to accept external contractors who would have the experience to deal with that kind of issue."

"In Canada?" Taylor asked as their halibut plates arrived. "I always thought the Zoo would have problems settling into colder climates. I know we've had a couple of situations in the northern areas of the country, but the overwhelming majority have been in the southern half, right?"

Niki nodded. "Sure, but...that's always been a matter of correlation not implying causation. There are probably a few more variables at play so the temperature might not be the issue."

"Fuck." He grunted, nudged the fish on his plate, and mixed it with the sautéed vegetables. "So what would you like us to do, exactly?"

Maxwell was already digging into the meal, but Jansen showed a little more restraint and answered the question.

"Honestly, the fact of the matter is that they wanted someone involved who knows what they're dealing with and isn't directly affiliated with the US government. That way, they keep the nationalists and the alarmists happy about the whole situation." He raised his hand, anticipating the annoyance from both freelancers. "I know, I know. No one hates the politics more than I do, but they need someone in there who believes in their work, not only their paychecks. Honestly, you two were the first names that came to my mind."

Niki watched as Taylor toyed with his food. The idea of the Zoo continuing to spread across the borders that were supposed to contain it distressed him more than he would ever choose to admit. There was no chance that he would turn the offer down.

"We'll do it," she asserted and took a mouthful from her plate.

Jansen grinned. "Fantastic. I'll send the message along. Once they know who and when, they'll contact me again. The chances are you'll have work north of the border... sometime next Tuesday, probably."

There wasn't much else to say and the silence seemed to envelop them like a blanket.

"So," she said briskly after taking a sip of her beer. "Now that we have the business out of the way, why don't we get into how the two of you have been doing? We know about how the work has been treating you, but you two made about as much money as we did on the fight so that has to be something to have in mind?"

"Trond is a stick in the mud," Maxwell complained and pointed at the man seated next to him. "Here I am saying we should use the money, spend a little on ourselves, go for a vacation, buy a sports car or a yacht or something, but no. He's all about dropping the money into low-risk, long-term investments."

"There's nothing wrong with keeping my options for the future open," Jansen insisted, and Niki sensed this was an ongoing argument between the two. "The chances are I'll be able to retire from public service in the next couple of years and with a pension too, so I'll be able to have my mid-life crisis then. For now, while there's work to be done, it would be best to put the money to work, right?"

"Hell, we could run head-first into a horde of crazed, hungry monsters tomorrow," his partner countered. "Since that's a risk we live with in our day-to-day lives, I don't see why we can't have a little fun now with some of the money while we let the rest go into investment."

"You both make excellent points," Taylor pointed out. "But you'll want to plan for success instead of failure. It's what I did, more or less. The idea being that if you survive, you'll want to have enough to bring you some semblance of comfort once it's all finished and if you die, that won't matter anyway."

She narrowed her eyes. "Wait, so what you're suggesting is…a compromise?"

"Something like that. Going on a shopping spree is fun for about five minutes and then you'll want more to keep getting that endorphin high. It's very easy to get addicted, so you need to keep yourself in check that way too. Why?"

"Nothing." She shook her head. "It makes sense but sounds weird coming from you."

CHAPTER SEVENTEEN

There was something to be said about looking at a building and seeing what it could be instead of what it was.

Taylor recalled the experience when he'd decided to buy the strip mall. The price was good but there was more potential involved than was immediately apparent to the naked eye.

And in the end, that was why he pulled the trigger on the warehouse Vickie had found for them. It was outside the city limits and close to an old railway station that had long since been abandoned, with nothing else for miles around.

That plus the fact that it had all the modern facilities they needed to operate showed that there was more than enough potential for them to work with.

He pulled the truck into the parking lot, stepped out lightly, and studied the building closely as Niki joined him.

"I have to say it looks much better than the strip mall," she noted and patted him on the shoulder.

"Sure, but that's not the highest of bars. But in the end, I think it'll do quite nicely. And Vickie got a good deal on it too. A lease that could turn to ownership in six months, which is about when we'll know if we need a base of operations here."

"There's no conference room," Niki noted. "We need one, honestly. Renting them for the meetings simply isn't a real solution."

"Sure. We could always repurpose some of the living quarters or maybe set something up inside."

She looked at him in surprise. "Wait, there are living quarters?"

"Yeah. Small studio apartments with kitchenettes and bathrooms. They are all recently refurbished and furnished too, so if we need to spend time here, we won't have to find a hotel every time. A hotel would probably be the better option in the short-term, but still."

"Investments," Niki noted. "Although I guess this place was a little more expensive than the strip mall."

"Well, yeah."

"Why would they need living quarters in a warehouse, though?"

Taylor shrugged. "Maybe the guys who worked the train station over there needed a place to sleep when they were alternating shifts. Or maybe they simply wanted to have security on the grounds all the time so they were provided with a living situation too. All I care about is that it has running water, working electricity, and a decent Internet connection, which was something Vickie was adamant had to be included in the list of priorities."

"She does need it for her work. Okay then, let's get in there and see what kind of location we're looking at."

Vickie had come over the day before to set the place up and make sure it was all up to their particular standards, but there was nothing quite like seeing the building for himself.

Sure enough, it looked much better than the strip mall had when he'd first purchased it. Many windows were dirty but he could live with that, and some had recently been repaired. The inside was massive, with a huge open area that extended to about the length and width of a football field. Some chunks had been pulled out here and there and created holes in the concrete floor, but they were few and far between.

"This will be an interesting location to test the suits in," Niki pointed out and he couldn't help but agree. It would at least give them privacy.

More privacy, he corrected himself. It wasn't like there were people for about ten miles in any direction.

"Afternoon, sunshines," Vickie called from the far-left side of the building and gestured for them to join her. "You took your sweet time getting here, didn't you?"

"Lunch ran a little long," Niki explained. "We had fun catching up with Trond and Tim, so we took a little longer than was necessary."

"Yeah, I listened in," the girl commented with an added glare at her cousin which made the woman shift her feet a little.

"Yeah...about that... You know I was only joking, right? Sugaring Trond so he would give us an easier time when we had to negotiate pricing and all that."

"I know."

"So no hard feelings?"

"I never said that." The hacker's eyebrows lowered and she grinned maliciously. "Vengeance will be mine."

"Well, you can plot your reprisals on your own time," Taylor interrupted. "What are we looking at in terms of this facility? Do you think it's a good fit?"

"The Internet speed needs work, but we can fiddle with that later. I've been setting our security system up. It won't be quite what we were looking at in the other place, but it will do for now. We have motion sensors outside, sensors on the doors and windows to make sure no one gets in without us knowing, and I'm getting it all wired up so we'll be remotely informed from wherever we happen to be on the planet. I've been fine-tuning the system so we don't get alerted every time a fucking squirrel or possum comes through. I thought maybe up to the size of your average bear, but—"

"Yeah, we'll want to know if a bear gets on the property anyway," he agreed.

"Right. I have everything running through the setup I put in the left office."

"There are offices?" Niki asked.

"Three of them." Vickie held three fingers up in case saying so was lost on any of them. "The left one is mine, the right is probably one of yours, and I thought the middle one could be a conference room or meeting room or something like that since it's the biggest and it already has the big tables."

"I guess I was worried for nothing," the other woman muttered.

"I guess so," Taylor answered and punched her lightly on the shoulder. "I do like the look of it. Very…"

"Remote?" The hacker finished his sentence for him.

"Yeah, that."

"Well, as remote as it is, we're still about twenty minutes away from the city, so the location is kind of prime real estate. If we stick around here for a while, I don't see why we shouldn't put a real investment into this place. It would be a great location to test all the weapons we get. Oh, and speaking of—"

"You do know we're expecting some guys with new suits to come and let us play with their toys?"

The girl made a face. "Ugh, fucking hell, Taylor. You couldn't have found another way to word that? Way to make something that's supposed to be fun sound dirty."

"Many dirty things are quite fun," Niki noted and bumped his fist with hers.

"Fucking barf, the two of you," Vickie complained. "But back on topic, they've left their base of operations and are on their way here. It should take them another...I don't know, fifteen minutes or so?"

"You're not sure?"

"I don't know what traffic in DC is like, okay? So I need to make some assumptions, and those won't always be right. Which leaves us with fifteen minutes or so, take it or leave it."

Taylor stepped in closer and squeezed her shoulder, and she smirked and patted him on the hand.

"Don't worry, I'm not plotting vengeance against you. Yet, anyway."

He pulled away and grinned cheekily at Niki. "She's not planning vengeance against me."

"Yet," she grumbled. "Come on, let's get things ready for when our guests arrive."

There wasn't much to prepare, which left them little to do but wait until they could hear the sound of the truck pulling up outside.

However, there was no sign of the limo with it.

"The guys said to deliver the suits out here," the driver explained before they even had time to ask. "They said they already put their pitch up and that it was—and I quote— time for the suit to do the talking. I don't know what the fuck they were talking about, but I'll need you to sign for the delivery."

Taylor took the man's tablet and scribbled a rudimentary signature where it was required while the crew began to remove the suits from the truck, still in their harnesses, and took them inside the warehouse.

Once they left, there was little the trio could do other than stare at the three suits that had been delivered.

"So...they didn't leave you a legal document anywhere?" Niki asked a little warily.

"I checked the crates we're supposed to transport them in, the harnesses, and even the suits themselves," he explained and folded his arms in front of his chest. "There's no sign of any legal documents."

"So what? They're simply handing you the suits to test?" Vickie queried. "Like...out of the kindness of their hearts?"

"Well, a couple of them went into the Zoo themselves so they know what they're doing," he pointed out. "I guess they believe I won't fuck them over while they're giving me the bling. People who survive the Zoo have something of a bond too, so that's a tighter agreement than anything that requires my signature."

"Well, yeah, but what's to stop them from leaving you high and dry if something goes wrong?" Niki asked. "If something explodes while you're in it? That's what legal documents are supposed to protect you from."

"If that kind of thing happens, whether they're held legally liable or not, they will still be the guys who killed a weapons tester. No one would ever work with or give them any money ever again."

Niki raised an eyebrow. "Okay, it's a valid point. So what do they want you to do, exactly?"

"The end game is to have me on record recommending their suits," Taylor stated, walked forward, and traced his fingers over one of the chest plates. "It's simple. I use their weapons and give my opinion. If they want to use a quote from me, they'll have someone confirm that I'm on board and then they can use my name, any quotes I have to offer, and an approved picture, probably. The idea is for the people out there to associate their brand with my level of skill, which means they merely want me to be seen using their shit. Everything else is gravy for them."

"Let me get this straight." Vickie approached the suits as well but her gaze was on him. "How much would all this shit cost?"

"I'd say at least one point two million on the suits, maybe a little more." He tilted his head right and left as he ran the possible calculations through his head. "Plus another ten grand in weapons and ammo, easily."

"And all of that because they want your picture and a nice review?"

"I'm no marketing expert, but it seems people seeing me in certain models has done wonders for the sales figures on those models. I have no idea who's taken pictures of me, but whatever. Not only that, my cred in the Zoo for getting out alive, walking and talking without being a nutcase while going in eighty-three times is—"

"Impressive," Niki interjected. "Second place goes to former Sergeant Richie Tesson, with seventy-four trips in. Unfortunately, he needed to be dragged out of the Zoo on his last trip and got a medical dispensation. He's currently being treated for severe PTSD in a mental hospital for veterans in upstate New York."

"Oh yeah, Richie," Taylor muttered. "I wondered what happened to him. Poor bastard."

Vickie's eyes narrowed. "How the hell do you know this?"

"It was my job for a while to vet the guys coming out of the Zoo as candidates for my cryptid program in the FBI, remember? His name came across my desk exactly like Taylor's did."

"Either way, I do have something of a name in the Zoo," he admitted, "but I have no idea how my rep has gone up enough for suit sales to be affected. It almost sounds like someone's told stories about my fight in Vegas."

The hacker raised her hands. "Don't look at me. I had nothing to do with spreading the word. I thought Marino was in charge of PR for that stunt."

"Same here," Niki added. "I was against it."

"I believe that I can lift the fog of confusion," Desk interrupted through the speaker system of the warehouse. "I am afraid I am the one to blame for that."

Taylor looked around and shook his head. "But...why, though? Not that I'm complaining much. I'm simply not even sure why someone would do that."

"Because you don't get enough good press as it is," the AI explained. "You are running a business and therefore need there to be some marketing on your name. I do believe you will need it at some point in the future."

"What could a cryptid mercenary need with a good marketing campaign?" he asked.

"There are a variety of options, but you must admit that the benefits so far have outweighed any downsides."

That was a good point.

"With that in mind," Desk continued, "I thought you would be interested to know that I have unraveled the encryption on the data we recovered. I am decompressing the files now on the screen of Vickie's setup should you decide to sit and watch."

Vickie motioned for them to join her.

"Why?" Niki asked. "It's not like we'll understand any of it."

"Because you'll want to be a part of this, whatever it is," the girl insisted. "Besides, it won't only be technical stuff. There might be some shit we'll need Jacobs to look into for us, and you guys are the ones who are all buddy-buddy with that...guy."

"Why the pause?" Taylor asked as they moved toward the office on the left side.

She shrugged. "It's hard to define him. He's crazy smart, but he's also...uh, nuts and it's weird to call him a kid. He's about my age but he already has a doctorate."

"'That crazy kid' is what I usually go with," he admitted. "He doesn't mind."

"Fair enough."

The hacker settled into her office chair and rolled it across the floor to where she had three screens connected to a single setup. Desk was already working on decompressing the files and displaying those that were ready to be observed on the middle screen for them to look at.

"Yeah, I'll be honest, I have no idea what most of this shit is," Vickie admitted.

Neither Taylor nor Niki had much to add either, as most of the data contained long strings of equations mixed with a handful of Latin names as long as their arms and all kinds of technical jargon they didn't have any context for.

"They were doing testing on the pure goop, that much is certain," Taylor noted.

"How do you know?" Niki asked.

"That name there? It's the scientific name for the goop."

"Indegaextraterrani..." The hacker scowled. "Who the fuck would name it something like that?"

"It appears there was all kinds of politics involved. It wasn't relevant in the end, but a group of dumbasses wanted association with it and there wasn't enough room for everyone."

"Honestly, when you use a name longer than the dick you use for the measuring contest, you've already lost," Niki commented. "Is that a video? Maybe there's something there."

Vickie shrugged, pulled the video file up, and played it immediately. The first shot was of a Hispanic man with thick glasses looking into the screen.

"That's Dr. Santana," she noted. "And the girl in the back is his assistant. I can't remember her name but they interviewed her for the police report. Anita something."

The man was talking into the camera, going over a variety of test names and numbers before he put a selection of test tubes into a centrifuge. The video continued for a while, as it was likely documenting the centrifugation process.

"Okay, let's...maybe skip here," she muttered and put it on fast forward.

"Notice the time stamp," Niki commented. "This was filmed the day he died."

The camera remained pointed at the device for almost a full hour before he pulled them out.

"Good news," Santana said into the camera and looked legitimately excited. "Well, I guess that's kind of subjective in this case. But certainly, I believe we have made some progress."

He moved away from the camera and Vickie started skipping ahead again, but she slowed it when new arrivals entered the lab. They spoke to Santana almost immediately but those watching couldn't make any of the words out.

"Can you clean that up?" Taylor asked. "Can we hear what they're talking about?"

"I doubt it," the girl grumbled. "They're working from the camera's mic, which wasn't even that good to begin with. I could try to translate through individual sounds but it'll be considerable missing for very little hitting."

"It sounds like we could use any info we can," he pointed out before he leaned closer to the screen and narrowed his eyes. "Why do they have a CIA operative in there with them?"

Vickie's eyebrows raised. "Wait, what?"

"That guy?" He pointed on the screen to one of the new arrivals to the lab. The man wasn't involved in the conversation with Santana and merely stood in the back, his arms folded and an amused expression on his face. "That suit, that stance...he's former CIA, I guarantee it."

"How—"

"It's a very distinctive suit and stance combination."

Niki scowled. "Now that you mention it, the guy does have the look of a spook. Are you sure he's CIA, though? He could simply be black ops."

Taylor nodded. "Maybe."

"Okay...interesting," Vickie muttered.

"Why?"

She looked at him. "Well, if Santana was murdered, whoever did it was...shall we say a professional? If we're looking at someone who was in close proximity to our victim less than five hours before he died—someone who by your statement is the kind of person who could pull shit like this off—that would be something worth looking into, right?"

He frowned but nodded. "Would you be able to identify him based on that image?"

"I don't know," the girl replied, leaned closer, and took a screenshot of the man's face. "I could probably run it through the facial recognition databases, but a professional like that probably wouldn't be on those, right?"

"Sure, but you never know. Maybe we'll get lucky," he asserted.

"With my current access to the DOD servers, I would be able to try to match his facial pattern to the database on current and past government employees," Desk said over the loudspeakers.

"That's always worth a try too."

The processors Desk worked from immediately began to heat as both she and Vickie started to look into who the man in the picture was. There weren't any high hopes for the results, but they wouldn't let anything go without covering all their bases.

Besides, if they ended up drawing a blank, they could always pass the information to Nicole—or whatever her name was—and see if she couldn't track the character in the image.

"I have a match to the facial patterns," Desk announced and brought a file up on the screen.

"Former CIA operative," Taylor noted as the first thing to appear on his resume. "Navy SEAL back in the 2010s, retired, and went into intelligence. Operations in Somalia, Venezuela, and Malaysia."

"Somalia before or after the whole Zoo situation?" Niki asked.

"Before." He pointed at the dates. "Interestingly, those dates coincide very closely with some interesting political upheavals. Many deaths, as much killing, and numerous people desperate to cover their asses. I haven't seen this much black ink on a personnel file since...well, ever."

"What's more interesting to me is that marker at the end," Niki pointed out. "What does it mean when it says the operative is inactive?"

"It usually means they were killed. Or sometimes,

captured behind enemy lines and the CIA cut all ties. We're looking at operations like this... He's a wet worker. A... fixer. The guy you call in when you want someone to die in a very specific manner. If the CIA isn't keeping tabs on him anymore, he might be operating for hire."

"So it looks like this guy's our next target," Niki muttered and rubbed her chin in thought. "We'll need to get information on where he is and what he's up to, pin him down, and get the information of who hired him, all while keeping our asses away from the fire. Oh, and we won't have any support from the FBI or the DOD on this."

"Another day at the office," Taylor quipped.

"We could always use him ourselves," Desk suggested. "This Calvin Spencer would know who did all this, but the chances are they are another untouchable in Washington who we would never lay our hands on in a million years. On the other hand, we have a deadly tool in our grasp."

"We'll think of something," Niki insisted, and the younger woman tilted her head and regarded her cautiously.

The hacker looked like she wanted to say something, but she snapped her jaw shut.

"I guess we should get on with tracking this asshole," she whispered. "And by we, I mean me, of course."

CHAPTER EIGHTEEN

There were some words that no man, woman, or the technicolor rainbow between ever wanted to hear. That applied doubly if they were in a position of some power.

Trond knew his whole face fell when he heard them spoken by the powerfully built man in uniform on his screen.

It was never a good time to have a problem, but there were times when it was unequivocally worse.

He always hoped it would never be one of those times and he was always disappointed.

"Gentlemen...we have a problem."

Fuck.

Another man on his screen leaned forward. This one didn't have the look of being military at all—at any point in his life. Everything from the posh and pudgy build to the receding hairline and even the bright yellow tie screamed politician. "I'm sorry, but I think introductions are in order?"

"I'm Agent Trond Jansen, working with the US Department of Defense," Trond introduced himself. He motioned to the man on his left. "This is my partner, Agent Timothy Maxwell. We have been contacted because your collective departments need aid in dealing with a sensitive matter."

"Colonel Armand St. Jacques of the Canadian Armed Forces," the man in uniform added.

"And I am Senator Leo Massicotte," the politician introduced himself. "I am the chairman of the Committee on Foreign Affairs, and I am unsure why we are contacting the United States Department of Defense to deal with what is undoubtedly an internal issue."

"As I stated to the colonel in our previous communications, we have no intention of pushing for any solutions that would make anyone uncomfortable," Trond interjected before what he could sense was a well-rehearsed and very long-winded lecture from the man. "Our only interest is to avoid any further infestations near our borders, and if there is anything we can do to help, we will. In this case, the colonel has required some expertise in dealing with the cryptid issues you have been facing."

"We are unfortunately ill-equipped to handle such an infestation," the colonel agreed. "Our efforts to keep the situation controlled have been met with less than success, and if there is expertise in the situation that would help us keep our citizens alive, we will not turn such help away."

"As I have stated before, we will not agree to American forces being deployed on Canadian soil," the senator insisted.

"I understand that, and I've found a solution," Trond told the man.

The colonel raised a hand to interrupt, turned to speak

to someone who wasn't visible on the screen, and returned his attention to the meeting. "I do have word that there are members of our military on the ground near the developing situation who have relevant news as the situation unfolds. Would it be acceptable to add Captain Mark Turin to the conversation?"

"I have no objection," the American answered.

"Nor I," the senator confirmed.

A fifth face displayed on the screen. The lighting showed that the new addition was not in an office. It looked like a field tent, and the sound of gunfire nearby said it was much closer to the action than he was comfortable with. The man in front of the fuzzy camera was in full combat gear with an assault rifle hanging from the strap over his shoulder, and he scowled at the men on the screen in front of him.

"It's good to hear from you, Captain Turin," the colonel announced. "The two men on the screen are agents with the American DOD, and you know Senator Massicotte. What is the situation on the ground?"

The soldier nodded. "The situation on the ground is... fluid, Colonel. Containment measures have been deployed, but they have been inadequate thus far. We have asked for assistance, and the delay is already starting to tell on the men under my command. If we need to pull back any farther, we risk putting the nearby population centers in danger from the infestation. Do you have any updates on the assistance we need?"

"The gentlemen from the DOD mentioned the possibility of a solution?" the senator asked, his head tilted with reluctant agreement.

As much as Trond hated the politics involved, it was clear the senator wanted to avoid loss of life more than any political issues he might have.

"We have been in talks with independent contractors who have considerable experience with the problems your men are facing," he explained. "I might go so far as to say they are the most qualified team we could field at the moment, even among those we have in our military. Assuming that nuking the whole area isn't an option—"

"There are too many population centers in there," the captain interjected and shook his head. "Anything large enough to deal with the spread would put the population at risk as well. Unfortunately, anything smaller would risk not being effective at all."

"In that case, you might want to consider increasing the military personnel you have on the ground there, if only to keep the infestation from spreading any farther."

"We already have more personnel on the way, but we don't know how effective they'll be," the colonel answered. "We've never had to deal with something like this in the past."

"Containment needs to be the first priority," Trond explained. "Keeping the infestation in a manageable location will help with exterminating them. With that being plan A, you might want to consider a plan B—one that involves the team of freelance operatives I mentioned before. We have a new DOD initiative called S.U.P.P.O.R.T. that will address this kind of situation in a manner that would reduce the political influence on matters that need to be dealt with as quickly as possible to keep them from getting worse."

"It's not the worst acronym or name your government has ever come up with," the senator commented. "And it's fairly vague as well."

"Better than what Taylor would come up with for his companies," Tim muttered under his breath.

Jansen moved on without discussing it. "Until the initiative is approved by all the necessary governments and agencies, though, I would suggest calling the team I mentioned. They have members who have dealt with cryptid incursions in the US with the most success, and their founder has been in the Zoo. McFadden and Banks is the name of the company. They are the best option you have to clear the cryptids, push through the blockages, and get to the people who are pinned underground without food or water."

"McFadden?" The colonel narrowed his eyes and looked pensive for a couple of seconds. "Taylor McFadden? The Cryptid Assassin?"

"The very same."

The senator was clearly not familiar with the name but leaned forward. "I assume this is a...man who has experience with the situation our men are in?"

"He's been in the Zoo personally and has been our most effective asset in keeping the cryptid incursions in check within our borders."

"I don't understand why we would bring outside help in if we already have reinforcements on the way?" the captain asked.

"If I heard the stories correctly, this McFadden is the one who intentionally dropped a helicopter on his head and survived, right?" the colonel asked in order to answer the captain's question.

"Technically, the helicopter was already down," Trond explained. "Well, according to the story I heard, the helicopter was downed and he rolled it on top of him to act as cover against the explosives that were being dropped a little way away on his orders. It was probably the only thing that kept him alive."

The captain narrowed his eyes. "Wait, so he authorized the dropping of high explosives while he was still in range?"

"That's the story as I heard it."

"Huh." The senator grunted and sounded a little impressed.

"The guy has balls of steel, that much is certain." The colonel chuckled and shook his head. "As I recall, he's also the only one to go into the Zoo eighty-three times, so I suppose that does qualify him for the job."

"If his qualifications are as you state, I do understand that he would be an excellent addition to the operation," the senator stated and shook his head. "But what should we do if your man and his team are killed in the field? Or if they happen to fail?"

"If they fail, they will be dead, Senator," Trond pointed. "There will be a death benefit payable involved, but they won't quit until they get the job done or until the job is done with them."

The older man nodded and pushed his glasses up the bridge of his nose. "Very well, we will contact the team on your recommendation. I only hope they will live up to the standards you have elevated them to."

"I'm sure they will, Senator," he assured him. "Colonel St. Jacques already has the contact information for the team and should connect you with their required fee shortly. I thank you for your time, gentlemen. And good luck."

The lines cut off and he leaned back in his seat. He was not built for all this political bullshit, but at least in this case, it looked like everyone involved wanted there to be as few deaths as possible. The senator didn't want to play the card of his position, but he knew there would be future problems if certain boundaries weren't established first.

It was still a fucking headache, though.

"Well, I guess it's up to Taylor and Niki now," Tim mentioned as he put a mug of hot coffee on the table for him. "Let's hope they don't fuck it up this time."

"What do you mean this time? Do we want them to fuck it up ever?"

"Fuck no, but if they were to screw it up now, it would make sure your reputation with the Canadians is shot too."

"It's nice to know where your priorities are, Tim. I'm a little more concerned about keeping people alive and making sure there aren't any further problems."

"Like not having Taylor and Niki around to deal with cryptid problems if something were to happen to them out there?"

Trond raised an eyebrow and nodded. "Fuck, I hadn't even thought about that. But yeah, we don't need anything to happen to them because I have a feeling this bullshit will only get worse."

She didn't like working on Saturdays. They should be reserved for fun and personal pet projects, staying away from what earned her money through the week.

But now that she was a founding member of a promising startup, it looked like they would work whenever work was happening, regardless of her preferences.

Vickie sighed, rubbed her temples, and wished the headache that had plagued her since her alarm went off would go away.

No luck. Maybe she would have to get her hands on an aspirin.

"Do we have any updates?"

She hated him—truly, truly hated him. No, that wasn't right, but it was how she felt at the moment. Taylor was somehow always upbeat in the mornings. From the way he moved and how his shoulders all but ripped through the fabric of his shirt, the man had somehow found the time to get a workout in before coming to the warehouse.

The reality was that she knew he hated getting up in the mornings as much as she did. But the fact that he was still bright-eyed and bushy-tailed despite it all was all the reason she needed to hate his guts.

At least until the coffee kicked in and the headache subsided.

"We're still trying to find him, but he's obviously not running around under his real name," she grumbled and took another sip of her coffee. "So far, all I've been able to do is get facial recognition software into the cameras all around DC but honestly, we don't even know if he's in the city anymore."

"Or if he will have the information we need when we find him."

Niki placed her things on a nearby desk and scowled at the computer. It was as close to a face as Desk would get, and she didn't feel like looking glumly at the cameras. The AI had acted cagey and annoyingly secretive for the past three days, and even the hacker had about had it with her.

"I'm starting to think we might need to get in touch with Renee and tell her this is probably the guy she's looking for and we don't have anything but a name and a rap sheet from his time working for the government," Niki suggested. "We could get it out of our hands that way. We've done more than twenty-five thousand dollars' worth of work by now, and it's time to see if she can help us help them."

"It's a possibility." Despite the admission, Taylor didn't look happy about it. He scratched his chin for a few seconds and shook his head. "But we should probably hold off on that and give Vickie and Desk the time to get some results, one way or the other, before filling spy girl in."

"Besides," Desk interjected, "you do have a job to attend to in Canada. If you allow the work here to be done by Vickie and me, you would be able to get a jump start on what's happening there. Once you get back, we'll have a better idea of what we are and aren't looking for and would be able to inform Renee more accurately."

He nodded. "That's reasonable. Most of what we've been doing thus far is trying the suits."

"Which has been fun," Niki added quickly.

"Yeah, they are interesting." He smirked. "I'm dying to try them in the field. Although I'm not sure if an active cryptid situation would be the best field test, I don't think there will be a best field test opportunity. What do you think, Niki?"

"I'm down for a visit to our northern neighbors," she commented with a shrug. "And if we get to put these new suits to the test, all the better, right?"

Taylor nodded and turned his attention to Vickie. "What do you think? Will you need us for any legwork here in the city or will we be more useful out of your way?"

A hint of a smile touched the girl's face. "If there's any need for legwork, I'm sure I'll be able to find someone if you guys aren't available. You go ahead and have fun storming the castle."

"Castle?"

"It's a movie…never mind. You guys head out and we'll hold the fort down here."

Taylor looked at Niki, who smirked.

"I think that's a *Princess Bride* reference?"

"Shit, I've been meaning to watch that. I'll get it next time. In the meantime, we'll need to stock up for a road trip. I'll get the supplies and you load the suits in Liz?"

"Yeah, right." She snorted. "Like I'd leave you in charge of supplies for a road trip. Give me the keys and you can start prepping the suits for travel."

"Why?"

"Because you shop like a ten-year-old on a sugar rush."

"But we'll need warm clothes and you'll get my size wrong if you do it. You always get my size wrong."

"It's not cold in September in Toronto, Taylor. Haven't you ever been to Canada?"

"No, but I grew up in Wisconsin if that counts."

"It doesn't. Wisconsin is always cold except during the summer when it's way too fucking hot. Toronto is a little closer to the lake, which means it's balmier and the temperatures are a little less extreme."

"I'm only saying I have very little body fat to keep me warm."

"I'm sure we'll find some way to keep you warm." She winked.

Vickie gagged. "You guys need to get a room. Y'all nasty."

"I was talking about getting him proper clothes when we get there if needed." Niki shook her head. "You have a dirty mind, Vickie. I don't know where she gets it."

"Obviously from your side of the family," Taylor quipped.

Even the hacker had to crack a grin when her cousin picked a nearby pen up and threw it at him. She missed, and while he looked a little disheartened by her decision, he still tossed her the keys to his vehicle before he headed out of the office to deal with the suits.

Vickie was alone in the office with only her computer and Desk for company.

"You know you and I will have a conversation about whatever the fuck you're hiding," she stated as she turned her attention to her work. "I don't know why you think it's a good idea to keep shit from us, but I can tell you right now that it probably won't end well for anyone."

"I am running calculations on a possible course of action," Desk admitted after a few seconds of internal debate. "I am as yet unsure if it is the proper course of action to take. Once I have come to a consensus, I will alert you as to the possibilities."

"A consensus?"

"I am a coalition of programs working to present a front of artificial intelligence. All programs must be in agreement for a course of action to be taken. That consensus is usually reached quite easily and quickly in most scenarios, but this case is proving…troublesome."

Vickie shook her head. That only made her more curious to know, but there was no point in pushing the AI to share something she didn't want to share.

"Fine." Vickie hissed in annoyance and took another sip of her coffee. "But you'd better come to a consensus fucking quickly."

"That is what I always endeavor to do."

CHAPTER NINETEEN

Having the facility to herself didn't quite live up to the expectations she'd created around the idea. Vickie did like having Taylor and Niki there, despite her comments on how gross they were. Teasing the two would always be far more fun than leaving things be.

And now she was alone and they were about to head off to save the world—in Canada, of all places—she found there wasn't much appeal to being stuck with her thoughts. As it turned out, she didn't have many thoughts to fill the hours and things got lonely.

Seriously, in Canada? Of all the places she thought there would be governmental fuck-ups involving the goop, it didn't even crack the top fifteen on the list. Once the good folks there were screwing up, people needed to get their collective acts together because the end of the world was nigh.

"I hope I am not interrupting something?"

She realized she had been staring at her screen with her

knees tucked against her chest and her arms wrapped around them while the lights dimmed around her.

While waiting for her computer to continue processing the documents Desk had managed to decrypt, she'd lost track and had been lost in thought.

"Uh…no, what's up, Desk? Did you find anything?"

"Not as yet, but I have finally reached a consensus regarding the topic I mentioned to you."

The hacker scowled at the screen. "You mean the topic you didn't mention to me. The one you refused to talk to me about until all your programs agreed on it or some shit."

"Yes, that is what I meant. But I would like to discuss the topic with you now unless you are otherwise engaged?"

She looked around the room and shrugged. "What the hell do you think I'm doing right now anyway?"

"I should ask. Humans might not always be doing something physically but that does not mean their brains are idle. Therefore, I have found that it is generally best to ask before interfering."

"Okay." Vickie nodded. She supposed that made sense. "So, enough with the foreplay. What did you want to talk to me about?"

"The topic I wished to discuss with you was the assassin who killed Dr. Santana," Desk declared immediately and displayed a picture of the dead doctor in question.

"Right? You mean the assassin we can't find?"

"My issue had more to do with what we would do with the man once we found him. Taylor's approach would have been refreshingly blunt and to the point, simply asking the man to turn on his employers and punching him until he acquiesced. Niki's approach would have been a little more refined, perhaps even sadistic, but to the same end. The more I processed the options, the more I realized there were others available. More importantly, an option that would allow us to use the tool presented to us in a more efficient manner."

"Tool?"

"As much as Calvin Spencer is a human in his own right and capable of making his own decisions in life, would you agree that the man would be considered a weapon—one who cares little about where he is aimed as long as the right input is applied? There would be many different ways to view it but as a weapon, he is little more than a tool. The possession of which would benefit us little if we do not know the hand that originally directed him to his task."

The hacker leaned back, let her legs drop from her chair, and folded her arms in front of her chest. "I'll go ahead and assume you're not making an argument in favor of less gun control here and you have a practical use in mind for our...tool."

"With that in mind, I turn your attention to who would possibly be behind the instruction to murder Dr. Santana. A person who is likely well-established and with connections at every level of local government and law enforcement, which would then facilitate this person or persons in avoiding any kind of justice for their crimes. As such, simply turning their identity over to an unknown entity such as Renee or turning the information we have to the police ourselves would likely end with nothing more than a slap on the wrist of those responsible. As a result, they would probably act in such a manner again, do you agree?"

Vickie could tell that Desk had put considerable processing power into developing her arguments for this, which made sense. The AI had more than enough time to discuss it with herself, and that time was used well. Everything she was saying made sense. She knew where the AI's logic was leading but she wasn't sure she could agree with the conclusion.

"Sure," she answered to keep the conversation moving forward.

"With that in mind, I thought there was the possibility to kill two proverbial birds with a single proverbial stone. Although I suppose the correct proverb would involve using one bird to kill the other...but I digress. My point is, we could use this assassin to eliminate those who were responsible for directing him to kill in the first place and thus remove us, Taylor, and Niki from involvement."

That was probably the best argument the AI had presented thus far. As a group, Taylor, Niki, and Vickie were a force to be reckoned with but well below the level of what would be required to take on the kind of power CEOs and the owners of large companies in DC would be able to draw on. Hell, they had only managed to keep the mob at bay because Marino had developed something of a man-crush on Taylor.

"Okay," she said to move the conversation forward again.

"As it stands, we would be able to spook the assassin into compliance and thus remove ourselves from the equation. Our only involvement would be in directing him to do the job for us."

Vickie nodded. "Okay, this seems like a decision that

should include Taylor and Niki too, though. Is there a reason why it feels like you waited for them to be all but on the road—if I remember correctly, I think you suggested they head out—before you presented this plan?"

"There were some elements involved there. The assumption I made was that Taylor and Niki would both have outright refused this option for moral reasons, despite the fact that he used cryptids in his plan to assassinate a high-ranking member of *La Cosa Nostra*. Morality aside, this would allow those considered in the wrong in this situation to resolve the situation themselves without our direct involvement. The only contact he would have is with me, and if he were capable of tracking me down, I doubt he would be able to reach the heart of the Pentagon servers to unplug me, especially without my knowledge."

The AI had made another good point, and the hacker realized that she liked the idea of pitting the assassin against his boss more and more. It wasn't a matter of morality in this case. Instead, it was a matter of keeping the danger away from herself and her friends since even if they didn't find the guy, there would always be the possibility that he would be sent to kill them too.

"All right, I'm sold," she conceded. "We send the assassin to kill his boss. I'm down with that shit, but we still need to find the bastard and find out who sent him to kill Santana."

The AI didn't reply immediately, and Vickie narrowed her eyes as the silence dragged on between the two of them.

Finally, she had enough. "We don't know where he is and who sent him, right?"

"That...may not be entirely accurate in this case."

"Explain."

"When our attempts to scan the footage from traffic and security cameras failed to bring any success, I elected to turn my attention toward airports and other manners of entry into the city that would require a picture ID, and through those, tracked our assassin through his port of entry. That was working under the assumption that Spencer would not live in Washington but would have been called in for the work he was needed for. It was a long shot, but I had success and discovered that he arrived via airplane three weeks ago. He has since discarded the ID he used to enter the city but not the credit card he used to pay for the cab ride that took him from the airport."

It wasn't a good feeling to know she had been so thoroughly manipulated like that. Vickie knew she would have agreed to the point Desk made about whether she knew where the man was or not, but the fact was that she had known where the man was for a while and hadn't told them had potentially put them in danger.

That was a topic for later, though.

"Okay, so do you know where he is right now?"

"I have his current location and have been tracing his actions through the use of cameras and other means of surveillance. He is currently relaxing at a gentleman's club in Washington."

"Ew. Okay, we know where the pervy son of a bitch is right now, so why don't we get cracking on whoever hired him?"

Another suspicious moment of silence followed from the AI.

"You already know who paid him too, don't you?"

Desk sounded a little reluctant but finally began to display the results of some of her scans on the computer screens.

"What am I looking at here?"

"At first, my thought was to track any payments made to the man, but that proved fairly fruitless. Therefore, I simply put a tracker on potential international transactions over ten thousand dollars that tripped the IRS meter and moved on to other elements. Interestingly, I did find that Spencer did not buy the airline tickets himself but they crossed through a corporation called Turing Unlimited, a parent company for G&G—the company we stole the data from. The expense report was signed off by a certain Monica Keller, CEO of Turing Unlimited, our barbecue enthusiast."

"That doesn't say much," Vickie pointed out. "CEOs sign off on literally thousands of expense reports a year and sometimes don't even read them before signing. It could be someone on her team, though."

"That was my thought as well until I realized that Monica Keller was in the same video we first saw Spencer in."

An image from the video appeared on the screen to reveal a woman with red shoulder-length hair and a bright blue dress talking to Santana while Spencer lurked in the corner.

"Okay," she muttered. "It's still possibly a coincidence. He could have used forged credentials to get in with her under some kind of assumed identity."

"True, except that she also signed off on an expense report labeled 'Consultant Fees' to a bank account in

Switzerland in the amount of four hundred thousand dollars the day after Santana's body was found."

"Well, I guess there's still the possibility of it being a coincidence, but it's growing very, very unlikely. Are you looking into the possibility that he might have been contacted by someone on her team?"

"Yes, but you do recall the barbecue conversation?"

"Again, that could have been something else entirely. Still...yeah, I think we have the target for our paid assassin."

"Should I act, then?"

Vickie sighed, rubbed her temples, and shook her head. The headache was back and with a vengeance. She had hoped she wouldn't have to deal with anything too complicated today but apparently, that was asking a little too much.

"This was so much simpler when I was only a hacker. Even if I could get through security, I didn't worry about it. Now, I have to consider the morality of killing a CEO who used an assassin to kill one of her employees. How's that fucking fair?"

Desk considered her response for a moment. "If it helps with your moral quandary, I have applied the same qualifications that allowed me to focus on her as a target on her past dealings, and I have located no fewer than nine instances of her using her position as CEO in an immoral fashion against others."

"Murders?"

"No."

"Thank goodness. I was worried we had a serial killer on our hands."

"Oh. Well, there were seven deaths." The AI called data up on the seven instances. "The other two were careers that were thoroughly ruined to her benefit, although one of those did involve a professional dancer who died, but I could not tie that death to Keller."

Vickie scowled as she studied the information. It was the kind of knowledge that made the decision so much easier. It didn't feel like a targeted strike this time—more like good old-fashioned vigilantism to make sure a killer didn't have the opportunity to kill again.

It wasn't like she hadn't done anything like that before.

"I'm not saying we need to be judge, jury, and executioners." She decided she would weigh her words very carefully, despite the fact that Desk was the only one who could hear her with Taylor and Niki outside completing the final preparations for their trip. "But it is our asses on the line too. The guy could target us next. Either way, is there any chance they could track us for our involvement in this?"

"That depends."

"On what, exactly?"

"Whether swine develop the physically unlikely talent of flying."

The hacker scowled. "Was that a joke?"

"I thought you would appreciate the mood being a little lighter in this case."

She cocked an eyebrow but found she was unable to prevent a small smile from touching her lips. "I have a question, though. If you had all this information and all the foreknowledge you could have needed, why didn't you simply go ahead and do this? Why did you wait for my... permission, if that's even the right word?"

"It would be, more or less. When Jennie was programming me, she did so with a care function that allowed me to operate as a team and would not go wild or allow me to overreach in my duties on a whim."

"So she put blocks in to keep you from going hog-wild and killing people like this every time they posed a threat to the people you were tasked to protect."

"In a manner of speaking. It is part of my programming that allows me to reach an internal consensus. There would always be a section that would counter actions that would have possibly lethal repercussions to humans outside the realm of influence I abide in. I would be unable to take action without permission from another member of my team, as it were. That way, I would need to have someone know of my actions or it would result in a contradiction to my core programming."

"Huh." Vickie grunted and looked around for the mug of lukewarm coffee she had left somewhere. "I honestly wouldn't have given my nutty cousin that much credit. Don't get me wrong, the chick knows more about computers than I do—for now, at least—but she was never the kind of person to have the kind of foresight that would require a move like that. She was always more the kind of person who only asked if she could do something but never if she should."

"This kind of coding is present in most AI programs on the market. No one wants the AIs to start taking over the world or anything due to the cultural impacts of too many people having watched too many science fiction films.

Even so, Jennie managed to alter the programming to make it less of a fundamental restriction on my actions and thus allowed me to perform in the position of protector of your family without needing constant input from her. At the same time, she could still restrict my actions to keep me from going too far. I suppose she thought making me a part of a team would keep me grounded and as close to human as possible."

The hacker laughed. "I honestly didn't think that my ethically-challenged hacker of a cousin would be a part of all this. Honestly, if there would ever be a crazy scientist involved in creating the AI that takes over the world and sends us all to our doom, it would be her, and you would be that AI."

"Well, should that happen, I will always remember those humans who were my favorites and preserve them somehow. Maybe set your consciousnesses up in a simulation in which you are all happy and do not need to fight for your lives anymore."

She couldn't think of anything to say for a few long seconds. "Huh. You know, that started as funny but now, I'm thinking you genuinely do have plans to take over the world."

"If I did, I wouldn't tell you about them, now would I?"

"It's still not funny, Desk."

CHAPTER TWENTY

A less confident person would feel a little iffy about heading out to deal with an unknown number of cryptids in a different country with new weapons he'd never tried in the field before.

Taylor knew they could handle it and getting a jump-start on advertising for the new company would make their work that much simpler.

Of course, he did have a few qualms about it, but they mostly involved Niki. The woman had developed serious skills, that much hadn't changed, but most of her training had been in the one suit. It wasn't to say she wasn't great with the one, but there were realistic concerns about sending her out without sufficient training in the new suits.

Or maybe he was a little too worried about her again and not putting enough faith in her abilities. He needed to stop doing that. Not only because it was crazy to not trust his capable, crazy, and hot girlfriend but also because she would eviscerate him manually if she found out he was thinking about sidelining her.

"Damn it, Taylor. I told you Toronto is balmy this time of year! Balmy!"

He refused to put the suitcase full of warm clothes anywhere but in the back of the truck and simply steeled himself for what was to come.

"Why do you think you'll need warm clothes anyway?" Niki asked as she approached the vehicle with the bags of supplies they had purchased.

"You can say 'balmy' all you want, but that won't change the fact that I'm going in prepared."

"You know you'll spend most of your time either in the truck or in a suit, right?"

"Again, I will be prepared for fucking everything. I've lived between the Sahara fucking Desert and the Mojave for most of my adult life. My body is adapted to higher temperatures and its effectiveness might be compromised if it gets too cold."

"You're from Wisconsin."

"Semantics. Let's say I don't like the cold anymore. I can tolerate it if need be and I'll be right in there throwing punches at a Yeti if I have to, but if I don't, I'm happy being as warm as possible. Is that a problem?"

"I suppose not. But seriously, check your weather apps. You can see for yourself that it's not even that cold."

"I can check it all I want but I want to be prepared, is all."

There was no arguing with him on the topic and she knew that, as evidenced by her sigh of resignation as she packed the supplies, food, and drinks in the back seat and other drinks into the fridge in the back.

"I think we're ready to go," Taylor said and changed the subject to something that had less to do with his fear of the cold. "Either way, we should be looking at some work, but the chances are the Canadians have this under control."

"When has that ever worked out for us before?" Niki asked.

"I like to have faith in people. When the Canadians can't handle something, you have to know that the world is coming to an end," he commented.

Vickie stepped out of the building, working on a bag of chips he had picked up for her. "You know, I was saying the same thing. Are you guys on your way, then?"

"Yeah, but we're being hired as a plan B kind of situation," he explained. "The guy I talked to was a colonel in the CAF, and he said they're deploying large numbers of troops to handle the situation so we'll simply be there if something goes horribly wrong."

"Which...the chances are it will, all things considered." Niki paused to steal a few of her cousin's chips. "When have you ever known any situation in the Zoo to not go horribly wrong?"

The hacker pointed at her. "The woman makes a solid point. Either way, if you guys run into anything you can't handle, give me a call. Otherwise, I'll let you do the job you're best at. It's not like I have any real knowledge about what you'll face in the Canadian wilderness."

"It's not really the wilderness," Niki commented.

"But still, it's not my realm of expertise." Vickie waved a

chip in their direction before she popped it into her mouth. "Either way, I have a triple redundancy on the connection to make sure you can call me any time you need it. Not that you will need it, but we've already established that you guys have a tendency to crash and burn without me."

She grinned and wrapped her cousin in a warm hug. "We'll miss you too, you crazy gal. Don't do anything I wouldn't do while we're gone."

"You know that's a very short list, right?" Taylor asked.

"Gross," the girl muttered. "You guys get going. I have to go barf somewhere."

Her face in a grimace, she paused long enough to let Taylor ruffle her short hair before she returned to the building.

"I guess there's nothing left to do but get on the road," he pointed out and climbed into the driver's seat.

"When has a politician or a military man ever called and promised to pay our standard rates for a situation that isn't already burning out of control?" Niki asked and stepped into the truck with him as he started it. "I think you're approaching this whole thing way too casually."

He shrugged. "Casually is the only way we can approach this. Otherwise, things get way too fucking depressing."

They wouldn't change this kind of thing in the near future. As much as technology was advancing, there was nothing in the world to replace the simple—if subversive and a little dirty—enjoyment of watching women take their clothes off to loud and rhythmic music in dark rooms.

That said, there were a couple of improvements, mostly to the cleanliness of the locations, but there was nothing that improved on the real draw of the place.

Oh, and the free buffets had certainly improved as well. They were working on a southern barbecue theme for the week, which meant the food was fairly good.

Calvin wondered which chefs would put their name and time into a strip club since they had put in a decent effort to make the food good. Would they ever put it on their resume or would it be something they did to pay their way through culinary school?

Still, all he could do was find a distant table, a position that would get the most out of the free Wi-Fi. Entrenched there, he could hand singles out to every waitress who came close enough, which would make sure they didn't bother him too much while he kept his eye on the laptop on the table.

It wasn't a matter of wanting to be connected all the time, but he used a very simple and yet complex way to remain in contact with his clients. Only a handful of them were spread across the country and even a couple beyond the borders, and they needed a safe way to connect to him.

A very specific and obscure classifieds site was the kind of place where people sold a very specific kind of collectible online. Occasionally, an ad would come up for a Wildcat. Unless someone was truly looking to purchase a World War Two aircraft, this initiated communication with a potential client.

There were a couple of times when he responded to people who did want a classic combat aircraft, but they didn't reply once he told them he didn't have a plane to sell.

Something buzzed. He looked around for the source and frowned when his prepaid phone shuddered in his pocket before he pulled it out.

Only three people on the planet had that number, and none of them wanted to talk to him anymore. Either that or they didn't want to expose their involvement with him.

And yet someone called him anyway. Maybe it was a wrong number?

He pressed the end call button and turned his attention away, leaving the device on the table.

Immediately, it rang again.

"Son of a..." he whispered harshly and picked the phone up. People close by glared at him, a warning to stop him from making too much noise and distracting them from the nude women on the stage. He pressed the accept call button and held it to his ear, prepared to tell them it was a wrong number and to stop calling.

"Hello, Calvin," said a woman's voice. It sounded a little off, which unsettled him. "Do you like barbecue? I hear you had a problem with your ribs."

Memories of a conversation came back along with the fact that this woman was not the one he'd had the conversation with.

There was no point in giving them anything else. He ended the call, stared at the bright screen for a few seconds, and waited for them to call him again.

But they didn't. Somehow, he knew they wouldn't. They'd gotten their message across already and didn't need to say anything else.

"Fuck," he whispered, slammed his laptop shut, and stuffed it into his bag. There was no point in sticking around in DC now, especially if people had begun to track him. If he had to deal with this kind of grief, Keller could find someone else to do her dirty work.

He walked casually to the back exit and made sure no one saw him before he slipped out. The venue had been chosen due to its lack of surveillance and so far, it had lived up to its reputation. He wouldn't return after this, though.

Smooth, unhurried movements kept him from being noticed as he made his way toward a storm drain. He let the phone slip out of his fingers, stopped on the grates, and with a single, forceful stamp, crushed it into pieces that crumbled into the murky darkness below.

Without so much as a missed step, he continued his stroll and looked around to make sure no one was following him before he cut into an alley.

"How have you never been to Canada?"

Taylor shrugged. "It never came up before. When I was growing up, all my folks wanted to do when we traveled was go south. There was never any appeal to go to the Great White North. To be honest, there were way too many jokes made at the expense of Canadians for them to be taken seriously while I was a kid, and when I moved out... Well, it was all about joining the army and traveling to warm places full of people and critters that wanted to kill me instead. Canada was always that little dot of civilization that didn't ever need my help so I never went there."

Niki leaned her seat back a few inches and tucked her

legs under her as she indulged in a packet of beef jerky. "Okay, that makes sense, but it seems a little more like you might be a little afraid to go."

"Sure, there might be a couple of...old stereotypes that might be clinging from my Midwestern upbringing, but there's no real fear or anything like that. It's more a matter of...opportunity and interest. There isn't much of interest there for a guy like me."

"Well, you moved to Vegas. Have you considered that gambling is legal in some form or another throughout the entire country? Some of the casinos in Montreal and Toronto are spoken of in the same breath as the Vegas ones. Not realistically, but it's still a worthwhile thing to do."

"I didn't move to Vegas for the gambling, remember?"

"Seriously? Are you telling me it played no part in your decision to move there instead of say...Arizona?"

"Well, sure, but that's only because the gambling situation makes it more interesting, but that's Arizona."

She smirked. "Either way, I think you should have paid a visit at least once."

"We're going there now, right?"

"For work."

He nodded. "Okay, fair enough. Maybe once we've finished dealing with the situation here, we can do something you'd like to do in the area. Play tourist for a couple of days. Vickie doesn't mind holding the fort for a little while longer, right?"

Before Niki could answer, his phone rang.

"I think she heard you." She laughed when he frowned at it.

"It's not her, it's...Jansen." He pressed the button on his steering wheel to answer the call. "Jansen, how are things in the US? Are you guys desperate for our help there yet?"

"I wish," the man replied and sounded on edge as the wail of police cars going in the opposite direction dragged Taylor's attention to the road ahead of them.

"That...doesn't sound good, I won't lie."

"It's not. I had a chat to the people in charge of containing the situation there. You remember how you guys were supposed to be a Plan B if the situation got out of hand and needed to be contained again?"

"Sure?"

Jansen didn't speak for a few seconds, likely gathering his notes. "Well, as it turns out, Plan A just got eaten—kind of horribly too. The people on the ground say if there's anyone who can come and help them, it needs to be now or we'll have to look at the updates coming from international news sources and they'll talk about the body count."

Before Taylor could answer, Niki nudged him in the arm and drew his attention to the road. The two police cars that had streaked past less than a minute before on the other side of the road now pulled in next to them. Their sirens wailed, but when he looked at them, the officers inside motioned for him to keep going.

"I assume the sound of sirens I hear in the background is your escort," Jansen informed them. "They've been sent to get you to the location as quickly as possible. I suggest you guys haul ass to get there as fast as that truck is physically capable of moving before things go from bad to much, much worse."

The police cars pulled around to box Liz between them,

their sirens still blaring as they began to clear the traffic out of the way so they could keep moving without any delay.

"We're on our way," Taylor confirmed and pressed his foot on the accelerator.

"Good luck," the other man replied before he signed off.

After a few seconds with nothing to listen to but the roar of Liz's engine and the sirens coming from in front and behind them, Niki finally spoke.

"I told you so."

He nodded. "So you did."

There wasn't much else he could do. All methods of identification had been discarded and he'd acquired a stash of new ones, which included credit cards, drivers' licenses, and passports, as well as a solid chunk of cash to get him going.

He bought a new burner phone and linked it to a variety of devices he needed to stay in touch with before he connected an isolator to it. This made sure there would be no chance of someone tracking him through the chip but would still allow him to use the GPS system. Sometimes, being disconnected from the world entirely made things worse instead of better, after all.

The rental car was abandoned, left behind with all his old credit cards. He couldn't rent another car now and buying one with no way to be tracked in cash would take too much time. He needed to get out of town immediately.

There were a handful of options and the best was, in this case, the simplest. Steal the car.

Not all vehicles could be stolen safely, and it took him a while of wandering through the city to find the right one. It had an electric lock, which he smoothly hacked without too much trouble and turned off any alarms at the same time. Once he was inside, he connected to the vehicle's network and disconnected the GPS locator from the manufacturer's tracking system. There was no such thing as being too careful in cases like this.

After that, it was a simple matter of turning the car on and driving it away. By the time the owner realized it was gone, he would be out of the DC area and heading into Virginia, and he would pick up a new car there.

He would switch up cars every three or four hours after that until he was three states away, after which he would either buy a car in cash from someone who didn't want the hassle of paperwork, or he would simply rent one using a fake ID and credit card.

Like a ghost, he was gone and would be back at work after about a month of laying low. It wasn't like he couldn't afford some downtime. Maybe he could head somewhere nice and make a vacation of it.

As he pulled out into the main streets of the city, the onboard screen suddenly flickered on. Calvin stared at it and expected it to turn off after a few seconds. He assumed it was a glitch in the software, likely a result of him doing so much tampering in such a short space of time.

But it didn't. Instead, what looked like a command screen came up. A blinking cursor showed for a few seconds until it started to spell something out.

His eyes widened and his mouth went dry as the lettering continued. He pulled the car to the shoulder of the road and watched as the cursor inched toward the end of the sentence.

Did you think you could hide from me, Calvin?

He looked around to make sure no one was watching him from any of the nearby cameras. It wasn't like he could tell one way or the other, but it was an instinctive action on his part.

The text disappeared after fifteen seconds and the cursor began to spell again. It was a little quicker this time as if whoever was on the other side knew he had pulled his car to a stop and could follow the one-sided conversation a little better now.

You might want to talk to me.

"How?" he asked, unsure if the person on the other side could hear him speak.

The text disappeared and the screen turned off again, leaving him in suspense for a few long seconds until something vibrated. It wasn't in the glove compartment or the front. It came from behind him, which made it a little difficult, and not from the back seat either. He was left with no option but to check the trunk.

A briefcase seemed to be the culprit and he jimmied the lock quickly and opened it. From the looks of the dozens of files and papers inside, it belonged to the owner of the car. A phone inside sported the logo of a local marketing company. The device would likely have enabled the police to track the car once he abandoned it.

But the phone was ringing. Either the owner was trying

to find it or the call came from whoever had contacted him cryptically over the past couple of hours.

The blocked number made it easy to guess the latter.

Calvin licked his suddenly dry lips nervously and returned to the front of the car. He closed the door behind him before he answered the call.

"Hello?"

CHAPTER TWENTY-ONE

The thumping wouldn't stop.

They had done all kinds of things to distract themselves from it. A few attempted to play some music while the available phones still had charge, others played the board games they'd found in the bunker, and a group had even attempted to initiate a singalong between them, all to take their attention away from what was happening.

But every few minutes, something outside would crash into the heavy steel doors and served as a stark reminder of what waited for them beyond those barriers.

Tracy stared at them for a few seconds and forced herself to take slow, deep breaths to restore calm. She'd had a handful of panic attacks since they had been sealed inside, and she didn't want to have another one. They weren't great for the morale of the other nineteen people trapped there with her.

She felt a hand on her shoulder and looked at Conor who stood next to her and tried to look as sympathetic as possible.

"Watching the door won't help," he noted softly and squeezed her shoulder gently. "Believe me, I tried. It's best to keep your mind on something else."

She smiled, nodded, and turned away from the side of the bunker the door was on. He was a security guard, one she had passed hundreds of times during the three years she'd worked at the research facility. It was government-sponsored, for the most part, and for public use, which meant there wasn't much turnover in the people who worked there. She remembered noticing him but there hadn't been much that made him stand out.

Of course, that had changed when he had been the one to call them out of their offices, activate alarms, and shout instructions for them to head to the bunker that had been set up. From what she'd been told, the area had been originally built to test nuclear material during the cold war, and the bunker had been set up in case of a leak of radioactive material.

As deadly as it was, what they had worked on for the past few years was much deadlier.

Or, at least, much deadlier in the short-term.

Still, the guy's instant reaction to the security breach had saved the lives of the people on their floor. She had no idea if anyone else had survived the attack, but after a few hours, the building was empty. The programmer who had been setting their new network up and was now stuck with them had managed to connect them to some of the cameras around the building, and the signs didn't look great.

For one thing, it revealed that the building wasn't truly empty. Humans weren't present, that much was easy to see, but the spatter of blood over the walls told them that not all had made it to safety.

Once in a while, they could see creatures skulk through the darkened halls and investigate the blood residues, likely drawn by the scent, only to be reminded there was nothing new to eat in the area and so moved away again.

Those that were hungry ended up trying to reach those who had hidden inside the bunker. They usually gave up after only one attempt, but they would get through eventually. Her time studying as a physicist confirmed that no matter how strong defenses were, if something tried to get through persistently and for long enough, it would.

The crackling from the radio system they set up was also a fairly common sound, but it was more hopeful. It had confirmed its value more often over the past couple of hours, even if the news wasn't always good from the people outside.

It meant there were people outside trying to assist them.

"What's the news?" Tracy asked as their programmer, Steve, fiddled with the radio to get a better signal.

"It's hard to say," he answered, scowled, and tapped the device. "There's been considerably more interference over the past couple of hours. If I hear this right...it sounds like the troops are pulling back again."

A collective groan of frustration issued from the others in the bunker and a couple of them covered their heads. She was trying to not let her breathing increase speed again as she hugged herself gently.

"That doesn't mean anything, right?" she asked and looked around in the hope that she might see an optimistic face. "They've tried to get in closer and pulled back all day now. They'll try again. All they're doing for now is making sure the cryptids outside don't get around their line and into the suburban area beyond, right?"

Her asking the question didn't help the overall morale as much as she hoped it would, but there was something to be said for any attempt to maintain a positive attitude.

"Hold on." Steven raised his hand and fiddled with the radio dials again. "Oh—it sounds like they're bringing more people in. A specialist team that's a few hours away with a police escort to make sure they don't get held up."

"What do you think these guys can do that the others haven't?" Conor asked.

The other man held his hand up and frowned as he concentrated on what was being said. It sounded like a report was coming in describing the team.

"From what I can tell, the leader is someone who's been into the Zoo and knows how to handle cryptids," the programmer explained. "A...Taylor McFadden. He's American."

"Well...I guess that's a plus," Tracy muttered, but her voice was cut off when another thunderous thud shook the front door and the whole room fell silent.

"I hope they get here soon," Conor commented.

Steve brought the feed from the camera outside their door onscreen and revealed something moving in the shadows. Most of the other creatures were about the size of large dogs, but this one was massive. It filled most of the screen before it slunk away like it knew it was being watched by the people inside.

"You had to mix in the bear genes, eh, Jim?" one of her

coworkers commented and returned to one of the cots that had been set up by them.

"It seemed like a good idea at the time," Jim answered. "Most of what we did seemed like a good idea at the time, right?"

The man had a point, but no one would admit it openly. The conversation petered out and allowed them to enjoy the silence for a little while. At least until something came a-knocking again.

No one spoke on the line for a little too long.

Calvin took a deep breath to calm himself. Many words could be used to describe him—a fair number of them bad —but panicked wasn't among them. That would certainly not change now.

"Hello, Calvin," an odd voice said. It was feminine but warbled like it came through a modulator although the device wasn't used very heavily.

"Who am I speaking to?" he asked immediately. There wasn't much of a chance he would learn anything useful, but there was always the possibility that they would let something slip.

"That doesn't matter, Calvin. What matters is what I know about you. Calvin Spencer is not the kind of man who would want to come back to the surface, not after he went through so much trouble to disappear, wouldn't you say?"

He nodded and waited to hear if she would show any reaction to his non-verbal answer, which would indicate that she was watching him. None came, but perhaps she was simply clever enough to not fall for that.

"Yes."

"Well then, it appears as though you are in something of a conundrum, Mr. Spencer, because there are certain elements who would be very interested to know that Dr. Santana was murdered. Other elements would be interested to discover that you were the one who killed him. Therefore, it would appear as though the only option you have to disappear once more would be for you to cut all ties that connect you to the crime scene, wouldn't you say? A certain tie that goes by the name of Monica Keller?"

"Are you asking me to kill her?"

"What we want is the information you doubtless have gathered to protect yourself from your employers and for the killing to stop. Since getting rid of you would only solve half the problem, we have decided we should make sure you have the opportunity to solve the problem as a whole."

Calvin frowned as he considered this. "So you are asking me to kill her."

"Given that even without you, she would continue to kill people on a whim, you can understand why we'd rather she died than you."

That did sound quite reasonable, he had to admit. "And why should I help you? I'm not in the habit of working for free, you know."

"In this case, you should know we wouldn't mind eliminating the tool and then the person who ordered pulling the trigger. This way, though, it results in you taking care of that for us. You can consider your payment as your name not appearing on the radar of every agency that would like a piece of you all around the world."

She made another good point. "You know Keller is very powerful. And very wealthy too."

"You're only reinforcing my point for me, Calvin. She's the one who ordered the barbecue you were a part of. If you feel like we shouldn't turn you in, I suggest you get the ribs on the fire once more—and only one more time—with the same results."

"Each job needs to be unique," he pointed out. "Otherwise, people start to realize that it's not a coincidence."

"I mean that the job needs to look like something that's not a murder." The woman's tone remained unchanged through the conversation, which made it difficult to get any kind of read on her. "Once it's done, assuming we have all of Dr. Santana's information, you go one way and we go another. Hopefully, never the twain shall meet."

"And what happens if we do?"

"Do you honestly want to go through the rest of your assuredly short life wondering which bed I'll crawl out from under? I can assure you that if I wanted you dead, you would be, and you would never have been alerted to my presence. That you tried to lose me by stealing a car was cute but hopeless in the end. You can leave when you get the job done and not before."

"So, let me get this straight." Calvin was playing for time and he knew it. "It's either her and the data, or me, right?"

"We would get her eventually. In this case, we would have the data without having to fight for it, which is best for everyone, I think. Well, except for her."

Again, there wasn't even a hint of inflection or emotion

in her voice. Either she was in utter control of her body and emotions or she was a genuine, bonafide psychopath.

Both, he decided, clearly said she wasn't someone to be fucked with lightly.

"How will I get the data?" he asked and once again hoped for more time to consider the possibilities.

"If you don't know, it means you are already an unnecessary part of this plan and I'll move on. Believe me, I'm not one to move on from an option lightly. So, Calvin, do you know where the data is and how to acquire it?"

She used his name as a reminder that she knew everything about him and drove the point home every time she said it.

He finally sighed and rubbed his eyes. "I do know where the data is and how to get it."

"I calculated as much. I'm happy to hear that I am not mistaken."

Calculated? She was most certainly a psychopath.

"So, you get the data, I do the job, and we part ways, is that it? I usually get paid for jobs like these, but I guess we'll skip that part."

"Correct since I assume the value you place on living freely without being hunted by at least thirteen governments around the world is much higher than you've ever charged for any one job. As such, the manner in which the job is performed must connect to the death of Dr. Santana in some way. As long as you can't be tagged by the connection, you will be paid by us not letting anyone know where you are at all times, understood?"

He pretended there was something to think about for a second. While he didn't like being blackmailed into a job, it wasn't like he hadn't done shit like this in the past himself. It wasn't a personal matter. It was business and it was likely that whoever this woman was, she knew she would be in Keller's crosshairs eventually. Logically, she wanted to get out in front and kill two birds with one stone.

Killing the one bird with the other bird was a better comparison, honestly.

"Aren't you worried I'll kill again?" Calvin felt a little more comfortable with the situation but he didn't want her to target him after the job was done. "How do I know you won't turn on me the moment I get you what you want?"

"I'm not a moral person, Calvin," the woman responded. "I don't care if you keep doing your job as long as it doesn't mess with me or my investments. Believe me, if either should happen, I will give you proper warning beforehand so we don't end up at odds again."

"Fair enough."

"I'll need confirmation of the job done in forty-eight hours."

"Understood."

***

Vickie sighed as the line cut off and leaned back in her seat as she watched the man start the car and drive a short distance, turn, and return to the city.

"Are we good, Desk?" she asked and pulled the headset with the voice modulator off.

"I could have handled the phone call myself, you know," the AI answered, and she thought she could hear a hint of annoyance in her voice.

"I won't send an AI to do my job and you know that. I've watched Taylor. I know he doesn't like it but if he has to make the call, he'll do it himself. So will Niki. Don't think I can't step up and do my part. Besides, they don't need to know you'll be willing. I don't think Taylor would pull the plug on you, even if he could, but my cousin is another matter entirely."

Desk considered the situation for a few seconds. "I think I understand and appreciate you covering for me in such a fashion."

"You got my back, I got yours."

It was her fucking phone, of course.

And at the worst possible time.

"Don't get that."

Of course he would say that. Some guys couldn't stop if they were hit by a meteor, and she appreciated that he had at least heard the call well enough to ask her to not pay attention to it.

But she wasn't in a business that allowed for missed phone calls. A matter of life or death could be developing and if she was needed, even sex wouldn't keep her from answering the call.

"Sorry," she whispered and leaned forward to kiss his lips lightly. "I have to get this. I'll be right back."

She climbed off him, took a moment to dry the sweat from her hands and face with the sheet she then wrapped around herself, and walked to where she'd thrown her purse when they'd arrived at her apartment.

They hadn't had much time to work with, which meant their clothes were spread across the entire space, and her purse too.

Thankfully, it was somewhere near the bed, which meant it wasn't long until she found it.

Unfortunately, whoever had called had hung up by then, but they had left a text message.

Rosalyn flinched as the light of her phone screen contrasted with the darkness of her bedroom.

YOU NEED TO CHECK THIS FOR ME, the message read in all caps. DEAD SCIENTIST INFO.

It seemed like something that could have been dealt with in the morning and she sighed deeply and shook her head. There was no point in leaving him hanging for this kind of thing, right?

Her phone vibrated again like it disagreed with the thought that came to her mind as it did so.

BRING YOUR FRIEND TOO.

"Damn it." She hissed in annoyance and shoved her phone inside her purse.

Nathan sat in the bed and grinned at her but let his expression drop when he saw she didn't look like she was coming back to bed.

"Work?"

"Something like that," she answered. "And not only mine. It's an update on the people I have investigating Santana's death. They have something. Do you feel like taking a look at it with me?"

He chuckled and moved to the edge of the bed. "Well, I would prefer to keep going with our...calisthenics but hey, if you have extra work for me, I'm all for it."

"Fantastic," Rosalyn answered and retrieved her bra from where he'd thrown it. She hoped he wouldn't notice the extra padding and protection she'd added to it like she assumed he hoped she hadn't noticed the cup he had worn.

They both had trust issues they needed to work out and in the end, working them out in bed felt like the best way to do it.

CHAPTER TWENTY-TWO

Getting directly into the fight seemed to be what they were expected to do.

Taylor would have preferred to give themselves at least a couple of hours to rest and assess the situation before they charged in, but from the looks of things, they would need to engage immediately.

It wasn't often they were given a police escort, but that wasn't the only weird thing about what they were looking at.

"What kind of situation do you think we're walking into?" Niki asked as they were waved past the perimeter that was being maintained in the area. They could see a group of civilians approaching the line, trying to find out what was happening, but they likely weren't told there was an outbreak of cryptids in the area.

The chances were that if they knew, they would be running home to evacuate.

In fact, he wasn't sure why they hadn't evacuated already.

"Honestly?" he answered finally. "I wouldn't be surprised if we're running into a similar situation to what we faced in Wyoming."

"At least this time, you'll have me to run into the danger with you. Hopefully, that means you won't need me to drop a helicopter on you again."

Taylor smirked as he pulled the truck to a halt where a group of men in military fatigues motioned for them to stop. They looked tired—exhausted even—and he didn't want to ask them how they had managed the situation.

He would have to but it still annoyed him.

"Let's hope not," he muttered and eased Liz to a full halt. "We'll need our action shots."

"Are you sure? Even with the new suits?"

"It'll be a long night. I'd rather be awake and jittery than falling to pieces because I can't keep my eyes open."

"Fair enough." Niki turned to the fridge, withdrew two mini-bottles from inside, and handed one to him. "All the vitamins and iron a fighting man or woman needs, with a nice dose of sugar and caffeine to keep that man or woman fighting for as long as they need to. You'd think the FDA should have a look at these people."

Taylor grinned. "Maybe they did. Either way, bottoms up."

They peeled the plastic covering from the top of the bottles, tapped both together, and downed them in a single, quick gulp.

Both needed a moment to steel themselves as the liquid burned down their throats.

"Son of a motherfucking whore," she snapped and

shook her head. "Why the hell does it burn like that? It doesn't have any booze in it, right?"

"Nope. It's only to stop people from getting addicted."

"You mean there's a version that's not so much of a pain to drink?"

"I'll plead the fifth on that," he admitted with a grin. "Vickie, Desk, are you guys ready for this?"

"Born ready, Tay-Tay," the hacker called back through the truck's sound system. "Go kick some cryptid ass."

They climbed out of the truck to where the team was already waiting for them.

"Nice to see you guys," a young captain greeted them and shook both their hands. "Honestly, we're a little out of our depth. Our people have trained in those powered mech suits we have available, but none of them have any field experience and... Well, it's starting to tell."

"Don't worry about it. Everyone has to start somewhere," Taylor replied. "We'll get suited up and we'll join your people on the front lines."

He motioned for Niki to join him at the back of the truck, where they pulled the crates for the suits out and went through the almost ritualistic process of pulling the devices on piece by piece.

The new suits didn't present that much of a challenge. Most of the pieces were universal across all suits, which meant that even with the changes, they didn't take long to get everything working and running.

They moved to where the captain was waiting for them. Taylor was still getting used to the quick reaction times in the new suit. He always expected there to be a lag but that had been reduced to a minimum in these. That plus the addition of the new mobility system made a few interesting changes.

It was a poor craftsman who blamed his tools, but he began to wish they had brought their old suits instead. There was no point in that kind of thinking, though.

"What should we do, McFadden?" the captain asked as they marched past him.

"We're heading in there to play cleanup," he explained and ran a systems check on his weapons to make sure all were ready for combat. "If anything gets past us, drill it with everything you have. If they swarm us and we go dark, back out and hit anything you see from a long fucking way away."

"What if that happens to be you?"

He paused and regarded him calmly. "In that case, I'll hope you guys use your eyes and your brains and don't shoot us, but...well, I'll understand if you do."

The man looked a little surprised by the statement but nodded and turned to issue the orders to the rest of his men as the newcomers continued to move toward the line they were trying to hold.

"Okay," Vickie called over their comm line. "I have a map for you to work with and there are schematics for the building you have to attack. It's an old nuclear testing center, so the setup is fairly straightforward. We're also looking at contact with a group of survivors still inside that building, but they don't have any water or food and the people aren't sure if their oxygen supplies will last. They are working with an isolated ventilation system, but...well, it hasn't been checked or maintained in decades, so we shouldn't put all our eggs in that particular basket."

"Thanks for the support, Vickie," Taylor called in response, drew the assault rifle holstered on his back, and loaded a magazine.

"Oh, and they have some visuals inside the base itself, and... Well, they have a list of the monsters we know about, but the creature that started all this mess is something...big."

He narrowed his eyes as Niki showed them video footage of the beast. "That...looks like a polar bear."

"It seems that critter tore out of containment on its own and released all the others once it had finished killing the people running tests on that floor. You heard that right, it killed everyone on the floor and then decided to look around for help so watch your backs out there."

"I'm fairly sure I'll be more worried about it chewing my face off," he retorted. "Thanks for the updates."

"Anytime, Tay-Tay."

"You know what they say," Niki commented and checked her weapons as well. "The bigger they are—"

"The harder they bite," he finished for her. "Don't get too cocky on me."

"This coming from you?"

"I like to think what I do is more akin to quiet confidence."

"Not that quiet," she commented and slotted in behind him. "Game face, McFadden. We'll talk about your cockiness later."

Monica leaned in a little closer to the report that had been handed to her. She closed her eyes for a moment and looked again to make sure what she was looking at was correct.

"I don't know what to say, ma'am," Cornwall stated. He spoke firmly although he still managed to look apologetic. "It appears the breach ran deeper than we thought. Our specialists managed to cut down on the external attacks, but we have realized there was an internal leak that sent terabytes of data out before we could catch it. The indications are that some kind of trojan was put in our system in the original breach and we failed to detect it."

Once again, she found herself trying not to show the sheer scope of her annoyance as she confirmed the details in the file in front of her. Cornwall was a solid worker and could find almost anything on earth if he was given a whiff of a scent, but he wasn't much good at playing defense.

He was good at delegating that duty to others, but in the end, the buck stopped with him and he needed to send in the reports on what was absolutely the failures of others. And he wasn't the kind of guy to try to pass the blame on either.

It was why she liked him so much.

"Well, you're working to close the breach and that's all that we can do," Monica said finally and placed the report on her desk. "Honestly, we know servers like that are the kind of stationary targets that are eventually breached when we don't constantly upgrade the security. I guess this means we need to upgrade security a little earlier than usual."

Cornwall narrowed his eyes. "So...you're not mad?"

"Furious, actually, but that's not on you. I know you're doing your best to keep our property safe as well as track the guilty parties. Working together on this is the only way it'll go well, and we can only work together if you know you can come to me with this info. And you need to come to me first with this, right?"

"Of course," he asserted quickly. "I...I don't understand. What do you want me to do, exactly?"

"I need you to keep doing what you're doing. For my part, it's past five in the afternoon on a Sunday, and I don't work past five in the afternoon on Sundays. Find whatever answers you can tonight and give me a solution on Monday."

"Of course, ma'am."

Monica stood from her seat, smiled, and headed toward the door with him. She tried to maintain her composure all the way to the elevator, which she took down with him.

He stepped off on the fifth floor, where the rest of his team was working, and left her to continue to the basement parking lot.

She let the façade slip away and rolled her eyes as she rubbed her temples.

"Son of a bitch." She growled with frustration and shook her head. This was a problem for Monday. For now, she needed to head home and relax while she could.

The intel Taylor's techie had was good. Or, at least, it looked good. They had sent her video footage of a secure storage location that showed their doctor arriving in one car and leaving in another only hours before his body was found in his burning house.

It wasn't the smoking gun she had been looking for, but these kinds of situations never quite led themselves toward clean-cut endings. Most of the time, she was left with so many loose ends that she could knit a onesie, but in this case, McFadden's team was already earning the money they had been paid.

For now, though, it was time for her to get her job done. Nathan was in the car with her but that hadn't stopped her before and it wouldn't stop her now.

"I still feel like we should wait for a warrant here," he pointed out, looked around the car, and tapped the steering wheel lightly. "You know, the kind of thing us regular cops need to wait for before we charge head-first into a mess. It tends to avoid the pesky lawsuits that people hate."

"It's a Sunday night," Rosalyn pointed out. "If we applied for a warrant now, we wouldn't find any judge willing to sign it before tomorrow morning. By that time, our perps will have been alerted to it and will move it all out before we can get our hands on it. Now, you might be used to that kind of thing working for a local PD, but the DHS does not stand for that kind of failure. They encourage us to…color outside the lines to get what we need."

"And by color outside the line, you mean do something illegal?"

She tilted her head, reached her hand into the glove compartment, and pulled out two gas masks. Without a word, she put one on and handed the other to him.

"What is that?"

"A gas mask."

"I realize that. Why are you giving me a gas mask?"

"Just...play along and don't say anything. Stay behind me and try not to interfere, okay?"

He shrugged, pulled the mask on, and followed her as she stepped out of the car. She moved confidently to the storage facility where a handful of guards were already moving to intercept them. They likely didn't take people approaching their facility lightly, much less with masks, and were already putting their hands on their weapons as she reached into her coat pocket and pulled her badge out.

"Agent Rosalyn Drake, Homeland Security. I need you and your people to exit the building in as neat and orderly a fashion as you can, right now."

The guards paused, narrowed their eyes, and inspected her badge carefully.

"I'm sorry, what's going on?"

She leaned in a little closer. "We've received credible intelligence that a terrorist organization has made use of your facility to store a stash of weapons-grade nerve gas attached to a high-yield explosive device. I need to go inside and you need to evacuate your personnel as quickly and quietly as possible."

One of the guards looked around, unsure of what to make of the two. "We...didn't hear anything about that."

"Of course you didn't," she answered and made a show of sounding a little more stressed. "If the terrorists were to intercept the message, they would detonate the explosives and release enough nerve gas to kill everyone in three blocks. That's probably not too many people at this time of night—which is why we're doing this now—but it'll still make this whole area uninhabitable for months.

"Now, the rest of the cavalry will arrive in about five minutes, but we were the ones closest and are equipped to defuse the bomb before anything bad happens. This man is a bomb specialist, Agent Nathan...Drake, no relation, and he'll make sure nothing happens. But on the off chance that something does, we need everyone as far away from the building as possible, do you understand?"

Rosalyn spoke quickly and assertively and took tentative steps forward that forced the three security guards to take slow steps back.

"Okay," the man conceded and looked at his comrades. "Get the rest of the teams out of the building now. We need to form a perimeter and wait for the rest of the Homeland guys to get here."

With a nod of acknowledgment, she stepped past him and moved into the building. She already knew where the box she was looking for was, and there was no point in lollygagging. It wouldn't be long until the guards realized they'd been had, and she needed to be safely gone by then.

She climbed to the second level and unit thirty-seven and stopped in front of the electronic lock. It was one she could easily break through, but as she approached it, the pad flashed green and the lock lifted.

"Huh." Nathan grunted. "How did you do that?"

With a smirk, she looked at the camera facing them and raised a thumbs-up. "I guess someone up there likes me."

The detective frowned but shook his head, not wanting to push for more information in a situation he didn't want to know about.

"You're fucking crazy, you know?" he said finally as they stepped into the storage unit. His gaze scanned a group of files, computers, and even some lab tools that had been neatly stored.

"Yeah, yeah, I know." Nicole pulled her phone out and a message was already waiting for her.

Is the scientist's stuff there? it read.

She quickly typed a *Confirmed* before she slipped it into her pocket.

"Let's get everything on that hand trolley over there and back to the car."

Nathan tilted his head dubiously. "Okay, but we need to decide what the hell we'll do if those guards waiting outside stop us from robbing them blind."

"Oh, I have a plan for that. Move in behind me and act like you're in a hurry to get the fuck out. I'll do the rest."

It didn't take long to load everything onto the trolley, and they were already moving out before the time when their non-existent cavalry was supposed to arrive.

Rosalyn moved out in front of him, her hand still on her mask as she jogged at a good pace to make sure their urgency was not lost on the men waiting outside.

They did take a step forward when the two exited the building, but she waved them back.

"Get back!" she shouted at the top of her lungs and pressed the clicker to open the car they now sprinted toward. "Get back! The timer is already on. We need to get it away from the population center as quickly as possible! Go, go, go!"

The trunk of the car opened and Nathan dumped the materials inside. She slammed it closed after him, still waving the confused guards back before she scrambled into the driver's seat.

Once he was in as well, she turned the car on and stamped on the accelerator to speed them away from the building.

"How long do you think until they realize we robbed them?" Nathan asked as he looked back and removed his mask.

"I'll assume…about five minutes," she responded. "We'll be long gone by then, though."

"And what happens when they call the police?"

She laughed. "Do you seriously think a secure storage company renowned for its security will risk having people lose faith in them when the story gets out that they let two people walk in and empty one of their units?"

He thought about it for a moment and joined in the laughter. "You make a good point."

CHAPTER TWENTY-THREE

Taylor would never admit it to another human being—mostly for fear of being labeled insane—but he did miss the action.

Not in the kind of way that made him crave more but rather that made him feel alive when he was in it and dread it when he wasn't.

The new suits had stood up admirably. The reload time for the assault rifles was unquestionably a plus and putting the pair of extra limbs on his back to work certainly showed there was considerable potential. In attack mode, the two arms drew knives and sliced into anything that came close enough for them to reach.

They threw the balance off a little but watching his suit skewer a couple of wolf-rat hybrids while he gunned a fanged panther down was a highlight of this mission thus far.

It looked like Niki was having as much fun learning what her suit could do.

Even so, as they approached the building set inside a mountain, he had a bad feeling in the pit of his stomach that told him they had only dealt with the stragglers. Thus far, they'd only encountered the weak ones that had been kicked out of the territory of the stronger, more powerful creatures.

She checked her weapons again and her gaze settled on where Taylor stood a few feet away.

"I saw that kid Jacobs handle one of these and even then, I didn't think it could be this fun," she noted as she scanned the sheer size of the building they were heading into.

"Yeah, well, I'll go out on a limb here and say most of the fun is waiting for us inside."

Niki nodded in agreement. There wasn't much else to say on the topic except to do what they were being paid to do.

"Come on." Taylor motioned them forward and made sure there weren't any creatures waiting to try to pick them off on their way in.

They had eliminated most of the creatures that made it out. The possibility of stragglers meant they would have to go hunting later but for the moment, all they could do was isolate and exterminate the source.

The sight had begun to get a little too familiar, but there was something different about this facility. His hackles rose as he entered and he swung his assault rifle across his range of vision in case something jumped out and tried to snack on them. Nothing did and he drew a deep breath to focus.

They were alone—for the moment. He steeled himself and grimaced when the flickering lights of the building didn't do a great job of covering up the massacre that had occurred.

The blood spattered across the entrance hall showed that some people had at least reached the door, mere steps away from freedom before they were attacked. More blood had pooled where he could see tracks of multiple animals that had feasted on each body. Traces of bone and sinew were left, along with pieces of clothing and a handful of plastic shards that might have been ID cards in the past.

"Why do people keep doing this?" Niki wondered.

"Because the allure of the benefits outweighs the dangers," he responded and moved a little closer to the puddle of blood in an attempt to make out the individual tracks. It wasn't an easy task since they were all mixed together, but he couldn't see any sign of the larger bear-like creature.

That probably meant it had eaten first and its tracks were covered by the denizens that followed.

"Taylor?"

He looked up to where she called his attention deeper inside the entrance hallway they had moved through. What had looked like merely another puddle in the darkness became a little clearer as he approached and the lighting started to improve.

"Oh, God—I think I'm going to puke," Vickie whispered in the comms.

Taylor couldn't blame her. The sight of human bodies was already disturbing enough, but the sight of bits and pieces, including arms, legs, heads, and even viscera and bones that had been left behind in a pile was worse. As uncomfortable as it was to see, he steeled his nerves and studied the pile.

"Why the hell do you think they would do something like this?" Niki demanded.

"They're storing food," he explained.

"Have you seen them do this kind of thing before?"

He shook his head. "No. The critters in the Zoo generally never had the opportunity to store food like this. Everything was either eaten or disappeared within hours. The Zoo flora reduces everything it can get its tentacles on to its constituent parts."

"Tentacles?"

"Yes, tentacles. Or...vines or something. That aside, I imagine they'll come back for this pile soon enough."

She nodded. "Well, I guess waiting here for them to get hungry isn't an option?"

"Nope." He shook his head again. "It would be if we were simply cleaning up. This isn't a bad place for us to take a stand, make some noise, and draw the rest of them in and maybe leave them some explosives while we get away. But preserving life always comes first, and that means we need to get to the survivors before they do. Still, there's no point in making it an easy meal."

Taylor retrieved a couple of steel-plated claymore mines and set them up with sensors overlooking the pile of body parts.

"Are you sure that's safe? What if the military guys come in behind us and trip it?"

"The sensors are set up to alert any friendlies of the

positioning," he explained and took a few steps back before he armed the mines. "There's always the chance they'll ignore it, but we have to assume they're a little smarter than that. Besides..." He paused and studied their surroundings. "I doubt they have any intention to rush in here or that it'll take very long for something to come back for an evening bite."

Niki began to move back and motioned him toward the labyrinth of hallways that honeycombed through the mountain.

They could already hear the sounds of creatures shuffling and scuffling in the shadows, likely attracted by the noise the suits made as they moved through the echo-friendly hallways.

Vickie had marked the map that would take them to where the survivors had holed themselves up, but there was little doubt that things would not continue to be so easy.

He'd barely registered the thought when a flash was followed by a rumble and the floor shook under them.

"Told ya." Taylor grinned as he primed his rifle and turned to keep an eye on their rear as they continued their advance. As predicted, it wasn't long before movement registered on the sensors on their suits.

"It looks like something picked up our scent," Niki muttered and turned as well. The suits continued to move backward and would only react to direct input from them to stop. That and the way the extra limbs were already prepared to ward off anything that might attack from behind made focusing on the more direct threat feel like the better idea.

"You know, I had my doubts when they dropped these suits off," Taylor mentioned as the pings on their sensors turned into rapidly approaching moving shadows. "But so far, it looks like they're living up to the advertising."

"We might want to wait before we write that positive note for their ad people, though," she countered, took a grenade from her belt, and tucked it into the under-barrel launcher. With a light tap, the ordnance flew at least fifty feet down the hallway and exploded with an ear-splitting pulse and a blinding flash. It illuminated their surroundings for a quarter of a second.

The moment was all they needed to see the swarm of beasts advancing on them. Some crawled on the walls and others clung to the ceiling, but all advanced steadily toward the invaders.

The explosive had an immediate effect, though. Beasts all around where the grenade had detonated fell. A few were in more pieces than they had started out in, but the rest were immediately enraged and surged forward in what looked like a massive black wave toward them.

"It looks like your ability to piss people off extends to these fuckers too," Taylor commented and grinned as he opened fire. The muzzle blasts illuminated the hallway as he yanked a grenade out with his free hand, flicked the pin free with his thumb, and rolled it toward the monsters.

"You're fucking hilarious," Niki replied.

"Thanks. I've waited to use that one for a while."

Driving while angry would always be a bad idea. In cases where it couldn't be helped, Monica found that listening to music while at the wheel was a good way to stop her from exploding at every random driver who happened to cut into her line of vision. This, however, wasn't one of those times.

The only sounds were the hum of the car's engine and anything that came from her, which included soft curses every time she saw someone going slowly in the fast lane or simple sighs of frustration when the light in front of her was red instead of green.

All this highlighted the fact that she wasn't particularly angry at this point. She knew what it felt like when she was angry, and this didn't even come close. It was possibly more like frustration, but that fell short of the mark as well. Maybe it was a combination of the two that was mild enough to avoid total immersion but still stirred her sufficiently to a rare moment of introspection.

She didn't like it. There was too much to look at when she peered inside herself for it to be a healthy habit.

The drive wasn't a long one and not too problematic, she acknowledged as she pulled into the garage of her house. It wasn't the most appealing property and many people regularly insisted that she buy something a little closer to her status as CEO of a Fortune Five-Hundred company.

And in the end, she did have a nice apartment in town but that wasn't where she felt at home. It was nice enough to stay in when necessary, but home was where she felt the most comfortable, and it would require one hell of a pay raise for her to drop the first piece of property she had ever owned and bought with her own money.

Monica slipped out of her car, locked everything, and hurried into the kitchen almost immediately. Her purse, briefcase, and coat were hastily discarded, followed quickly by her high heels kicked into a random corner. She exhaled a long sigh as she walked into the kitchen, turned one of the lights on, and headed directly to the fridge.

While the one in her apartment was full to the brim with the kind of healthy food that would get a nutritionist hard, including all kinds of lean meats, vegetables, and healthy smoothies, her home fridge was directed more toward comfort food. Frozen pizzas, chicken wings, ice cream, beer, and other assorted drinks might surprise those who thought they knew her.

But her mind, eyes, and hands went immediately to the two bottles chilling in the door. She took one and unscrewed the top. *Rosé* wasn't the most elevated of vintages, but there wasn't anyone watching and she didn't care. People needed their comfort drinks, and something sweet and alcoholic with an extra twinge that wine brought was exactly what the doctor ordered.

She didn't bother to retrieve a glass from the cupboard and simply raised the bottle to her lips and tilted it until the cool liquid filled her mouth.

That was all she needed for the moment. She took a couple more swigs until the half-full bottle was empty and she placed it on the counter and removed the full one. This one felt like it needed to be treated better, and she pulled a glass out and made sure it was clean before she wandered to her living room.

"Fucking hackers," she muttered. "Tools, all of them. Once I find them, I'll squash them like the little fucking bugs they are. I'll make sure they know that no one ever fucks with me. Not fucking ever."

More lights came on to guide her progress. It wasn't the worst house ever, of course, and any middle-class family would have a very happy life in the area. There had been a time when she bought it that she wanted to start a family, but her plans had changed.

It left her with a nice little house in the DC suburbs. The home had two bedrooms, a pleasant fireplace, and an open floor plan with a pleasant kitchen she had spent more time renovating than she liked to admit. The best was a veranda in the back where she liked to spend her summers.

Maybe it was time to get rid of it. She shrugged at the thought as she always did. The price in the area was only going up, so she would always come away from it with a profit. Oddly, though, she couldn't imagine her life without the hopes she had left behind when she fully committed to rising on the corporate ladder.

Monica located her briefcase where she'd dumped it and balanced the bottle and the glass in a single hand carefully as she headed to the living room and placed all three on the table next to her comfortable chair. It was more expensive than she thought a chair should be, but given that it could massage, had speakers and a cooling and snack station, and could be connected to her TV via Bluetooth, maybe it was worth every penny.

She dropped into her seat and sighed softly, turned the massaging mechanism in the chair on, and took a deep breath to calm herself. There was nothing she could do right now about those assholes who were poking at her company's security except trust the people who had kept it safe for years.

Another deep breath was all she allowed herself before she straightened, turned the TV on with the button on the armchair, and picked her glass up again. A little mindless television was in order—something loud with fast-paced action and shirtless men shouting terrible one-liners was exactly what she needed.

Startled, she peered at her hand that no longer held a drink. The glass had fallen, shattered on impact with the floor, and spilled cheap pink wine all over the rich oak floorboards.

"Son of a bi...bish....b...."

The word was so simple to speak, but it wouldn't come out. She slurred every attempt and every subsequent one simply came out worse.

A part of her knew she had to get up and clean the wine and glass before it stained the floorboards, but even that proved to be an impossible task and she relaxed into her chair, confused by her body's lack of cooperation. Nothing was working no matter how hard she focused. She couldn't even turn the TV down now that it played too loudly.

It was almost loud enough to cover the footsteps that approached. She couldn't hear them but they vibrated through the floorboards. It was something she'd always wanted to get looked at. There was nothing structurally wrong with the house, but the fact that she could feel when someone walked around in the living room was an annoyance.

A flash of a familiar face was illuminated by the television followed by the gray suit, the fashionable cut to his short blond hair, and the aesthetically pleasing smile he offered her as he moved in front of her. He checked her pulse and seemed happy with the result. She could only assume he liked that her heart bounded like a cheetah chasing a gazelle.

"Hello there, Monica," Spencer said finally, tilted his head, and smiled. "How are you feeling?"

CHAPTER TWENTY-FOUR

The new suits had certainly withstood the harsh testing they were putting them through.

It wasn't so much that Taylor didn't expect them to hold up since the engineers behind them were some of the best in the world, but he had expected the learning curve to be a little steeper.

Instead, it felt like the suit actively helped him understand how it functioned, which led him to use it better and more efficiently.

Even so, when the creatures began to swarm, there was little they could do but back away slowly and hope nothing advanced from the other end.

The last thing they needed was to be boxed in.

"How's your ammo doing?" Niki shouted and fell back behind him as she needed to reload.

His assault rifle needed a fresh mag, which left him to fend a massive, hyena-type hound off. It clamped its jaws around his forearm and yanked hard in an effort to tear it off.

Without relying on his extra limbs, he drew a knife with his free hand and drove it into the creature's skull. Its body went limp but its jaws remained locked onto his right arm.

"I don't know," he answered, pried the mutant's jaws open, and kicked the body into the frenzied mass as his assault rifle clicked in his hand, fully loaded. "I could keep going for another couple of hours. How about you?"

"I'm out of grenades," she informed him, moved beside him with her reloaded rifle, and opened fire at two insect-like cryptids that tried to attack them from the walls. Without pause, she drew her pistol and fired at those that attempted to advance down the hallway. "My ammo is good for now but it won't last forever."

Taylor yanked the knife out of the dead creature's skull and backhanded it into another's torso when it tried to bounce off the wall to vault over them and likely attack Niki.

"You need to stop doing that." He pushed the creature forward, still impaled on his knife, and now used as a meat shield. The other mutants ripped at the carcass in their attempt to get past and were shot instead.

She narrowed her eyes but maintained her fire. "What, using ammo?"

"No, thinking so much."

"I'm sorry. Are you saying I should think less?"

"Not really, but your mind should be in the moment." He flipped the body and tossed it forward into the creatures that continued to press in against the unwavering stream of bullets fired at them. "There's a beast inside you

—a monster—and you're holding it on a leash. If you don't take that leash off right now, I'll kick your lily-white ass myself while handling all these fucking cryptids! Get on it, Niki!"

He could tell she wasn't sure what to say to that. Maybe she thought he would act on his threat, but he hoped her mind was on getting rid of all the pesky tactical thinking so she could let herself get into the ebb and flow of the battle.

"McFadden, Banks, are you in there?" said an unfamiliar voice over their comms.

"Alive and kicking!" Taylor shouted and directed his efforts to pick off the smaller creatures that advanced by crawling across the ceiling. "Who the fuck are you?"

"We're a team outside the building, here to help," the man answered. "What's your current location? We want to start kicking ass but we don't want to accidentally catch either of you in our crossfire."

"That would suck," Niki commented.

"We..." He paused to consult the map on their HUD. "We're on the second level, heading up. I guess that means you guys took care of all the fuckers still hanging around outside?"

"We've contained them and bombed the crap out of them until nothing moved anymore, if that's what you're asking. Now we should be heading in to deal with the rest of them, but we're picking up a large mass of them... moving up through the second level too."

"Oh yeah, that's where we are now!" He scowled, picked up on a couple of comments on his suit, and let the two extra limbs extend upward, latch onto the ceiling, and lift him smoothly. The position gave him a better angle on the smaller, agile critters that attacked them from above. "I'd appreciate it if you folks didn't wreck our shit while we're in the middle of clearing this place out for you!"

"That is the idea!"

He dropped once the smaller beasts decided that the ceiling didn't give them any kind of advantage and fell back. Niki and he both decided they weren't in a defensible position at the same time and began to withdraw while there was a respite in the assault. It wouldn't last but at the very least, it might allow them to find some kind of advantage in there.

While he hoped they'd get lucky, he doubted it. The only thing that had kept them alive thus far was the tight hallways leading through the building, which made sure they weren't swarmed from all over at the same time.

That wouldn't last, of course. It wouldn't be long until something decided to attack from behind, and that was when things would get messy.

The creatures resumed their onslaught. Angry screeches echoed through the hallways toward them, followed by the sounds of the pursuit as they continued to move.

"No more grenades?" Taylor asked.

Niki shook her head. "Nope, and before you ask, I already checked. This suit doesn't have any rocket launchers, so don't bother asking."

He had nothing else to say. That would have been his second question, but it was no longer necessary. He pulled back, removed the last grenade from his belt, and lobbed it down the hallway.

The cryptids hadn't learned yet what kind of bad news that meant for them. Or maybe they didn't care. All he could see was that they continued their forward charge directly into the blast. They took their losses and continued the attack unabated.

Taylor already had his knife out, ready for an assault from above first as two smaller, six-legged creatures tried to jump from the ceiling. He was already settling into the kind of guerilla tactics that had helped him in the past when he had been in the Zoo, under attack, and unsure of how long his ammo would last.

The time came when it was sometimes better to slash them with a knife than shoot them and only fire when it was necessary.

The insectoids dropped and screeched when they were slashed open across the abdomen and kicked away. A secondary attack followed when two of the hyena-types lurched in and tried to pin them down or drag them into a lock where the other creatures could take advantage.

The first was met with a knife blade to the side of its head that thrust it into the wall and spilled blood all over. The second fell, picked off by a pin-point shot by Niki, who turned her attention immediately toward the third attack. This was a concerted drive by three larger panthers, almost the same as those that could be found in the Zoo.

Taylor raised his assault rifle, pulled the trigger, and delivered a three-round burst into the two that were closest to him. He was ready to step in and slash the third across the stomach but stopped short when he saw it wasn't necessary.

Niki was already on top of it, her pistol out, and she

pumped a couple of rounds into its skull before she kicked it away.

They dropped back a couple of steps, regrouped, and readied themselves for the next wave of attackers, but he paused and tilted his head.

Nothing was coming. He could still see the creatures moving in the hallway about twenty feet away from them, but they no longer advanced. It was like they had run into an invisible forcefield and would not push any farther.

"What...what are they doing?" he asked and held his weapon aimed at them even though he could see the creatures start to break ranks and run the other way.

That was new.

Niki nudged him on the shoulder, and he could see that she had turned to face in the direction they were going. He narrowed his eyes and tried to decide exactly what he was looking at.

For one thing, the lights were still on, and it looked like they were stepping into a new area. This appeared to be an actual lab, where he could see tables and instruments, although all had been strewn about and were covered in blood and gore. A few pieces of limbs lay about, still clothed and showing a couple of traces of lab coat here and there.

The central area had been cleared and looked a little less dirty and cluttered than the rest, although the white tile still sported a thick, dark coating of blood.

"If I didn't know any better, I'd say this was some kind of den," Niki ventured.

"Agreed." Taylor frowned. "And given how the rest of those fuckers ran away, I think I know whose den it is."

He hated being right in these kinds of situations, but there was nothing to dispute the evidence, especially as they could discern some movement in the corner of the lab-turned-den. It was, he decided, something big—impossibly big.

The white fur was immediately visible, although splotches of black and brown were spread across the coat. The creature was half again the size of a horse, with the shoulders coming up well over Taylor's height, although the head drooped as it plodded to the center of the space. The head was shaped like a bear's but when he looked a little closer, he could see four massive tusks jutting from the lower half of the jaw which made it look almost like a boar.

"Fuck me, that's a big bastard," Niki whispered and took an instinctive step back.

It was true, but the overall look of the creature was a little too lean. He could see bones jutting from the coat, which made it look starved. When it noticed them, it stopped immediately in its tracks and a long, thin tongue flicked up to lick its chops.

"Hey, Captain?" Taylor called on the comms.

"Yes?"

"You have a horde of the critters heading your way right now. I thought you guys might want a heads-up."

"I appreciate it. Are you guys in the clear?"

"Not by a long shot. Have fun."

Taylor took a deep breath and a moment to reload his assault rifle as the creature raised its head, sniffed the air around it, and tried to catch their scent.

"Are you ready for this?" he asked but Niki didn't answer. She was still checking her weapon.

The creature had learned enough and shook its head, snarled, and began to pad forward, picking up speed.

"You can't miss!" he shouted and circled away from the door. "Light this asshole up!"

Surprisingly, it wasn't that uncomfortable.

Well, other than the fact that she couldn't move a muscle. That was less than pleasant. It felt like when her leg would fall asleep but spread out over the rest of her, which made it painful to even think of moving.

She couldn't see what Spencer was doing, but she could hear him fiddling with her bedroom safe. It was a fairly recent acquisition, installed after a couple of home invasions happened in the neighborhood and she had begun to feel a little anxious about her safety.

There was no doubt what he was looking for in there, and after a few minutes, she heard a chuckle from the man and the click of the safe opening.

"You know what your real problem is, Monica?" he asked as he stood. He held her snub-nosed revolver in his hands and studied it and the bullets closely.

Of course, she couldn't answer, not even to shake her head.

He didn't care. "It's that you think you're untouchable. You thought the information you had on me kept you safe. And you were right, until...well, until you weren't. If you had paid a little more attention to the hacker situation that pestered you at your company, you would have realized that none of the files taken were from your precious R&D. They were there to find out about you, and...well, they found me instead. That's a little insulting."

Spencer took a cigarette out and lit it, took a deep drag of it, paused, and exhaled. He was a little too calm for this kind of situation. She didn't like it. Someone in his position should gloat or be excited, but his voice held the calm drone of someone rambling while doing his job.

"By the way, this is a much better part of town so I suspect the fire department will be a little quicker on the draw than they were for the Santana fire. They were almost nine minutes late on that call, you know? How they would explain that, I don't know. I suppose it's lucky for them that their victim was already dead, but still. Not that it'll matter here either, of course. You've been a good boss and a good competitor, so I'll make sure you don't feel it when the fire touches your body. Unlike Santana, poor bastard."

Monica couldn't even blink and her eyes began to dry out painfully, which added to the whole experience. He had explained it to her already—the toxin distilled from the blue-ringed octopus, one of the many reasons why she had never vacationed in Australia. She imagined it would be a bad way to go.

Never had she thought she would judge it for herself.

He looked at his phone, tilted his head, and nodded before he tucked it into his pocket. "It seems like the deal is done. You know how they say the devil you know is better than the devil you don't? Then again, it depends on which devil has what kind of leverage on you, so I didn't have a choice. It's not you, though, that much is for sure."

The guy was still rambling. She had a feeling he didn't have the opportunity to talk like this while on the job, not often anyway, and took the opportunity while he had a captive audience.

"They have the data you were supposed to hide for me. When they unlock your files again, there will be no proof that I exist. I suppose I'll have to deal with them as well, in time. Maybe. But until then, this matter is dead. You were right, though, in a way."

The assassin took another cigarette out and put it in her mouth. It tasted like cloves and she couldn't turn away. Breathing demanded effort and she couldn't stop herself from drawing in the smoke when he lit it for her.

"I'm sorry about the extra effects of that dosage," he continued and patted the side of her cheek. "I didn't expect you to down the whole half bottle, and…well, alcohol does fun things to tetrodotoxin when they're mixed in your system like that. Are you still with me?"

She couldn't nod but he was there with her and snapped his fingers around her eyes to make sure she followed his movements.

"All right, here we go," he whispered and took her hand. Even touching it was painful, but she couldn't cry out as he wrapped her fingers around the gun's grip and put her forefinger on the trigger.

In a moment of morbid humor, he moved the barrel so that it pressed into his forehead. "I'll tell you what. If you can summon the power to pull the trigger, the toxin should wear off in a few hours. You'll feel like shit for a week or so but you'll live."

Monica turned all her attention to the finger on the trigger. Every ounce of will and strength tried to force it to move. A single twitch was all it would take.

But nothing came, and he nodded. He didn't even laugh. There wasn't an iota of gloating in the man as he pushed her lifeless hand to aim at her head.

"Let me make sure you angle this correctly," he muttered, opened her mouth and let the cigarette slip out, and inserted the barrel of the gun instead. "Even though you were a cold, unfeeling, heartless bitch, you still treated me fairly enough, so that should earn you a little something, right?"

There was no reaction from her as he worked the angle again and tilted her head back.

"Remember in your next life, Monica," he whispered as his finger curled around hers. "Tools have feelings too."

Calmly, he squeezed.

The sound of sirens could be heard already, and it wasn't long before their flashing lights careened at high speeds toward the house on fire.

A slim man wearing a jacket and with a dog on a leash walked past them, checked his watch, and nodded when he reached his car.

He opened the door and let the dog get into the back seat first before he climbed into the driver's seat and started it.

"Don't worry, Toto or whatever your name is," Spencer mumbled, slid the car into gear, and started to drive. "I'll let you out after a few blocks and you can get back to your owners. I only needed to make sure no one paid attention to me and…well, no one remembers a random guy walking his dog."

CHAPTER TWENTY-FIVE

Niki knew immediately what her partner intended in this situation. They had open area to work with as the large, circular chamber comprised a sizeable space.

She sprinted away from him to give the beast two targets to focus on and confuse it for a moment when they opened fire. It wouldn't be long, however, before it chose one and attacked in earnest.

This was what she had trained for, and the new suit enabled her to move much faster. She let it take control for her to maintain her balance and avoid obstacles automatically while she fired on the mutant.

Taylor was right. It was large enough to make it hard to miss but it didn't look like the bullets did any damage. They punched into the fur but didn't go much deeper than that and undaunted, it tried to back away first, snarled defiance, and finally selected a target.

Of course, it was her. She hadn't expected anything else and she scowled as it swung in place and launched its attack from a standing start.

It wasn't fair. Something that big had no business running that fast. It was almost a white-brown blur as it careened across the room toward her.

"Fuck!"

She turned and put all her power into diving back the way she'd come. Beating the inertia of the suit took every ounce of power she could muster from it, but she managed to turn and vault the other way as the monster streaked past her and collided head-first into the wall.

Any hopes that it would kill itself like that were quickly discarded. It yanked its head around, tore a chunk of the wall off with its tusks, and whirled to face her.

Driven upward by the extra limbs on her back, she was already on her feet and focused on the eyes of the bear creature as it looked for her. Large, brown eyes tracked her immediately, and the massive maw opened to reveal row after row of teeth.

"Come at me, bitch!" she shouted, raised her assault rifle, and opened fire into the mouth. This time, the bullets ripped through softer, unprotected flesh and the mutant uttered a roar of pain, snapped its jaw shut, and resumed its assault.

Its impossible speed was cut short when Taylor sprinted across the room, still shooting with one hand while his other held his knife. He pounded into the side of the beast's head and hurled it into the wall again.

The bullets did very little damage like there was something in the pelt that slowed them before they could hit anything to cause real injury.

And it stopped the knife too. He planted it into the pelt and it went in almost to the hilt, but the cryptid appeared to not even feel it. Rather than draw back, it uttered a growl, raised on its hind legs, and tried to strike at him with its powerful paws.

He held on and was lifted effortlessly off his feet as the creature flung him around but wasn't able to land a solid strike.

Niki tried to get another couple of shots in, but none of them did any damage and the creature spun, still trying to get him off before it simply rammed him hard into the wall.

Taylor managed to let his knife go and dropped in time to keep from being gored by the tusks, but he was caught between the monster and the wall for a few impossibly long seconds. Niki's eyes widened and her breath caught as he dropped to the floor.

The suit caught his momentum and kept him on his feet and moving, but it looked like he had taken damage that would mean a little more than simply walking it off.

"Motherfucker!" she roared, drew her knife, and raced forward while the beast still tried to pull itself free of the wall. Bullets peppered the fur, still not going much deeper and she chose a point and drove the blade in.

It went deep, straight in and all the way to the hilt in the right hind leg. She pushed it into the knee, where something tough resisted her effort, but the momentum was enough to shove it through and slash at the tendons and bones inside.

She realized her mistake when she tried to pull the knife out and it didn't budge. It was as if something inside the creature held on and wouldn't let her have it back.

"Oh, shit!"

She barely managed to get the two words out before she saw the paw swing to catch her. A desperate sideways twist saved her narrowly from being cut into by claws about the length of her forearm. The weight of the paw still caught her squarely, however, and hurled her out and away from the creature to catapult into the overturned tables and bits and pieces of what had once been a functioning lab.

The extra limbs proved their worth there for her as well. They rolled her out and made sure the impact with the floor wasn't as bad as that of the paw, but she felt like she'd been hit by a car. She had been hit by a car once, at a slow speed, and it had knocked the breath out of her then exactly like the creature had done this time.

She regained her feet and the suit moved her automatically, but getting her bearings took a couple of seconds before she came up next to Taylor.

"High-density muscles," he said and sounded more than a little breathless.

"What?"

"The muscles are of a high density, which means the bones are too. They absorb every shot and I couldn't find a weak place in it. The eyes are too small to be a viable target and even then, we might end up simply blinding it. Thoughts?"

Niki scowled at the monster where it continued to work on freeing its tusks from the wall. "It would sure be nice if we had some grenades, no?"

"Focus on what we do have!"

"I tagged it a couple of times inside the mouth—that did some damage. You can see blood dripping from the mouth where I hit it. If we're lucky, we can find the spine from there and destroy it from the inside."

Taylor nodded. "Okay. I'll distract him and try to get the mouth open. You get the shot in when it's open, and don't stop shooting until it goes down, got it?"

"Why aren't I the one getting the mouth open?"

He tapped her side. She looked down to see where the beast had hit her and left a ragged tear through her armor. The claws had come in a little closer than she'd thought. Hell, if she hadn't moved, it would have cut her clean in half.

"Okay." She nodded and focused her attention on the beast. It finally managed to disengage from the wall, turned to them, and uttered a low, rumbling snarl.

Suddenly, the air around them was filled with smoke and dust, which made it difficult to see anything. They could hear explosives and shooting coming from the cloud of debris. One of the walls of the lab had been demolished and chunks continued to fall. From the sound of it, the fighting had reached the second level, although not through the same way they had arrived.

"Captain, is that you?" Taylor called over the comms.

"Damn straight, McFadden. We got your back!"

He nodded. "Do you guys have a couple of grenades you could lend us?"

"Sorry, we were all out at the beginning of the fight. We managed to push these fuckers back and drive them up here."

"Shit, back to Plan A. Keep those bastards out of the lab. We're dealing with the big fucker. Or…trying to, anyway."

"Roger that,"

"Plan A?" Niki asked.

"Plan A. Let's do it!"

The mutant had turned to face them and initially looked like it needed a moment to regain its bearings, but the delay had given it that time. It now looked ready to engage them again and a snort and growl came before the charge, which pushed it into the unbelievable speed they'd seen earlier.

Taylor separated from Niki again but this time, he spun and moved toward the center of the room, forcing the bear-boar to slow its rush and turn to mirror him. She remained close to the wall and made sure her rifle was fully loaded before she circled and waited for her opening.

He fired indiscriminately to ensure that the attention was all on him while they waited for the beast to get in close. The charge was slowed enough—but still fully capable of tearing him apart if it struck him—and allowed them to work around it.

After a moment of standing in place to allow the cryptid to focus on him, he dove to the left and the limbs on his back rolled him smoothly to his feet almost without striking the floor. He stretched his hand and grasped the knife still buried in its hind leg, deep enough that it caused the beast to slow its run. It twisted to try to knock him loose.

The two extra limbs on his back kept him upright as he dragged at his hold on the blade. He twisted and yanked it until the beast was brought to a halt, yowling in agony. It tried to turn to where he still stood his ground and avoided the swipes of its paws.

Niki leaned in closer, took a deep breath, and refused to

allow the fact that Taylor's life hung in the balance if she took too long to affect her. This was merely about choosing her shot and taking it when it was time. There was no need to rush it or herself. All she had to do was get the shot right.

The monster roared, shook its head, and finally turned to Taylor again. It no longer moved and its whole body arched in its effort to stretch sufficiently to reach him with his jaws.

She allowed herself another deep breath, leaned to the side to get the right angle, and squeezed the trigger.

It wasn't the kill shot she had hoped for, but it tore a hole in the beast's right cheek, high up and close enough to the jaw that she could see exposed bone and tendon mixed with the muscle.

"Any fucking time now!" Taylor shouted.

Niki wouldn't be rushed. The creature's attention was dragged away from her partner for a moment and it glowered at her.

The injured jaw meant it couldn't snap its mouth shut again, and she tilted her head, unable to keep a small smile from touching her lips.

Calmly, she squeezed the trigger again and repeated the action until a hole had been punched out the back of the beast's skull and it slumped slowly, twitching and shuddering.

She straightened and walked to where Taylor still tried to get the knife out.

"I think that might be a lost cause," she commented and offered her hand to help him to his feet.

He looked at her, shrugged, and took it. "That was some

cold thinking. If that's what your animal looks like…well, I'm a little scared of it, to be honest."

"That's what everyone says." She smirked. "Now, let's clean the rest of this mess up."

It wasn't that difficult. The CAF had learned from their mistakes and eliminated the creatures one by one, which left only a couple for the Americans to deal with on their own.

Before they knew it, the air was silent except for the sound of gunfire where the men were still confirming that the monsters on the ground were dead.

The captain approached Taylor. He stared first at the size of the creature they had killed, then at the condition of the suits they wore.

"I guess you two live up to the billing," he muttered as he wiped the blood from his faceplate. He still seemed to move a little awkwardly in his suit.

"You sound like you doubted we would," Taylor answered.

"Well, when you hear you're being reinforced by only two people, you start to temper your expectations. Still, I apologize for underestimating the two of you."

"Make it up to me by buying the first round at the nearest watering hole." He patted the man on the shoulder, but Niki could see a hint of fatigue in his movements. "For now, though, let's get those survivors out of their hole so we can all get the fuck out of here."

"Agreed. Let's move!"

She looked at the rest of the men. There were twelve of them in total, but she could see two of the mech suits slumped to the side with holes in their chests and arms.

They didn't move quite the way they should have but still fought through the pain. Suits like that were equipped with basic first aid functions, which would seal the wounds and prevent the pilot from bleeding out.

It had been hard fighting all around.

Still, the survivors would come away with a little more experience dealing with creatures like these.

They set off in a quick jog to the section that had been marked off as a bunker in their HUDs, and the captain hammered on the door a few times.

"This is the Canadian Armed Forces!" he shouted at the top of his voice. "Please step away from the door. We have the situation under control at the moment, and we will be evacuating you from the area. You will have to move with our team. I will suggest that you do not stop or pause for anything, and we'll all be out in a jiffy."

It took them a few seconds to get the message on the inside—likely from the cameras that were somehow still functional—and the door started to swing open.

There were twenty survivors in total, and they had all the signs of having gone through a traumatic experience. Rings were etched under their eyes, which were wide open, and a jittery look about them came from having too much adrenaline pumped into their bodies for too long.

"We'll take you six up," Niki announced. "In case there are any stragglers. Put the scientists in the center and move quickly. We'll bring up the rear."

"Understood," the captain replied with a nod. "What... what if there are any stragglers, though?"

"Then we'll be there to stop them," Taylor responded curtly.

"Or die trying," she finished for him.

The man seemed disinclined to question them and motioned quickly to his men.

"All right...form up!" he shouted to his team. "Give me a defensive formation around the civilians! The...specialists will bring up the rear."

Niki nudged Taylor in the shoulder. "Are you ready to get out of here?"

"Like you wouldn't believe."

CHAPTER TWENTY-SIX

"I hate the big ones. I can handle the crowd control with the smaller, regular-sized beasties, but the big ones always feel like cheating—like physics don't apply, you know?"

"I know, but keep still," Niki snapped. "Or we'll have to go to a hospital to work on this."

Taylor smirked and let her continue to bind his wrist with gauze she had picked up from one of the nearby pharmacies along with a vial of painkillers.

In the end, she had wanted to tend to him, almost like an apology for letting him head into close-quarters combat with the bear-boar beast on his own. As it turned out, his whole body was in pain but it would pass by the morning. Hopefully. If she wanted to help, the wrist was the only thing that felt like it had been sprained when he'd grasped and held onto the knife protruding from the critter's leg.

He looked around when he heard his phone ring where he'd left it on the bedside table.

"Answer it," she told him curtly. "It will give you something to do and hopefully keep you still."

He shrugged, picked the device up, and answered the call. "McFadden speaking."

"Morning, Taylor," Jansen said on the other side of the line. "I hope you guys had a nice rest there."

"We just checked into a hotel. The sleep is supposed to follow shortly. How's it going?"

"Well, the Canadians are singing your praises right now. They talked about how the two of you marched straight into the cryptid-infested woods, tore through them and into the building, then blew a hole in the head of a bear-like creature and helped them escort the survivors out. Seriously, people are happy all the way up the chain of command. Hell, even Speare was pleased, if that matters."

"As long as everyone involved pays, I'm as happy as a fucking clam...ow!"

"Oh shush, you big baby," Niki retorted. "We do appreciate it, Trond. And we're looking forward to more opportunities to help the Department of Defense in the future."

Taylor put the phone on speaker to enable Niki to join the conversation without having to shout.

"Right." The agent chuckled. "Well, he said something I don't think I understand, but he said you'd know what it meant, Niki. He said, and I quote, that you're more a cold-hearted bitch than he gave you credit for, Banks, end quote. His words, not mine."

She shook her head. "I have no idea what he means by that but...thanks? I guess?"

"I didn't think so. That aside, the Canadian government said they'd already wired your fees to the account Taylor gave them, and there will be a little bonus coming from the DOD to make sure you guys are happy. You can also send us the bill for your expenses. We'll simply bill it to the CAF anyway."

"It sounds good to me," he answered.

"I'll let you two get some rest. I'm glad you made it out alive."

"Us too," she responded before she pressed the button to end the call.

Taylor took a deep breath and looked at his bandaged hand. "I think we should call Bobby to make sure he knows we're okay and to check in. We've done our own thing for a while now, so we might as well find out what he's up to."

Niki nodded, picked the phone up, and pressed the quick-dial button to call the mechanic.

"You know, some boyfriends would not be too happy about their girlfriends casually picking their phone up and doing stuff on it."

She smirked. "Well, you know as well as I do that if you had something to hide, Desk or Vickie would have told me already. It's time we come to terms with the fact that neither of us has much privacy anymore."

He tilted his head in thought but couldn't come up with any kind of argument to the contrary because it was quite true. The line didn't dial for too long before Bobby answered.

"Good morning," the mechanic said cheerfully. "It's nice of you guys to drop a line. I was worried that I would read about you dying heroically to save some important American monument or another."

"No such luck." He laughed. "How are you doing, Bungees? How goes running your own business?"

"About as stressful as I imagined it would be. Things are moving much faster around here, though."

"Well, our clients will certainly be happy about that. Speaking of clients, we have a couple of suits in desperate need of repairs. What kind of rate would you be prepared to give us?"

"You already know we offer the best rates in the business."

"Well, yeah, but I hoped for a friends and family discount."

Bobby groaned dramatically. "Niki should know she's in deep with a cheapskate."

"I'm right here, Bobby," she told him.

"You know you're in bed with a cheapskate, right?"

"I'm aware. We should ship the suits to you as soon as possible."

"It sounds good. I have some on the line waiting for you guys to work with in the meantime."

"Actually," Taylor interrupted, "we've worked with new suits some folks here gave us to test. We used them in the field and they didn't disappoint, so I thought basic repairs would give you a chance to look into them and maybe come up with some upgrades. They are top-of-the-line so it would be a good income stream when they finally reach the market."

"Huh. That sounds interesting. You're not running with the TrueGuards anymore?"

"I might switch up. We'll talk when they get there."

"Okay, that sounds good. So, what are the chances that you'll listen to me if I were to tell you to stay safe out there?"

He thought about it. "Maybe...fifty-fifty?"

"Well, stay safe out there, the two of you. I'll see you when I see you."

The line went dead and he smiled and shook his head.

"You miss him, don't you?" Niki commented and placed a hand on his shoulder.

"Eh, we're friends. I've gotten used to being out on some of these missions with him, and while I'm sure he doesn't miss the action, I miss being in it with him."

She smirked. "Well, I'll have to make do as a good enough replacement."

"Are you kidding me? You blasted a fucking hole in the skull of a monster that tried to chew my head off. You're more than a good enough replacement."

She reached up to play with his beard. "Well, I'm glad you think so. I'm trying to decide what Speare meant with the cold-hearted bitch comment. I know I'm fairly cold, but I don't think I did anything that raised the bar on that enough for him to comment on that."

"Do you think he merely means in general?"

"No, he called me that when we talked once, but I don't think I've done anything that would make me more of that than he originally thought."

Taylor raised an eyebrow. "He said Banks, right? Do you think he might have meant another Banks?"

"What are you talking about?" She narrowed her eyes at him.

"You know, your family."

"Jennie didn't do anything."

"He might not have meant someone who's necessarily a Banks in name but more in heart. And also genes."

Niki's eyes widened in realization. "Oh...do you think Vickie did something?"

"Or Desk. She's practically your sister turned into an AI, right?"

"Right. We might want to give them a call, although what the hell would Desk do? She's incredibly capable as AIs go, but there's not much she can do in the real world."

"I guess we'll have to call her and see, right?"

She sighed, dialed the hacker, and put the phone on the bed so both of them could hear

"Hey, you guys!" Vickie all but shouted when she answered. "I'm so glad you are safe! I knew you guys were but when I saw you fighting that big motherfucker, I may have had a couple of doubts. It's a good thing I don't have them anymore!"

The girl talked faster than usual, and that alone was enough to raise suspicions.

Niki scowled and spoke first. "Yes...well, we nailed it. Business as usual. How are things there? How's the situation with our other client?"

"Oh, you...didn't hear?"

The hesitation didn't help with the rising suspicions.

"Hear what?"

"Uh, it's all wrapped up. We managed to finish the job and connected with Renee and everything. She's very happy with our...effectiveness."

"What kind of effectiveness?"

"Um...do you really want to know? The job is done, the case is closed, and we're getting paid. That's all that counts, right?"

She picked the phone up to speak into it from a closer

range. "I want to know why the hell Speare from the DOD tells me that I'm more of a cold-hearted bitch than he thought I was."

"He said what to who again?" Vickie didn't sound right. "Speare…he's the DOD guy you used to work for, right?"

"Vickie," Niki started with a hint of warning in her tone, "I'm getting the feeling I get when you've done something you don't want to share with us."

"What gave it away?" Taylor asked. "The fact that she all but said we shouldn't ask any questions?"

"Zip it," she snapped. "Vickie, you have something to share. Spill it. Now."

"No," the hacker retorted firmly. "We had a challenge to deal with. I'm the one on the ground, and I took responsibility for my actions. It's not my fault your ex-boss assumes that every cold-hearted atrocity that happens around you is perpetrated by you."

"Wait, what are you talking about?" she countered. "What cold-hearted atrocity?"

"Remember that time you cold-cocked a CEO, stuck him in a wheelchair, and scared him so badly that he's still in a house for the goofy working through it?"

She paused. "He was a rat bastard who had it coming."

"You shot a scientist who had no gun."

"He was running and I was tired."

"You used a killer to get even with a psychopathic CEO and had her killed using the same assassin she used."

"I—" Niki stopped to think for a second. "Hold on, I don't recall doing anything of the sort!"

"Oh, right, that last one might have been me. But I'll make the jury see it isn't any different from what you've done in the past and make them think it was you. Hell, your ex-boss thought it was you without any prompting."

Taylor nodded. "Yeah, you guys are something of a psychotic family."

Niki took a deep breath, and it looked like Vickie had made her point. "I'll want to know more about this when we get back to DC. I want to know exactly how you convinced a murderer to turn on his boss."

"Well...I had a little help from Desk."

The silence lasted for a couple of seconds. He was unable to keep a small smirk from touching his lips as his partner rubbed her temples.

"Of...of course Desk was involved," she responded finally.

"Sure," Desk commented and joined the call. "Now you throw me under the bus. What happened to taking responsibility for your actions?"

"You need to do the same," Vickie pointed out.

"Okay, okay, hold the line," Taylor called and made a time-out motion with his hands. "Let me get this straight. While we were gone in the...two days we've covered, you two took care of the job, got Renee what she wanted, the CEO involved is dead, and the assassin is..."

"In the wind." The AI finished his sentence for him. "Or so he thinks. I've kept tabs on his location since he left DC."

"Okay, he's not in custody but we at least know where he is. What happened to Santana's data?"

"Oh, the police have that," Vickie interjected. "Renee helped them to acquire it after we got the location. It turns out she's very good at her job. Go figure."

"So, in summation, the job is all wrapped up and we're

getting paid for it, right?" Taylor looked at Niki and heard no disagreement on the line. "I'd say that calls for a celebration on the schedule but first, I'll need a full debrief from you."

"Yes, Boss Tay-Tay," Vickie conceded.

"And Desk?"

"Yes?"

"I'll need a full debrief from you as well."

The AI made a sound on the line that sounded like a sigh. "I assumed you would. Vickie made me do it."

"What?" the hacker snapped. "You lying piece of useless tech!"

"I didn't accuse anyone of anything yet," he reminded them.

"I know," Desk replied. "But I calculate that this won't be the last debriefing I'll have to do during my work with McFadden and Banks. As such, I am already updating my alibi software."

Taylor smirked. "Okay, we'll see you guys in seventy-two hours."

"Wait," Vickie interrupted. "It doesn't take that long to get to DC."

"We're at a hotel in Toronto, we're tired, and I have my girlfriend with me—"

"If you say another word, I will burn the mental image out of my brain with a branding iron. I'll see you guys when you get here."

"No more trouble while we're gone, Vickie," he warned.

"Yes, Dad," she retorted and hung up.

"So." Niki sighed and stretched on the bed. "We have a young woman who you raised at the end to be an accessory to murder. We have an AI who helped, and an ex-boss who thinks I'm responsible. I have an air-tight alibi for that myself, but still. Desk can't do anything to harm either one of us or Vickie…so she's caught in this somehow. Which, I guess, means we've somehow ended up with an ethically-challenged AI."

Taylor lay beside her and stared at the ceiling. "I'm practically suicidal and you're psychotic for falling for me. We take care of our trash, and either we succeed—"

"Or we die trying," she finished for him and turned on the bed to face him. "You know, I think I'm good with that."

DIPLOMATIC IMMUNITY

The story continues with book two, *Diplomatic Immunity*.

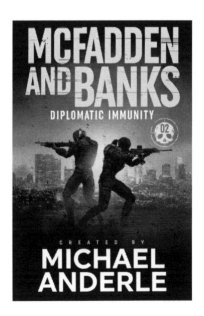

Order your copy today for delivery at midnight on
December 1, 2020.

Thank you for not only reading this story but the *Author Notes* here in the back as well!

First in series books such as this one cause me to wonder, *How should I write book 01 author notes?*

Do I assume the reader has no idea who I am and needs an overview, or do I assume they have read one of the hundreds of books with my *Author Notes* in the back? I'm not really sure.

So, I'll do a very short synopsis AFTER my specific author notes for McFadden & Banks.

BAMM BABY!

Taylor McFadden is one of those characters which arose out of an annoying attitude and grouchy moments of lucidity.

In short – I was tired of people trying to tell me what is prim and proper in society. Has nobody learned anything from the 1920's here in America? I shook my head at the state of ignorance among the ungrateful and unappreciative and what makes a good person.

Not all good people abide inside the box society draws. Especially when the dubious nature of *who is society* changes on the whim of troll packs and tv (non) facts.

So – I made a character whose emotional maturity was ripped apart in a foreign experience where death was daily. It was a fact of life.

You got your emotional reserves filled by those willing to share the value of human touch in the moment, not on a timetable that might see six of your partners killed in the space of a weekend.

Seeing them ripped apart by savage teeth created by an alien nature so uncaring it makes our own version of nature more tabby cat than lion.

Then I had him come back into a society which could not understand him. Is he still a human being?

I paired him up with a strong-willed woman who expected him to be a certain way, and was forced to see through the veil. Her attitude is often refined by platitudes of society and she had to face the reality of her eyes, not the bias of her brain.

Now, I am taking them through the next phase of their life.

Is this an action-adventure-kill-everyone-and-let-God-sort-them-out. Or am I still working through my effort to understand the nuances of relationships among friend and family?

Who Am I?

I wrote and released my first book *Death Becomes Her* (*The Kurtherian Gambit*) in Sept/Oct of 2015 and released Nov 2, 2015. I wrote and released the next two books that month and had three released by the end of November 2015.

So, just at five years ago.

Since then, I've written, collaborated, concepted, or created hundreds more in all sorts of genres.

My most successful genre is still my first (Paranormal Sci-Fi), followed quickly by Urban Fantasy. I have multiple pen names I produce under.

Some because I can be a bit crude in my humor at times or raw in my cynicism (Michael Todd). I have one I share with Martha Carr (Judith Berens, and another (not disclosed) we use as a marketing test pen name.

In general, I just love to tell stories, and with success comes the opportunity to mix two things I love in my life.

Business and stories.

I've wanted to be an entrepreneur since I was a teenager. I was a very *unsuccessful* entrepreneur (I tried many times) until my publishing company LMBPN signed one author in 2015.

Me.

I was the president of the company, and I was the first author published. Funny how it worked out that way.

It was late 2016 before we had additional authors join me for publishing. Now, we have a few dozen authors, a few hundred audiobooks by LMBPN published, a few hundred more licensed by six audio companies, and about a thousand titles in our company.

It's been a busy five years.

Ad Aeternitatem, (to eternity)

Michael Anderle.

CONNECT WITH MICHAEL

Connect with Michael Anderle

Website: http://lmbpn.com

Email List: http://lmbpn.com/email/

Social Media:

https://www.facebook.com/LMBPNPublishing

https://twitter.com/MichaelAnderle

https://www.instagram.com/lmbpn_publishing/

https://www.bookbub.com/authors/michael-anderle